The Presence

Charlene Neil

The Presence

Charlene Neil

Affinity
eBook Press
NZ

2015

The Presence
© April 2015 by Charlene Neil

Affinity E-Book Press NZ LTD
Canterbury, New Zealand

1st Edition

ISBN: 978-1-92-732863-7

Editor: Nat Burns
Proof Editor: Alexis Smith
Cover Design: Irish Dragon Designs

Acknowledgments

I would like to extend my sincere gratitude to everyone at Affinity eBook Press for publishing my story. If not for all of you, I would still be an aspiring author. I have learned a lot from you and will be forever grateful for that.

Dedication

To my children, thank you for always supporting me and my decisions, no matter what my crazy head came up with.

To my mother, for always believing in me.

To my father, for always pushing me a step forward.

To my sister, for being my best friend.

Table of Contents

Prologue

1901, The Anglo Boer War, South Africa

"Papa...Papa...*Papa*!"

The voice echoed from far in the distance, starting low and growing louder, as Catherine woke slowly from a deep sleep. Arising in the mornings was harder each day since her husband, Joshua, left to fight in the war. Life wasn't the same without his arms around her when she awoke and without his soothing voice when she needed comfort.

Catherine had a daughter to think of, however. Exhausted, she yawned and dragged her heavy body out of bed, and went to the window. She pulled the curtain aside. A dark and gloomy sky greeted her, matching her mood. She glared down at Carrey, her four-year-old daughter, who was standing in the front yard. She tried to focus her eyes on the clock by her bedside table. Six-thirty in the morning.

"Papaaaaaaaa!" Carrey called out again. It sounded as if she'd squeezed the final bit of air out of her lungs.

Catherine grabbed her robe. She wrapped it around her bare shoulders and shuddered. Her thin gown offered little protection from the cold. She turned too fast and kicked her toe into the sharp edge of the bedroom door.

"Ow...." She limped down the hallway. "Carrey!"

She raged breathlessly on her way down the stairs with only the echo of silence greeting her. She skipped every second step in order to descend as fast as she could, groaning every time she put weight on the throbbing toe.

She opened the front door and shoved the screen door aside. When she let it go, the loud bang against the rotted wooden doorframe echoed loudly. There was no one else for miles of their farm in Hoekwil, but sound travelled far in the frosty space of nothingness. The icy chill whipped her long light-brown hair around her face. She gasped at the sudden hit of freezing cold, and the frosty air burned down her throat. She took Carrey by the wrist and pulled her inside to the kitchen where it was warmer. And more protected. Catherine feared that if the British soldiers were in the vicinity, their lives would be at stake.

The instant they set foot inside the house, the weekly newspaper on the table caught her eye. Catherine dreaded the published list of perished soldiers. She knew the army would have sent her a telegram if anything had happened to her husband, but it was possible the telegram was delayed. The nausea that she felt every week at opening the newspaper maneuvered its way up her gullet. *Joshua.* She hadn't had the stomach to open the newspaper yet, even though it had arrived the day before.

She tried to refocus on her daughter and crouched down to Carrey's height. "What were you doing outside by yourself, especially at this time of the morning, little missy?"

"I'm waiting for Papa." Carrey spoke very well for her age.

"You know it isn't safe out there all by yourself. How many times must Mama tell you that?" Catherine had heard so many gruesome stories of the English soldiers taking women and children to concentration camps where they received no food or water and were beaten and neglected.

Hair stood up at the back of her neck at the very thought of that happening to her only daughter. For this reason, they had lived in concealment since Joshua went to fight in the war. At night, they'd not lit a single candle and had closed all the curtains just in case somebody was passing through.

"But I thought I saw Papa out there, Mama. I went outside to show him the way home. I don't think he saw me, though. He was too far away. But he looked like the man in the photo you showed me." Carrey's hair was much darker than her mother's and long, all the way down to her tiny waist. Long dark lashes decorated her big green eyes. She had her father's mouth and hair, but her eyes were Catherine's.

"Honey, how do you know he looks like Papa if he's so far away?"

Before Carrey could say anything, movement out of the corner of Catherine's eye caught her attention. She craned her neck to look in the direction of the door. The door that was still wide open. Fear clenched her heart like a fist. The man who stood there was not Joshua.

Chapter One

Present day, Sedgefield, South Africa

By three that afternoon, it felt like every pet owner in Sedgefield had needed Kayleigh Gibbs's veterinarian assistance for a medical emergency. By the time Kayleigh left to collect her eight-year-old daughter from school, she was exhausted but not complaining about the influx of patients. Since opening her practice, business had been slow.

She spun her black Jeep Wrangler out of its parking space before another worried pet owner could have the chance to spot her.

She understood the slow start of her practice. Carl Jones, just down the road, had been the only veterinarian in town for years and it seemed that most people did not accept the change of vet readily. When the townsfolk saw she was up-to-date with her equipment and techniques, they slowly started to accept her and bring her more business. Dr. Jones could hardly see anymore, and Kayleigh secretly dreaded the day he would remove an animal's bladder instead of its uterus.

The wind felt cool on her face. Kayleigh loved driving in the Jeep with the top down. It made her feel free. She switched from the radio to the current CD in the shuttle and selected her favorite song. A rhythmic beat flowed through the sound system, and she pumped up the volume.

As she drove, she thought of the lack of young people, let alone men, in this town. Kayleigh wasn't interested in men, really, and she'd had her fair share of bad experiences, enough to know men didn't know how to make her happy. She'd never felt the butterflies and so-called spark she'd heard about in the conversations she'd endured in school and university.

If true to herself, she realized she enjoyed her freedom. Besides, having a man around would tip the scales, and cause a disturbance in her perfect equilibrium.

Sarah was already standing by the gate when Kayleigh pulled into the schoolyard. Sarah placed her foot on the huge back wheel and hopped into the Jeep without opening the door.

"Hi, Mommy."

"Hi, sweetness. How was your day?"

"Awesome! We had a party in class because it was Zia's birthday. We ate cake and sweets and drank soda."

"Great. A sugar rush. Plus caffeine." Kayleigh shook her head.

All the way home, Sarah controlled the music in the car. She loved singing along to *"The Girl Next Door,"* a song by a local group, which she played twice before they reached home.

"Lunch box and juice bottle in the sink. Schoolbag in your room," Kayleigh called out to Sarah as soon as they entered the house. Sarah had the annoying habit of dumping her schoolbag on the couch.

"All right, Mom." Sarah sighed loudly before she did as she was told.

"Homework?"

"Nope. I finished all my homework in class."

Kayleigh studied Sarah. "Homework is for home. Like it says. Home. Work."

"The teacher said it was all right. She was done with class and told us to do our homework. Then we could have the whole weekend off." Sarah sang the final three words as she spun around on one foot.

Kayleigh grabbed *The Edge,* the local newspaper, and slumped onto the nearest breakfast nook stool. Her feet were killing her from all the running around today. She leaned over the counter and gazed through the rental listings. She felt her cell vibrate in her back pocket. Retrieving it, she looked at the caller ID before flipping it open.

"Hello, Bag," she said to her best friend, Lindsay Norris.

"Quit calling me that. I'll undo my wife's leash and let her attack you."

"You know you *earned* that nickname in college." Kayleigh smiled.

"So I had about five bags when I moved into the dorm room, big bloody deal. You didn't seem to mind borrowing most of my clothes."

Kayleigh laughed. "More like twenty bags, Bag."

Lindsay chuckled. "Moving on. Are we still on for tonight?"

"Most definitely. Babysitter's arranged. The works."

"I got the tequila, you bring the beers and the oranges. You know tequila tastes better with oranges than with lemons," Lindsay said.

"I do know and I will. How many people are coming?"

"Not too many, just a few of Judy's college mates and an old friend from high school. The poor chick recently relocated here from Cape Town, and she doesn't know a single soul. Lord knows why she moved to this small town."

"Any attractive guys?" Kayleigh asked with a hint of sarcasm.

"Sure, there's Bennie and Paul. Queens. You might like them."

Kayleigh giggled. "Perfect. See you later, Bag."

"Stop it."

After ending the call, she returned to reading the newspaper. "Two-bedroom apartments, six-month contracts, needs some work, blah blah blah...."

All of them were the same, and Kayleigh wanted a long-term lease. Besides, the prices were sky-high. She knew the owners never extended the short leases because of the town's proximity to the sea. The owners made a fortune renting to the December influx of holiday comers and kept their houses open for that purpose. She'd be damned if she would move again anytime soon.

The wind blew in through the open window and lifted the bottom corner of the newspaper. She placed her elbow over the paper to keep it still. Her long brown hair hung loosely over her shoulders and brushed against the top of the newspaper. With a swift movement of her right hand, she flicked her hair over her shoulder as she reached the lower part of the newspaper. With a loud and frustrated sigh, she moved her elbow to look at the rest of the page, when a listing in the bottom corner caught her attention.

"Four-bedroom house on large farm to let. Hoekwil." The rental was half what she was currently paying on her lease. "Wow. What a bargain."

She'd been looking to get a bigger place before she and Sarah got cabin fever. Without taking her eyes off the advertisement, Kayleigh grabbed her cell phone and dialed the number of her estate agent, Graham.

Chapter Two

1895—Hoekwil, South Africa

The day Catherine Jones met Joshua Botha was the best day of her life. She'd met Joshua, an Afrikaner farmer's son after the usual Sunday church service. His face was pale, enveloped by a thick shrub of dark hair. He looked so handsome in his black suit, and when he spoke to her, she nearly choked on her coffee. When he greeted her in Afrikaans, she struggled to respond since she'd only arrived from England a year ago. There had never been the time or the need to learn the language. Besides, her parents would've had a stroke if they discovered that she was interested in learning Afrikaans.

"Ek is Joshua, aangename kennis. En jy is?"

"Ek is... uhm... I'm sorry. I don't really speak Afrikaans. My name is Catherine. How do you do?" Catherine extended her right hand, which he took gracefully and kissed with the lightest of touches, as soft as a butterfly wing.

Joshua smiled up at her when she blushed at the touch of his lips on the back of her hand. He continued the conversation in broken English, but they managed to communicate very well. Whenever he was unsure of a word, he would utter it in Afrikaans, and if she understood his meaning, she would translate the word to English. As they spoke, they learned much about one another and that they had quite a lot in common

Catherine was quite eager to see Joshua again, and when he asked her to tea, she accepted immediately. He invited her to his house, where the servants prepared scones with fresh cream. At twenty and still living with her parents, lying to them and telling them she was visiting friends, wasn't easy the first few times. They trusted her and had no idea she was seeing a Boer. The conflict between the Boers and the British in the late 1800's was bordering on war. Her parents would never allow their daughter to even interact with an Afrikaans-speaking settler, let alone be courted by one.

After a mere month of secretly dating, Joshua and Catherine sat in the field one afternoon, on his farm, enjoying a picnic while watching the sunset behind the distant mountains. Joshua looked dreamily at Catherine. "I love you."

Catherine gasped in surprise and reached for his hand. "I love you, too. With all my heart."

"Will you be my wife?"

Tears sprang to her eyes as she flung herself into his arms. "Yes!" she cried. "Of course I'll marry you."

"You make me so happy." Joshua held onto her for a long while. "What do you think your father is going to say?" His English had improved a lot since he'd been with Catherine. He didn't stutter much anymore when he spoke to her.

"My father will probably disown me, but I love you, Joshua, and I want to be with you, whether I have my father's blessing or not."

†

"Father, we love one another," Catherine pleaded.

Her father boiled with anger. "No daughter of mine will marry one of your kind." He glared at Joshua.

Joshua swallowed hard. "Sir, I own a farm which I inherited from my parents. I am well off financially, and I promise to take good care of your daughter."

Red-faced, Arthur Jones pointed to the door. "Get out of my house, you Afrikaner scum. And don't you ever contact my daughter again."

"Please, Father. I can't live without him. He's the love of my life." Catherine grabbed at her father's blazer and sobbed. "I beg you, please don't force me to choose."

Arthur froze for a second while he stared at his daughter in anguish. He then pushed her away from him. "Then get out of my house. I never want to see you again. You're no daughter of mine."

"Arthur, can we at least sit down and discuss this first?" Elizabeth, Catherine's mother, looked petrified when she spoke. She gripped his arm. "This is my daughter. Please don't make me lose her."

"You have no right to intervene, Elizabeth. Sit down and keep quiet. I'll deal with you later." Arthur yanked his arm free and violently shoved her away. Elizabeth fell backward but stopped herself from hitting the floor by grabbing onto the arm of the chair. She pulled herself into the chair and sat down quietly.

"Mr. Jones, I beg you, please don't do this to your daughter. She has so much respect for you, sir. Please give us your blessing."

"Get out!" Arthur shouted and turned his back on them.

Elizabeth hugged herself and rocked in the chair as sobs shook her body.

Joshua took Catherine's hand and tugged her gently toward the door. Catherine gave her mom a desperate look as she followed Joshua.

.

Chapter Three

Present day

The steep dirt road leading up to the house offered a bumpy ride. At the end of the road loomed a mammoth, wooden, two-story house, which seemed to climb its way up the clear blue sky. A shiver of excitement ran down Kayleigh's back. Since she'd moved to Sedgefield, being unsettled had left her with a constant hollow feeling in her chest. Now, it was as if the futility drained from inside her to make way for a new purpose.

Graham, the estate agent, had already arrived and stood waiting beside his motorcycle. His grey hair was short and neatly cropped, perfectly styled even after removing his helmet. He looked like a brand new doll—straight from its box—right after removing the elastic band from the plastic hair.

"Hi, Graham," she called out to him as she and Sarah stepped down from the Jeep. "Why on earth didn't you tell me about this place?"

"I didn't think you'd like it." He appeared a little contrite. "You said you wanted something small, just for the two of you."

"Cheap, Graham. Not small. Cheap. This is perfect." She reached for Sarah and held onto her hand.

He raised his hands in gentle protest. "Now, before you jump blindly into anything, you have to take a look-see first. Especially since it's a long-term contract. I don't have any history on the house. It only became available recently, and I haven't had time to check it out yet." He spoke with a smooth English accent as he lifted a plastic container from the carrier of his bike and removed a bunch of old rusted keys.

"Wow, Mom. It's so cool." Sarah was about to run toward the house, but Kayleigh stopped her, still holding onto her hand.

"Let's wait for Graham, honey."

The grass around the house was long, but Kayleigh felt sure she could manage.

"All of this will be trimmed before you move in, so just ignore it, Kayleigh," Graham mentioned as he saw her looking around the yard.

Don't have to mow my own lawn? Great. She was completely mesmerized by the house. Sarah hopped in anticipation beside her.

Graham cleared his throat loudly, which got her attention, and Kayleigh turned toward him.

"Hoekwil is only eighteen miles from Sedgefield," he said. "Close enough to your practice and Sarah's school."

"I can already see us living here. That's a good sign, right?"

"I hope you're right." He continued in what she assumed was his estate agent voice. "This house is built on a massive smallholding, which had been divided into smaller pieces of land…"

Kayleigh struggled to listen to his detailed description of the land. Like her daughter, all she wanted to do was get a look inside.

"You needn't worry about maintaining the land. A farmhand and his family who live on the other side of the farm, which is about three hundred yards from the main house, care for the property. You may use the land if you'd like, but the owner promised to maintain it and to continue paying the salaries of the staff who reside here. One condition of renting the place is that you can't ask them to leave." Graham turned his attention back to the long grass around the house. "It's been raining quite a lot these past few weeks, which is probably why they haven't trimmed your lawn."

"Sure, of course." Kayleigh nodded.

With her free hand, Kayleigh cupped her eyes to block out the sun and looked out over the land as far as she could see. In the distance, she saw the small rondavels, the African-style huts, traditionally built with raw materials.

"I don't have a problem with that." She looked back at Graham, and then down at Sarah. "Shall we?"

Unlocking the front door presented somewhat of a challenge for him. "The lock is sticking I think it needs oil or maybe we should change them instead," Graham said as he struggled with the key. He finally got it unlocked and as he stepped into the darkened hallway, dust clouded his boot and lifted into the air. "Place needs cleaning." He coughed. "Oh, and painting." He motioned toward the peeling walls. "This might be the reason for the low price. The place is not in excellent condition. Do you want to continue or have you seen enough?"

"No turning back now. I love it." Kayleigh was very enthusiastic about the bargain. With Sarah in tow, she proceeded ahead of Graham as he did his slower, closer inspection of the house. Kayleigh let go of Sarah's hand, and Sarah skipped into the house. The long, narrow passage gave birth to a huge entertainment room with a fireplace. "Nice and cozy, I've always wanted a fireplace."

"You don't have to worry about a thing. My team will come in to clean up, paint the walls, and fix anything that needs fixing."

Graham had been her estate agent since she'd moved to Sedgefield, and he handled most of the rentals in the area. She knew him quite well and was well aware that he always made very pretty promises when trying to close a business deal. She knew that the house would see no cloth nor a paintbrush unless she did it herself. Unfortunately, he was the only rental estate agent in the immediate area. Lucky for her, she'd never been a lazy person, and hard work had never put her off.

She continued down the passage and reached the kitchen, which resembled a typical farmhouse kitchen. It was massive. The old-fashioned coal stove oven needed a good scrubbing, but looked in very good condition, and Kayleigh could imagine herself cooking a Sunday roast in it.

She ran her fingers over the surface of the stove. "Oh, man. This is so fucking cool." Kayleigh didn't even bother to censor her words, because Sarah had already gone off in her own direction.

"Mom!" Sarah shouted from the staircase. "Language!"

"Sorry, Sarah." Kayleigh covered her smirk with one hand.

The banister of the staircase gave a little as she leaned on it for support, but that didn't bother her at all. She hadn't been watching the Home Renovations channel all this time for nothing. The house had three spacious bedrooms upstairs and one smaller bedroom downstairs. The main bedroom had an adjoining toilet, but unfortunately, the only shower was on the ground floor, adjoining the smaller bedroom. One of the rooms had its own bath, which was the room Sarah claimed as hers. It was right at the top of the stairway, just off to the right. Kayleigh noticed a door at the top of the landing, which, no doubt, had been installed for extra safety.

After Kayleigh had seen the top of the house, she called down to Graham. "Sold, Graham. I want this place. It's perfect." Her mind rushed on with possibilities. *Maybe I can even buy it if my business maintains its current pace.*

Since the house was empty anyway, she was able to move in at any time. Kayleigh decided that by the end of next week, they would be the new occupants of number twenty-five, Hillview Road, Hoekwil.

†

Valerie Marx, Kayleigh's usual baby-sitter, was a young, twenty-year-old woman with no children of her own. Always punctual, she arrived at six sharp. "Hi there, Kayleigh. Where is my young superstar?"

"Valerie," Sarah called from where she sat by the dining room table. "I have the cards ready. Come on. Hurry."

"Okay, okay. Hold your horses." Valerie winked at Kayleigh. "Have fun."

"You too. Thanks for looking after her. I won't be late."

"No problem at all. You haven't been out in ages. We'll be fine."

The air was warm, so Kayleigh put the soft top down. She drove through the small town to Cola Beach where Lindsay and her life partner, Judy, lived. She was on her way to their house warming party—they'd finally bought their own condo near the beach.

Lindsay worked as a general practitioner at the local medical suite. Kayleigh met her at the faculty of Veterinary

Science of the University of Pretoria, where they'd both initially studied to become veterinarians. After the first year, Lindsay had discovered her real passion was with human health instead of animal science, so Lindsay left and went to medical school instead. They'd clicked immediately, however, and maintained their friendship. Kayleigh thought back to their college days as she drove. About how they'd used to hang out at the gay clubs and how the girls used to chat her up. She remembered enjoying the attention, which was why she'd always tagged along. Lindsay and Judy had a great mix of friends. Gay, straight, bisexual... whatever. They never judged people.

"Earth to Kayleigh," Lindsay called from the door when Kayleigh walked up the driveway. "Hello, darling." Lindsay immediately hugged her, and as Lindsay pulled away, she took the beer from Kayleigh.

"Who are you calling darling, huh?" Judy said as Kayleigh followed Lindsay inside.

"Oh, don't you worry, Judy, she wasn't talking to me. She was talking to the beer." Kayleigh opened her arms to Judy.

Judy laughed and embraced her in a tight bear hug. "You're officially our first guest to arrive. Welcome."

"Thanks. It's about bloody time we have a party. What took you guys so long? Hey, Lindsay. Before you hide the beer, pass us one, please. Don't be so stingy."

They walked toward the patio which boasted a bar, which, like the glass-walled house, overlooked the ocean.

"Breathtakingly and stunningly beautiful." Kayleigh sighed wistfully as she took in the ocean view. "Did I tell you guys how proud I am of you?"

"Only a million times." Lindsay came out on the patio with a cooler in her left hand and a bottle of tequila in her right. "Don't mind me. I can manage on my own," she said with a sarcastic twist in her voice as she plopped the tequila bottle down on the bar.

"Ah. My favourite. Patron." Kayleigh sat down at the bar and faced the bottle.

Rebecca Steward opened the trunk of her car and pulled the large cooler that was filled with everything Judy had asked her to bring. She slammed the trunk shut. She'd been staying in Sedgefield for a month and had been too busy settling in to come visit them. Even when she received Judy's call inviting her to their housewarming party, she'd almost declined. All she wanted to do was stay at home and be alone. The move had left her exhausted.

Rebecca sighed as she examined the long double driveway. She counted ten parked cars. She had parked on the left side of the drive planning to be the first to leave. If someone wanted her to move her car so they could leave, she had an excellent excuse to go.

"Rebecca. Finally. The last to arrive as usual. You'd better not be the first to leave," Judy said and waggled her finger at her. Then she grinned before hugging her in a vice-like grip and kissing her cheek.

"Hello, Judes. How've you been?"

"Very good, as you can see." Judy waved her hand toward her new house.

"I'm so happy for you. It's beautiful."

"Come, meet our friends. Here. Give me that box. It looks heavy."

"Sure, but don't drink it all in one go."

Rebecca followed her to the spacious patio where she found an empty bar stool and sat down. She stretched out her long, denim-clad legs in front of her. Everyone shouted quick greetings as Judy introduced her to the crowd of strangers. Rebecca's gaze lingered on the stunning brunette with the sexy green eyes. The woman, Kayleigh, sat on the opposite end of the long patio bar as she downed a shot of tequila. Rebecca grinned at the way she pulled a face when she sucked on a piece of orange after swallowing the drink. The orange must have been sour because when she looked up, her eyes were watering. They locked gazes for a few seconds while the rest of the world seemed to stand still. Rebecca could hear the silence ticking away in her head as the woman smiled tentatively and took a sip of beer.

"Kayleigh's straight. Don't you dare," Lindsay whispered in her ear when she hugged Rebecca from behind.

"How are you doing, girlfriend?" Rebecca squeezed Lindsay's arm and accepted the beer she offered. "Thanks." She sipped from her beer before looking up at Lindsay. She tried to offer up her best, reassuring smile at Lindsay's inquisitive expression. "I've been fine. Really. Fine."

Lindsay parked herself in the stool next to her and leaned her back against the bar. "Why haven't you been to visit?"

"Been busy settling in and opening my new business."

Lindsay touched Rebecca's arm. "Glad you're finally here where we can look after you."

"I don't need looking after," Rebecca said, a little sharper than she'd intended. She softened her expression. "Really. I'm okay."

Lindsay turned away with a wave of her hand. "Yeah. Whatever you say." Then she glanced back. "Just know— we're here for you."

"I know. Thanks."

While Rebecca listened to her friends argue which whiskey was the best, her gaze wandered back to the pretty brunette at the end of the bar. Her long brown hair caressed her firm breasts over her tight white top. She was in perfect shape. Her stomach was flat and appeared muscular beneath the skintight material. She wasn't really talking to anyone, so Rebecca decided to take the plunge.

Kayleigh sat by the bar as she poured her second tequila for the evening. She took a pinch of salt, downed the drink, and felt the bitter burn sliding down her throat before she sucked on a slice of orange. The sweetness of an orange made the tequila more palatable. Still sucking on the fruit, she looked up and caught a blue-eyed newcomer staring at her. Something about her clear blue eyes took Kayleigh's breath away. Or was it the tequila? The heat crawled up her cheeks in a never-ending blush. In her attempt to lose the redness in her face, she turned her eyes away and took a long drink from her beer. She'd missed the introductions while she was busy drinking her tequila and didn't know anything about the woman. Kayleigh felt the air crackle between them, noting that the woman could probably enter a room full of strangers and instantly command attention.

Fascinated, she watched as the woman picked up a bar stool and walked toward her. Their eyes connected once again while she placed her chair right across from her, making Kayleigh tense. Trying not to be too conspicuous, she inched her chair back.

"I'm Rebecca. Hi." The voice was low and husky, but it was the eyes that caught her attention. She felt as though they could reach into her soul.

"I'm Kayleigh. Hi. I'm straight. Sorry." Kayleigh nearly bit her own tongue off when the words slipped out. Since lesbians were always hitting on her she thought it was the best way to avoid getting into a situation she would struggle to get out of later.

Rebecca choked on nothing and started laughing. "Why would you say something like that? Did someone tell you that I'm gay?"

Kayleigh breathed out a sigh of embarrassment and frowned. "I'm so sorry. I guess I assumed that if you're friends with Judy and Lindsay, uh.... Well, I'm happy to meet you. Please forgive my rudeness. I'm not a homophobe..." She slammed her eyes shut before opening them and meeting Rebecca's eyes, eyes that twinkled with amusement. "I'm rambling, aren't I?" Kayleigh could feel her face heat up. "Sorry."

Rebecca laughed. "The pleasure is all mine." She extended her hand. Kayleigh took it with a smile. "Going with your logic since you are friends with Judy and Lindsay you have to be a lesbian. So why are you telling me you're straight?" She grinned.

"No...that isn't what I meant at all...oh, sometimes I just should keep my mouth shut."

Rebecca once again smiled. "Let's start over. Now, tell me. Is the tequila to share?"

"Of course. Excellent. No one else wanted to have shots with me and I was beginning to feel like a total idiot." Kayleigh took the bottle and poured two shots. Rebecca raised a shot glass and held it up in salute before tossing it back. Kayleigh followed suit and sucked on an orange. She handed Rebecca a slice and when she took it, their fingertips touched for a brief moment, sending a tingling sensation up Kayleigh's arm.

"How long have you been in these parts?" Rebecca asked before she bit into the juicy orange slice.

Something about Rebecca's deep voice was very intriguing. "About two years now. You?"

"Only about a month. I wouldn't have moved here if it weren't for my separation after ten years of bliss."

"Oh." Starting a conversation about exes would eventually lead in her having to share her own drama and that was the last thing Kayleigh wanted. Changing the subject, she asked, "Where are you from?"

"Cape Town." Rebecca rested an elbow on the bar and leaned forward while maintaining eye contact. "You?"

Kayleigh could feel Rebecca's breath on her face and shifted in her stool. "Johannesburg, Gauteng."

"What made you move here?"

"Caught my husband in bed with another woman." *Oh, nice, Kayleigh. So much for not sharing. Shit.* Now she *had* to talk personal issues.

"Jerk." That was all Rebecca said. "Another shot?" She took the bottle and poured two more shots before handing Kayleigh her glass. "Here's to those who love us and fuck those who don't."

Kayleigh laughed. "Cheers to that," she said before downing her tequila. The liquid went straight to her head. She needed to slow down or she wouldn't be able to drive home.

"So, where do you work?" Rebecca asked.

"I own a veterinarian practice in town." Kayleigh blushed when she saw the surprise on Rebecca's face. She peered down at her beer to cover her embarrassment. People always made a big deal out of it when she told them what she did for a living.

"Wow," Rebecca said. "Not just a pretty face."

Kayleigh felt her blush deepen. "Uhm… so what do you do?"

"I own a CD store in town. Just opened it the other day, and the customers are few if not non-existent." Rebecca sighed and took a sip of beer.

"When I first opened my practice, business was extremely slow. Happy to say that lately it's really been picking up. It'll happen, don't worry too much."

They spent hours talking until Rebecca had to move her car so that the others could leave. The crowd thinned and soon, everyone had left but them.

Lindsay and Judy joined them with mugs of coffee for each.

"Thanks, I sure can use this," Kayleigh said and Rebecca nodded in agreement. "Can I help you clean up?"

"That would be fantastic," Lindsay said.

They all started clearing away glasses and plates.

Kayleigh and Rebecca took as many glasses as they could carry and packed them into the dishwasher. Kayleigh felt Rebecca's eyes on her back and straightened before turning around to find Rebecca's face inches from hers.

"Oops. Apologies." Rebecca took a step back to allow Kayleigh to pass.

"It's late. I guess I'd better leave or the babysitter is going to start charging double," Kayleigh said as she slipped past Rebecca... but not before she felt the heat from Rebecca's body. She walked to Lindsay who was busy wiping the kitchen counter. "I haven't had so much fun since college, Lindsay."

Judy walked in with the remaining glasses, and Lindsay helped her load the dishes. "Thanks for having me, guys," Kayleigh said. She hugged Judy and Lindsay and shook Rebecca's hand.

"Are you both sure you're fine to drive? You're welcome to sleep over," Lindsay said.

"Yes, I stopped drinking a while ago, and the coffee really helped," Rebecca said. "Besides, my house is just down the road. How hard can it be?"

Kayleigh smiled. "And I'm two miles away. I'll be fine."

On the short trip home, a shiver coursed through her body as her thoughts returned to Rebecca and those passionate blue eyes.

†

The next day was Saturday. Kayleigh's hangover didn't help in rousing her from bed, but it was time to prepare the new house and begin moving in. Flashes of memory from the previous evening came back in short spurts and pieces, and she tried to fit the puzzle back together. She thought of Rebecca and wondered if she'd ever see her again.

Kayleigh and Sarah took all the necessities to the house to start the big clean up. As excited as Kayleigh was, her daughter was positively bouncing with energy. After so many different small apartments, the bigger living space, and an actual house was welcome for both of them.

Kayleigh parked her Jeep in the sandy driveway and removed the cleaning materials from the trunk. On the way up the rest of the drive, she noticed with relief that the lawn had been mowed.

"Wow, Mom. I love this house. It's so cool!" Sarah exclaimed for what seemed like the fiftieth time since their first visit. Her sneakers left small puffs of dust clouds in her wake as she rushed to the door.

"Wait up, Sarah." Kayleigh hurried to catch up with her.

They spent the remainder of the weekend cleaning. By Sunday evening, the house was spotless and move-in ready. Kayleigh had even had time to strengthen the staircase railing with brackets and wood glue that she had purchased from the local hardware store.

During the week that followed, Kayleigh spent every evening packing all their belongings into boxes. By Friday, everything was packed and ready for the moving company to transport to the new place. Judy and Lindsay took a half day off work, and helped her move. By Friday evening, everything was in their new home, and Kayleigh was exhausted. After Judy and Lindsay left, Sarah came to her where she stood in the kitchen, unwrapping glasses and placing them in the cupboard.

"Mom, please can we just be normal this weekend? Go to the beach, watch some TV?"

"I only have one word for you...." Kayleigh paused while she grabbed her cell phone and dialed Mr. Delivery. "Pizza."

"Yeah!" Sarah did her happy dance around the kitchen with her school uniform still on, the green skirt lifting while she spun around like a ballerina.

Kayleigh hung up from ordering the pizza and pointed Sarah toward the stairs. "Go take off your school uniform and put on your pajamas."

About thirty minutes later, the pizza came. Kayleigh carried it out to the expansive patio that overlooked all of Wilderness. The house, which sat on top of the mountain, offered a stunning view. Kayleigh breathed in the salty smell of the sea that carried to her on a soft breeze. She sighed in contentment. She glanced over at her daughter who'd just finished off her third slice of pizza. Sarah shifted in her seat and rubbed her stomach.

"Ate too much, did you? Don't fade on me during our first date now." Kayleigh grinned and sipped some bubbly. At times like these, she missed having someone in her life. Maybe it was the big house or perhaps the champagne. Sarah was great, but having an eight-year-old as the only company wasn't always easy.

Kayleigh wondered sometimes if true love existed. It sure hadn't in her marriage. She'd divorced her husband two years ago after catching him in bed with his secretary. Angry and hurt, she'd resigned from the animal hospital where she was working, and left. All their friends had sided with her husband at the time, agreeing with him that he had reason to cheat on his wife, due to her extremely long hours at work. She really only had one true friend, and that had always been Lindsay. Kayleigh had been fantasizing secretly about staying close to her best friend and opening up her own practice long before she caught him cheating. It took a lot of courage for her to make such a massive change in her life, but she finally cut all ties, took Sarah and her Jeep, and moved across the country from Johannesburg to start a fresh life in Sedgefield.

Kayleigh took another sip of champagne as she thought about how she'd used her life savings to open the practice. She'd struggled to make ends meet at first, but with the increase in business these past few months, she was optimistic everything was turning around. Now, with the new house and the lower rent, she would be able to have more freedom with the extra cash in her pocket.

Sarah's voice shook her from her thoughts.

"Tristan brought me flowers at school today, Mom. What should I do? I don't like him."

"Flowers? How sweet. God, what I wouldn't give for some flowers from someone." Kayleigh winked.

"I don't like him. He's fat."

"Sarah, that's very hurtful. I've taught you better than that. I hope you didn't say that to him."

"No. I took the flowers and chucked them in the nearest trash can."

"Sarah! I'm sure you hurt his feelings. What did he do?"

Sarah gazed down at her hands in her lap. "He cried and ran away." She turned her attention back to Kayleigh with tears in her eyes. "I felt really bad. I won't do it again. I promise."

Kayleigh tipped Sarah's chin up. "You need to treat others as you'd want them to treat you, okay?"

Sarah nodded.

Kayleigh ruffled her hair. "I think you should apologize to him on Monday, don't you?"

"Okay, Mom," Sarah said.

†

Rebecca got home Friday after yet another quiet day at her new store. She immediately went to the fridge for a cold beer. It'd been a week since she had anything to drink. Tonight she needed it. She twisted off the cap, and with her heavy black boot, she kicked the fridge door shut.

"Damn these locals," she muttered to herself as she took a seat by the kitchen table.

She pulled her phone out of her jean pocket and dialed Judy's number.

"Hey, sweetie," Judy answered after the third ring.

"I'm moving back to Cape Town."

"No. You're not. Take a deep breath and tell me what's wrong."

Rebecca heard Lindsay asking questions in the background.

"No customers. Not even one." Rebecca sighed into the phone. She raked her hand through her short, dark hair and her long bangs flopped back down over her eyes.

"Just give it time. They will warm up to you, promise," Lindsay said.

"I'm putting you on speakerphone, Beck," Judy told her.

"That's cool, mate. Hi, Lindsay." Judy and Lindsay did everything together. Sometimes, she was jealous of their strong relationship. "If I don't start getting customers soon,

I'm doomed." She sipped from her beer as she sat back in her chair, long, lean legs stretched out before her.

"And you will get customers. Don't worry too much. Have a free hotdog day or something," Judy said. "Kayleigh struggled when she first opened her practice and now her business is booming."

"Speaking of Kayleigh, how is she?" Rebecca tried not to sound too interested but wasn't sure she pulled it off. A vision of Kayleigh's vivid green eyes popped into her mind.

Lindsay interrupted her train of thought. "She just moved into a new place this week. Been hectic."

"Hey, bud, she's off-limits," Judy chimed in playfully. Still, Rebecca heard the serious undertone.

"Look, guys, I know I went through a phase of sleeping around after Maria, but that phase is over. This is the new Rebecca Steward. Watch this space."

"Nothing wrong with enjoying your freedom. As long as it's not with my best friend," Lindsay said. "She's so straight, it scares the lamp poles."

"Oh yeah, guys, speaking of straight, I kind of let her think I'm straight." Rebecca confessed like a guilty child. "I didn't really lie…well, only if you think omitting the truth is the same as telling a lie."

At first, there was complete silence from the other end. Seconds passed with no response, and then there was a cough from Judy. "Why would you do something like that? You're as gay as they come, chick. It doesn't get gayer than you. It took you years to jump out of the closet and shout surprise! Why would you want to climb back into that dark hole again? That doesn't make sense."

"It just kind of happened. I know it was probably wrong to let her think that, but, well when she introduced herself, the first thing out of her mouth was she was straight. I was just messing with her, and well, then it just was never brought up again. Please don't blow my cover, guys. I'd like the chance to explain, tell her myself. I really like this girl... as a friend," Rebecca quickly added.

"If you plan on seeing her again, you'd better tell her, Beck. The truth always comes out and bites you in the ass if you wait too long," Lindsay said. "You know what a big mouth I have. I might slip up."

"Don't you dare, Lindsay," Rebecca warned.

"Then don't mislead my friend. I'll slap you senseless."

Rebecca snorted. "Says the person who won't even hurt a fly."

After hanging up, Rebecca flipped on her music system and cranked up the volume before carrying her beer outside.

Chapter Four

Two weeks had passed since Kayleigh met Rebecca at the house-warming party. Kayleigh and Sarah were settling in their new house, and it was starting to feel like home. Kayleigh kept busy with renovations. She'd had some cracked windows replaced and some of the old carpets cleaned. She'd even managed to fix a few leaking faucets. She kept all the slips to give to Graham, so it would come off her rent the following month.

The neighborhood was peaceful, and even though the sea was five miles from her window, she could still hear the waves crashing in the distance.

On Saturday, as Kayleigh was waking, she heard Sarah talking. It sounded like her voice was coming through the far end of a tunnel. Disoriented, she opened her eyes and squinted around in a daze, wondering for a second where she was. As soon as she recognized her surroundings, her lips curled upward and she stretched. The wooden floor felt clean, smooth, and warm under her bare feet when they touched the floor. She walked down the passage to Sarah's room. It sounded as though she was talking to one of the dolls that she loved so much.

She glimpsed Sarah through the partially opened door. She was sitting on the wooden floor, her favorite doll clasped in one hand and a Barbie doll in the other. It appeared she was playing a mommy-and-child game.

"Morning, sweetie," Kayleigh said softly.

Sarah jumped up at the sound of her mom's voice. "Mommy!" She lunged toward her and hugged her around her waist.

Kayleigh returned the hug and looked down into Sarah's eyes. "If you help me make sandwiches, we can take a drive down to the beach."

Jumping up and down, Sarah shouted her delight. Kayleigh knew she could pretty much talk Sarah into doing anything for a trip to the beach.

They sang and danced around the kitchen while they packed the picnic lunch. Sarah made a big jug of juice with ice blocks and packed some plastic cups for them, while Kayleigh made peanut butter and apricot jam sandwiches. To round off their picnic, some Twinkies and fruit were added.

The trip to the beach took only five minutes in traffic. Kayleigh picked a spot as close to the water as they could get without getting everything wet. Luckily, the beach wasn't too crowded, but there were many body-boarders about. Kayleigh kept close watch so that Sarah didn't get hurt. There was not a single cloud in the sky, and the sun was brutal. The cool seawater was very welcome.

They spent the whole morning on the beach. By the time they'd eaten their sandwiches and their snacks, they were both turning red, and Kayleigh decided it was time to head home. It felt as though sand had entered every single orifice—she was ready for a nice, refreshing, cold shower.

"One more dip, Sarah."

Sarah whined as Kayleigh began collecting all of their stuff so they could leave. She glanced up. Her heart did a flip-flop when she noticed a very familiar woman with short dark hair walking up to them. Her penetrating, clear blue eyes were luminous in the sunlight.

"If it's not too late, can I offer you some sunscreen?" Rebecca asked as she showed a large bottle of SPF 40. Her eyes scanned over Kayleigh's body with obvious appreciation.

"Hi," Kayleigh said, taking the bottle from Rebecca and rubbing some lotion onto Sarah's shoulders. "Thanks," she said as she returned her gaze to Rebecca's heavenly blue eyes.

Sarah started to take off for the water.

"What do you say, Sarah?"

Sarah came to a halt, thanked Rebecca, and then bounced through the sand toward the sea.

"How have you been?" Rebecca asked in her low, sexy voice. "Here. Let me help you." Rebecca took the sunscreen and applied it liberally onto Kayleigh's shoulders. Rebecca's breasts were only inches away from her face.

"I've been...busy." Kayleigh cleared her throat, while trying to calm her rapid breathing. "How about you?"

"Ugh," Rebecca grunted. "I've had a week from hell. Remember my CD shop that I told you about?"

Kayleigh nodded.

"No business. Nada. Do you know about the new music store in town? I mean, do you actually know where it is? Because no one else seems to have found it."

"Yes, I know where it is," Kayleigh lied. "Sorry, I've been busy moving and I haven't had a chance to pop by." She didn't want to offend Rebecca by admitting that she hadn't even noticed the store.

"That's right. I heard you moved. Well, up until today I've had a total of *zero* customers." Rebecca emphasized the point by shaping her fingers into a zero sign. "Unless you want to count the ten CDs Judy came to purchase this past week. I'm sure she bought them out of pity."

"I had the same problem when I first opened my practice. It took me a year to get the locals to trust me with their pets. It's a shame Judy didn't go buy a pet to bring me business at the time."

Rebecca laughed. "She's such a good friend. I can actually see her doing that." She shook her head. "A year? No, I can't wait that long. I'll be doomed by then. No income, with all these expenses. God help me."

"Sarah and I will pop in some time," Kayleigh said, making a mental note to ask Lindsay about the location of Rebecca's store.

Rebecca gave her a brilliant smile. "I'd like that."

Wow. Even her teeth are perfect. "Well, we'd better get out of the sun. It was good seeing you, Rebecca."

"Nice seeing you too, Kay. Is it okay to call you Kay?"

"Sure."

After saying their good-byes, Kayleigh and Sarah headed back to the Jeep.

†

The road home seemed longer than it had when they'd left. Dehydrated and sore from the sun, Kayleigh could feel a headache coming on. She asked Sarah to stay in her room and play while Kayleigh took a late afternoon nap. Kayleigh took a quick, cold shower, locked all the doors, and went up to her room, falling asleep instantly and sleeping like a log.

Kayleigh woke and stretched. It was evening and her room was so dark that she couldn't make out her surroundings. It took a few seconds for her eyes to adjust just as she noticed it was raining. The smell of the fresh rain on the ground entered her open window and filled her senses with its relaxing rhythm and soothing effect.

As she pushed herself up on her elbows in her bed Kayleigh groaned. Her shoulders burned. Never again would she go to the beach without sunscreen. Guilt overwhelmed her when she thought about Sarah's sunburn and for leaving her daughter alone for such a long time while she'd slept. It was a relief hearing Sarah's voice drifting down the hallway. Wearing only panties and an oversized t-shirt, Kayleigh got out of bed and yawned as she sauntered toward Sarah's room.

The ceiling was leaking like a colander all over the floor, making her step over and slip in at least three puddles before she reached Sarah's room. She opened the door and the voice trailed away. Kayleigh frowned—the room was completely dark. Confused, she flicked on the light switch, finding Sarah fast asleep in her bed.

"Sarah?" She whispered, hoping her daughter would jump up and exclaim surprise!

I'm sure I heard her talking.

She shivered as she tiptoed to Sarah who was snoring softly. "I didn't know you talk in your sleep."

Kayleigh pulled the blankets out from under Sarah and covered her sleeping body. Kayleigh's gaze swept across the room and absorbed every inch of the room. The difference in temperature was uncanny. It was much colder here than in her bedroom, even with her window open.

Chapter Five

1896

Joshua and Catherine had a small wedding in a tiny chapel in Ruigtevlei. A few hours later, he carried her over the threshold of their new home. The house, on their farm on top of a mountain in Hoekwil, overlooked the whole of Wilderness. The sea, about five miles away, was also visible. Joshua was a sheep farmer but also had a couple of cows, chickens, and a large vegetable patch to keep them and their farm workers well-nourished at all times.

Catherine giggled when he dropped her down onto the bed and fell on top of her. He kissed her feverishly while he undressed her. She looked beautiful in her wedding gown, but now he seemed in a hurry to see the new Mrs. Botha, with her light brown hair and her brilliant green eyes, out of it. She kissed him back with so much passion that it made the hair stand up at the back of his neck. They made love for hours that night until, exhausted, Catherine begged him to stop.

They lay in one another's arms and talked through the night. When they finally managed to fall asleep, it was already dawn.

"I've arranged for the staff to do all the farm work so I can spend a whole week making love to you," Joshua told her later, when they awoke.

Catherine only smiled and pulled him closer.

"Are you happy, my love?" he asked Catherine on their fifth night.

She leaned on her elbow to look down at him. Her hair spilled over her shoulder as she caressed his cheek. "I'm the happiest I've ever been."

"And your parents?"

Catherine furrowed her brow. "Yes, I miss them. But here is where I belong. With you. I have no doubt about that."

He groaned with relief and pulled her into his arms.

Chapter Six

Present day

Rebecca sipped a beer while she sat on her deck. She thought back to her trip to the Wilderness beach that morning. She'd closed her store and had planned to watch the whales but she'd changed her plans after seeing the familiar Jeep. Kayleigh and her daughter were easy to spot. They were both burnt red by the sun. Rebecca caught herself smiling at the thought of Kayleigh and immediately tried to put her out of her mind.

Rebecca's house was just down the road from Judy and Lindsay's and she'd popped by earlier, after leaving the beach and visited for a few hours before returning home. Darkness crept up the ocean now as evening was settling in. She sighed in contentment, enjoying her own company and that of the Tsar's hops.

Her mind returned to Kayleigh who, with her wild, hungry green eyes and her damned straightness was nothing but trouble. She knew it and the very thought of her made Rebecca's stomach twist in knots.

"Rebecca, you don't want to go down this road," she mumbled.

†

Monday, back at work, business was hectic, which was excellent for Kayleigh's finances. By midday, she'd made enough money to cover the entire month's expenses. After closing the practice at lunchtime, she decided to visit Rebecca before fetching Sarah from school. Earlier she'd called Lindsay to find out the location of Rebecca's CD store. To her surprise, the store was directly across from her own practice. When she spotted the small, earth-colored sign for the store, she knew why she hadn't seen it before. Kayleigh made a mental note to look into neon signs for Rebecca as a welcoming gift.

Why am I so nervous? Her heart pounded away in her chest, leaving her breathless as she pushed her way into the store. Holding onto the door, Kayleigh admired Rebecca's slim features while watching her unpack a large box of CDs.

Rebecca's eyes shot up when she heard the door open and saw Kayleigh entering her store. She flashed Kayleigh a big grin. "Well, hello, neighbor." Rebecca straightened her back and groaned, causing her breasts to press tight against her T-shirt.

Kayleigh had to glance away at the sight and the orgasmic sound that Rebecca made while stretching.

"I'm happy you came," Rebecca said as she dusted her hands off by slapping them on her jeans. "I needed a break. Can I offer you some coffee?"

"I have a better idea. Let's go to Forest Lodge. I have the munchies today."

"It must be from all the sun this weekend. A severe overdose of Vitamin D."

Kayleigh laughed. "You could say that again." She rubbed her shoulder, still feeling the effects of the sunburn.

"I could actually use a bite to eat. I didn't realize it until now, but I'm starving."

"Good, then you must try their eisbein. It's massive, with lots of crispy fat."

"What? You figure that I look like I eat loads of saturated fat, huh?" Rebecca slid her hands along her narrow hips.

Kayleigh laughed at the gesture. "Actually, you look like you need it."

✝

The Forest Lodge restaurant sat behind Rebecca's store on the next street over.

"Let's see if we can get an inside table that's by the window," Kayleigh suggested as they walked up to the restaurant.

"Sounds good to me," Rebecca said as they walked inside. "I've never been here before."

"You'll love it."

Once seated, they each ordered the famous eisbein and a salad. Kayleigh ordered an extra meal to take home for Sarah.

After the waiter disappeared behind the doors marked No Entry, Rebecca looked across the table at Kayleigh. "How *is* the sunburn, by the way? I noticed you rubbing your shoulders in the store."

"Ugh. You don't want to go there. My skin feels as though a cheese grater scraped against it all night."

"I'm sorry I didn't get there sooner." Rebecca glanced down, and Kayleigh noticed her gaze resting on her chest.

"Me too. Look." Kayleigh said as she unbuttoned two of the top buttons of her shirt. She shifted the material aside in order for Rebecca to see the damage.

Rebecca inhaled. "Ouch. Painful."

"Then why are you smiling?" Kayleigh slapped Rebecca's arm playfully before she buttoned up her shirt.

"Didn't know I was. Sorry." Rebecca blushed.

The waiter returned with their food.

"Thank you," Kayleigh said with a smile before they both started digging in to their meal.

"You were right, this is delicious," Rebecca said after she swallowed a mouthful.

"I know, right? Sarah and I come here regularly. Their burgers are enormous. Next time we come here, I challenge you to finish one of those."

"Next time?" Rebecca stopped chewing for a short moment. "I'd like that."

Kayleigh warmed at the affectionate look Rebecca gave her. "Of course next time. Aren't we friends?"

"Well, I did give you sunscreen, so technically we qualify."

Just as they'd finished eating, the waiter brought Sarah's take away meal. Kayleigh reached for the bill, but Rebecca was faster. She snatched it out of the air and shoved her credit card in the waiter's hand.

"On me," Rebecca insisted.

"Hey, come on. I invited you. Besides, I made enough money today to invite the whole of Sedgefield for lunch."

"Yeah, yeah, yeah. Don't be such a show off." Rebecca's tone was playful as she waved Kayleigh's hand off. "You don't even have enough money to purchase yourself regular sunscreen, but you have enough for a big, fat eisbein?"

"I'm never going to live this one down, am I?" Kayleigh leaned forward in her chair enjoying the easy way they talked to one another. "Next time I'm paying. But for now, I want to be your very first customer for the day. Take me to your store, and I'll buy Sarah a CD."

Rebecca reached across the table and brushed Kayleigh's hand with her fingertips. "Lunch was my pleasure." She held Kayleigh's hand briefly before quickly withdrawing it.

Kayleigh slowly pulled her hand off the table and looked at her watch before gasping. It was nearly three and time to collect Sarah from school. She would only have a few minutes to find a CD.

After she followed Rebecca to her store, Kayleigh quickly browsed the CDs. She was sure there was some sort of a virus brooding somewhere inside her body since her hand still tingled from where Rebecca held it. She felt feverish as she scanned the shelves. She finally picked out a CD that was one of Sarah's favorite groups along with another one for her Jeep.

Rebecca smiled as she rung up the purchase. "Thank you," she said handing Kayleigh the bag.

"You're welcome. I've got to run or I'll be late picking Sarah up."

Kayleigh left the store and headed toward her Jeep. She hopped in, inserted one disk into the shuttle, started the engine, and then drove off to school to fetch her ultimate reason for living—Sarah.

†

Kayleigh smiled at her daughter and gave her a quick hug after she hopped in the Jeep. "How was school?" she asked.

"It was okay."

"Here, I picked this up for you." She handed Sarah the CD.

"Wow, can I listen to it now?"

"I have to go back to the clinic and order some stock. You can listen to it there."

Once they arrived back at the clinic, Sarah immediately popped her new CD into the stereo system that piped into the rooms. She sat at the counter and settled down to eat her meal. Ordering stock took Kayleigh two hours. Now that her practice was picking up pace, she needed to think again about hiring an assistant soon.

Kayleigh kept glancing at the door, trying to convince herself that she was waiting for more clients—she knew better. She was hoping for a visit from Rebecca. Something about this new friend of hers was very real and very different from all the other friends Kayleigh had ever had.

She couldn't stop thinking about lunch and the way Rebecca's eyes intrigued her. Kayleigh shook her head. It wasn't her eyes, but rather her friendly personality and the intelligent conversation that drew Kayleigh to her.

"Mom, please can I go and look at some of the other CDs?" Sarah whined after a while. "I'm bored to death just sitting here."

"Sure, sweetie. Just give me a second. I have to walk with you." Kayleigh swiftly counted her supplies in the fridge while marking down which stock she needed to order, then she closed the fridge, grabbed one of her business cards from the counter, and accompanied Sarah to Rebecca's store. During the short distance to the CD store, Kayleigh's heart rapidly picked up pace. She took a sharp intake of breath before entering the store.

†

"Hi, Sarah," Rebecca said as they entered the store.

"Hi," Sarah said. "May I look at your CDs?"

"Of course you may."

"Do you mind?" Kayleigh asked Rebecca. "You can just give me a missed call when she's done, so I can come fetch her." Kayleigh handed Rebecca her business card. Their fingers brushed as Rebecca took the card. Kayleigh steadied herself as she felt her knees weakening at the slightest touch.

"Absolutely. Sarah can stay for as long as she wants. Not a problem at all."

"Thanks. She's got nothing to do, and it would really help if she could kill some time here." She felt scrutinized as she spoke, and blushed.

✝

Once Kayleigh returned to her practice, she continued with getting the order together. She had hardly started counting when the doorbell chimed. Kayleigh turned around quickly, only to find Kenneth Berkley, a cop from the K9 Unit, walking in with his German shepherd. He brought his dog, Diesel, in every now and again for a check-up, always asking her out on a date before he left. Because she had no real feelings for him, she always declined his offers. He, on the other hand, never gave up. She disliked men who couldn't accept no for an answer. Nevertheless, he was a client, and she adored Diesel.

"Hi, Doc." Kenneth grinned at her as he entered. His brown moustache was so long that it was lower than his top lip. It looked like it must be taking jabs at his tongue every time he licked his lips. He had a nice body, probably kept fit from all the running around with his dog.

Has no-one ever told you how unsexy that moustache is? She thought to herself. *Trim it, at least, for heaven's sake. You can see yesterday's eggs for breakfast stuck between those hard facial hairs.*

"Diesel!" Kayleigh called as she bent down to scratch him right behind the ears where he loved it so much. Diesel's tail was a blur as he leaned into her legs.

"I just wanted you to check his hips again, Doc. He's struggling to get up in the mornings."

"Okay." She gave him a quick glance, avoiding too much eye contact, before giving Diesel all her attention again. "Come, boy. Let's see." She led him to the exam room.

Kayleigh palpated Diesel's hips, poked and felt them from every single angle and Diesel didn't show any sign of distress whatsoever. She turned to collect his x-rays from the cupboard and put them up against the x-ray light. She couldn't see any abnormalities.

"Do you want me to take more x-rays, Kenneth? This is the third time I've taken them and I find nothing unusual."

She wondered, seriously, if the poor dog would grow an extra eye if he endured any further radiation exposure. Kayleigh wasn't sure but wondered if he was lying about the dog having difficulties with his hips in order to get her attention. Her experience with men was that they would spin any crap story just to get into a woman's panties.

"Actually, I was hoping I could take you out for a steak or something," Kenneth confessed, finally.

As if she didn't see that one coming.

She suppressed herself from rolling her eyes. "Kenneth, you shouldn't use Diesel to pick up chicks, you know. You'll confuse him, and he's a dog of the law."

"Come on, just one date, and you'll see I'm quite a catch."

Kayleigh tossed the thought about inside her head for a second or two. She had thought she was done with men, but maybe going out on a date would be a good idea after all. Maybe she was just sexually frustrated. Casual sex was something she never indulged in, but it was possible that this was exactly what she needed. The thought of having it with Kenneth was nauseating, though. Nope, not in this lifetime.

"Can I call you on that? I have your number." She pointed toward the computer on her desk before leaving the exam room and leading them to the reception area. She needed to think this through thoroughly before she made the wrong decision. Imagine how hard it would be to get rid of him after a date.

He stepped closer and took both of her hands in his own, while Diesel wagged his tail. There was a minute of awkward silence as they stood there looking at one another. Kayleigh breathed a sigh of relief when the bell rang. Sarah came rushing in. Kayleigh let go of Kenneth's hands and turned toward her daughter. For a brief second, she caught a glimpse of Rebecca, who must have accompanied Sarah, through the glass door. When she looked again, Rebecca was gone and a feeling of disappointment filled Kayleigh.

"Mom!" Sarah exclaimed as she ran toward her, "There are so many cool CDs there. Please can we go there some time with your wallet?"

Sarah shot Kenneth a quick glance before she crouched by Diesel. "Hey, boy, I missed you." Sarah scratched him behind the ears. Diesel closed his eyes as his tongue bungee jumped from his open mouth.

"We'll go in just a moment, sweetie."

Kenneth's face dropped as he put Diesel's leash back on. "I guess I'll wait by the phone for your call then."

Kayleigh watched him walk out of the office with his shoulders slumped. Men.

"Can we go now, Mommy? Please?" Sarah bounced up and down.

"As soon as I'm done, baby. I have stock to order, remember? Otherwise, I'll have to use a pan to anaesthetize the animals next week. You know the bang over the head method?"

Sarah giggled. "You wouldn't."

"Here, let me show you how it's done." Kayleigh took her cup and chased Sarah around the counter. Sarah laughed and ran into the examination room. By the time Kayleigh had finished ordering stock, it was dark. She called Sarah from the back, who had kept herself busy drawing pictures of Diesel, and locked up shop. She took a deep breath and then headed off to the CD store with Sarah by her side. Much to her disappointment, the doors were already locked, the lights were off, and Rebecca was nowhere in sight.

Without saying goodbye, Kayleigh thought miserably. Disappointment crawled through her veins, although she knew she had no right to feel that way.

Embarrassed by her own reaction, she turned to Sarah. "I'm so sorry, sweetie. We should've come earlier." They walked to the Jeep and as Kayleigh unlocked the doors, Graham approached on his scooter. He slowed down to a stop and lifted the visor of his helmet.

"How's the new place?" he asked, his words muffled by the piece of the helmet that still covered his mouth.

"Loving it." She beamed at him. "Do you have any idea if the owners want to sell? If they're interested, I'd like to have first option."

Graham removed his helmet. "I have no idea. I'll find out from him and let you know."

"Oh, and by the way, the roof leaks. We need someone to come out real soon."

"Of course. I'll contact the owner and inform him."

They continued their chat for a while longer about the deposit and minor points concerning the contract. Graham agreed again to contact the owner to send a contractor to her house as soon as possible. After they said their goodbyes,

Graham left on his motorcycle, and Kayleigh and Sarah proceeded to their house.

✝

When Kayleigh unlocked the door, Sarah snuck past her down the hallway and sprinted straight up to her room.

"Don't run in the house!" Kayleigh called out after her. That was rule number four in their book of rules.

Kayleigh went to the bathroom and stripped for a shower. After their big lunch, neither of them would want dinner. Kayleigh thought they'd have some ice cream and sit outside on the patio until it was bedtime.

Kayleigh stepped under the shower spray and thought again about Rebecca. She wasn't used to thinking nonstop about her friends. She felt like a child with a new pet or toy. Rebecca's a new friend. It was normal to think about a new friend all the time. Wasn't it?

The warm water from the shower felt great on her tired muscles. After she'd lathered herself down with soap, she closed her eyes and allowed the water to soak her face and her hair. She lifted her chin toward the spraying water. An image entered Kayleigh's mind of Rebecca stretching, her breasts pressing hard against her T-shirt.

Okay... where did that come from?

Kayleigh shook away the image as if she was shaking away the water in her hair. Instead, she focused on how sweet, sincere, and full of energy Rebecca was. Those thoughts were much safer.

The unexpected feel of a clammy, claw-like hand on her neck made her jerk around in terror. The pressure on her neck was unmistakable. It had felt exactly like an icy human hand, but there was no one there. She leapt out of the shower and grabbed a towel to cover her body. Water ran down her skin and pooled on the floor. Fear gripped her insides. She reached for the sink, where she heaved and gagged into the drain. Her legs shook violently, and she struggled to stand without them giving way from underneath her. Lifting her head from the basin, she raked her surroundings again—her eyes wide with dread.

"Oh, my God. You've *gotta* be fuckin' kidding me," she whispered to the emptiness that surrounded her. She grabbed her gown and wrapped it around her, not caring that she still hadn't dried off. She turned off the water before she left the bathroom and hurried to see if Sarah was safe. Kayleigh's heart was beating insanely fast, her chest aching from hyperventilating. She paused for a moment at the foot of the stairs to catch her breath and ease her dizziness. She pushed back another wave of nausea.

"Sarah?" she called out, as she scuttled up the stairway. Sarah wasn't in her room. Kayleigh panicked. "Sarah!"

"I'm in the kitchen, Mom!" Sarah called back from downstairs. "I'm making you some tea."

Kayleigh breathed a sigh of relief as she turned toward the kitchen, water still dripping from her long hair. Sarah was standing on her tippy toes, reaching for the tea bag jar. With the jar finally in hand, she turned around to face her mom. "Jeez, Mommy. You look like you've just seen a ghost."

Kayleigh collapsed in a chair and tried again to control her breathing. The last thing she wanted to do was scare Sarah. "Tea sounds great, love. Thanks. Just let me pour the hot water. I don't want you to get burned." She managed to keep her voice calm, even though her heart was still slamming away in her chest.

She got up on shaky legs and added two spoons of brown sugar with cold milk before adding the hot water. She was in desperate need for some glucose to soothe her nerves.

After stirring it, she sat down again and started downing the warm liquid. It took her only a minute to finish the tea. When she looked up at Sarah, she saw that her daughter was staring at her as though she'd gone nuts.

"It was so delicious, I couldn't stop," Kayleigh said, before she placed the empty mug down on the table.

†

Kayleigh spent half the night tossing and turning and the other half placing buckets around the house. The house was obviously not rain proof, and between that and the problems getting settled, she hardly got much sleep. When her alarm went off at six o'clock the following morning, she struggled to get out of bed. The bags under her eyes were a dead giveaway. She splashed her face with cold water, brushed her teeth, and went to Sarah's room to wake her, only to find an empty bed.

"What now...?" Kayleigh descended the stairway to the kitchen. Sarah was up and fully dressed. She sat at the kitchen table with drawings scattered in front of her. Kayleigh frowned and looked down at Sarah, who was in an obvious trance. She seemed to be drawing the same picture repeatedly.

"What are you drawing, honey?" Kayleigh asked. Not wanting to startle her, she gently touched Sarah's shoulder.

Sarah stopped scribbling suddenly, leaving the trance as her eyes shot up to look at her mother. As Sarah's eyes darted around the kitchen, it was obvious to Kayleigh that she clearly had no idea of where she was. Sarah's gaze went down to the pictures she'd drawn, and she frowned. "I don't know, Mommy. I came down to have breakfast, and...."

Kayleigh picked a few pictures up off the table and stared at them. They were all the same—a square with a half-moon handle on one side of each square.

"You mean you didn't know you were drawing these?"

"I'm sorry, Mommy." Sarah was close to tears.

"It's all right, my angel." Kayleigh placed the pictures back down on the table and bent to embrace and comfort Sarah. Kayleigh was close to a breaking point. All she ever wanted was a bigger house—not all the supernatural crap that obviously accompanied this one.

✝

It was just before eight o'clock when Kayleigh entered the CD store. With insomnia leaving her vulnerable, her heart pounded in her throat when she spied Rebecca.

The shop itself looked magnificent. Rebecca had been working on it. She'd stacked all the shelves with CDs and had hung paintings of music legends. A big sign that read Wall of Fame hung on one wall. She'd placed three couches of different colors around the shop. Their funky green, red, and orange colors made the place look very hip. Music blasted from massive speakers mounted next to the CD shelves. Those few changes would definitely put the CD shop on the map. And soon.

Rebecca spotted Kayleigh and lowered the volume on the music system. "Oh, my goodness, woman. Pardon me for saying so, but you look awful. What the hell happened?"

"Thanks," Kayleigh said, not hiding her sarcasm. Then she burst into uncontrollable sobs.

"I didn't mean to...." Rebecca rushed up to her, placed an arm around her, and guided her to the red couch. "Sit down. Tell me now. What happened?" Her voice was gentle. She placed both her hands on Kayleigh's shoulders and pushed her down onto the couch, sat down next to her, and placed her arm around Kayleigh. "Did someone hurt you? Tell me, I'll go and fuck their shit up for them," Rebecca said, her voice laced with anger.

"No, no... it's nothing like that... I can't tell you... you'll think I'm totally wacko....," Kayleigh managed to stutter out around her sobs.

"Try me." Rebecca got up, went to the door, and locked it. Then she pulled a tissue from the counter before she sat down next to Kayleigh again. She handed her the tissue and gently put a hand on Kayleigh's leg. Kayleigh tried hard to maintain her composure and to control her breathing. Wiping her eyes and her nose, she looked up at Rebecca.

"I think my house is haunted." She shook her head as she realized what she must sound like. "First I heard Sarah talk while she was fast asleep, then something touched me in the shower, but there was no one there. This morning, Sarah was in a trance drawing weird pictures without knowing it." She went on to explain all the incidents in detail, while Rebecca stared into her eyes.

"I'm sure there's a logical explanation for all this," Rebecca said finally. "Maybe you're both just tired from the move. Besides, it's a very old house. Old houses tend to croak a lot."

Kayleigh laughed at the term. "They croak, you say."

Rebecca gave her a quirky smile. "Yes, croak. Do you want me to come home with you tonight? I can have a look around for you. Debunk everything for you." Rebecca's voice was full of concern. "I'm a skeptic, so I'll find the reason for all these experiences."

"I sound like a real coward, I know. But I just can't say no to that offer right now. I'm scared shitless. I have a child for heaven's sake, and I'm so frightened that something could happen to her."

"Kay, no problemo. I shalt accompany thou to su casa later." Rebecca grinned at her.

"Oh, but I close doors at three pm. You close at five, right?"

Rebecca nodded.

"Can I give you directions and then you can come by for dinner and a drink?" Kayleigh's voice shook. She always asked friends over, why should this one feel so different? "Or I can come and pick you up so you don't have to drive on an unknown road."

"I'll be fine, thank you very much. You haven't seen me drive that Mini Cooper of mine though hills and trees before, have you?" Rebecca paused and swallowed loudly before taking a deep breath. "I'd drive through fire for you, Kay."

†

Immediately after Kayleigh left Rebecca's store, she went for a quick visit at the estate agent's office, which was only a block from her practice.

She took a few breaths to calm herself down before entering his office. "Hi, Graham."

"Kayleigh, I was just about to call you. So glad you popped in."

"I hope it was with regards to the roof. It needs fixing today, or else Sarah and I are going to need other accommodation."

"I actually have a contractor ready to go fix it now."

"Great. There's no one at the house today. Can I just leave my keys with you?"

"That would be perfect. I'll have them back to you by this afternoon. This guy is very good and he has a whole team who helps, so it will be all done by this afternoon. I'll go with them so you needn't worry about anything.

Kayleigh, I'm really sorry, I had no idea the house was in such a bad state."

"As long as it can be repaired, I'll be happy, Graham. I really don't feel like moving again so soon." As she was about to leave, she remembered. "Oh, and please ask your contractor to check the insulation. One of the rooms is very cold."

"Will do, Kayleigh. See you later then, love."

"Thank you. See you later."

Chapter Seven

1896

"Good morning, sweetness," Catherine murmured as they awoke. She rolled over and with her fingertips, touched Joshua's muscular and tanned back. Joshua turned around and slid his hands up and down her slender back.

"Happy one year anniversary, my lovely," he said and kissed her. He reached to the bedside table and took something out of the top drawer. It was a gold chain with a golden locket in the shape of a heart. He struggled for a short while with the clip before he opened it and Catherine bent her head so he could place it around her neck.

"This is so beautiful," she said looking at the necklace. She gave him a long warm kiss. When she opened it, she saw two photos inside, one of her and one of him.

"It's symbolic of our love. Whenever you get lonely, I want you to open it and remember this day."

She beamed at him. "And when would I ever get lonely, my love? You're always around." There was a twinkle in her eyes before she added, "Do you mind if I remove the photo of me and replace it with a photo of me with our baby instead?"

"Well, of course not. One day when we have a baby, we will have a photo taken with all of us and I'll have it fitted for you." He noticed the expression on her face. "Wait a minute...."

Catherine grinned at him and nodded.

Joshua grabbed her and pulled her close. "We're going to have a baby!"

"Oh yes. Congratulations, my love!"

"I love you, more than life itself," he whispered and kissed her.

"I love you too, my husband. Together forever."

"Always and forever." He gently placed his hand on her stomach. "How long have you known?" he asked as tears welled in his eyes.

"I went to the doctor last week. I'm so sorry I didn't tell you sooner, but I wanted to wait for the perfect moment to surprise you. You can't imagine how hard it was not to blurt it out on so many occasions."

"This is wonderful news. How are you feeling?" He jumped out of bed before she could answer. "I must feed you and the baby. Come now, my love. I'm going to make you a hearty breakfast."

"You know we have servants for that, dear. Besides, I think Evelyn might be a better cook," she said, teasingly.

"I'm going to take such good care of you." He knelt by the bed and touched her stomach again. "I'll get Evelyn to scramble you up some eggs and make toast."

Chapter Eight

Present day

I'd drive through fire for you, Kay....

That remark replayed in Kayleigh's mind all the way home. She took a deep breath to shake it off as she unlocked the front door.

The day at the practice had dragged on. Kayleigh hoped she'd given all the right injections, though she double and sometimes tripled checked each time. With all that was going on at her house, and the thought of Rebecca coming over later, she couldn't keep her focus on work. At three, Graham had returned her keys and promised that the leaks had been sealed. He was a bit pale when she saw him and she wondered if anything supernatural had happened while they were at her house.

After closing for the day, she'd stopped at the store to buy the ingredients for the chicken a la king she was going to make, plus a bottle of wine for them to enjoy on the patio. Sarah was very excited that the CD-lady was coming for a visit. So excited in fact, she helped her mom clean and cook dinner without any of her usual fuss.

With the previous encounter in the bathroom still on her mind, Kayleigh barely managed to set aside her fear long enough to step into the shower. Thoughts of Rebecca and the dinner she'd planned helped get her mind off the spooky events, however. She was grateful for the temporary diversion. She finished showering, relieved that nothing happened to scare her witless again. After she brushed her teeth, she helped Sarah shower and then got dressed. Sarah had insisted on wearing a fancy white dress with matching sandals for this special occasion.

Now, it was Kayleigh's turn to pick what to wear. She stood in front of her closet and frowned, before choosing a pair of ripped jeans and a tight green top. Her cleavage protruded above the low dip of her top, but she felt like showing the girls off and didn't want to think about the why. To add some height, she slipped into her black leather boots with the two-inch heel. She rubbed some anti-aging cream under her eyes, added some eyeliner and mascara before brushing her hair so that it lay across her slim shoulders. With a final look in the mirror, she was satisfied with the results.

Sarah watched her from Kayleigh's bed. "You look so beautiful, Mom."

"Thanks, sweetie pie. You look prettier than a princess does. Got a date I should know about? Travis, was that his name? Or Tristan?" She winked at Sarah.

"No! Ewww! Boys drool!" Sarah wrinkled her nose.

Kayleigh giggled. "That's what you say now. Wait 'til you get older."

Sarah's compliment pleased her. She caught herself wondering whether Rebecca would also like the way she looked. It was nice to have a friend who was all alone like herself. A friend who understood what life was about when you had no one else.

As she was on her way down the stairs, the doorbell rang and Kayleigh's heart skipped a beat. She breathed in deeply before opening the door with shaky hands. She was nervous, and afraid of making a fool of herself in front of Rebecca.

"Hi." Rebecca greeted her with a smile. But then her lips faltered and her eyes widened. Her gaze went from Kayleigh's face, slowly down her body, and back up. "You look so sexy," she whispered.

Kayleigh blushed. "Thanks. What a nice compliment." She breathed in Rebecca's scent before taking in her appearance. Jeans hugged Rebecca's perfect figure, and her black turtle neck sweater fit her like a second skin. Kayleigh's mouth suddenly went dry. "You don't look so bad yourself."

Rebecca waved the bottle of wine she was holding. "Maybe this will help our nervousness."

"Oh, great," Kayleigh said. "You brought the entrance fee." She took the bottle and stepped back so that Rebecca could enter. "Now we can be drunk when we piss the ghosts, or whatever it is, off."

Sarah came rushing down the stairs. "It's the CD lady!" She ran up to Rebecca and hugged her waist.

"You can call me Aunt Rebecca, if that's okay." Rebecca glanced at Kayleigh for approval. "Look what I have for you, kiddo." Rebecca removed a CD from her bag.

Sarah shrieked. "Oh, thanks so much," she said as she immediately ran and shoved it into the hi-fi system, pressing play. With the volume at almost full blast, Sarah started dancing to the beat.

Kayleigh flashed a grin in Rebecca's direction and shook her head. "And that's what I'll be listening to for the rest of the month." She motioned for Rebecca to follow her. "Come with me. Maybe it will be quieter in the kitchen.

"I'm sorry. I should've asked you first if it was okay—"

"No, no, no, it's fine. I actually promised her the other day that I would buy her another CD, but with all the drama, it slipped my mind. It's a very sweet gesture, though. Thank you."

Kayleigh set the bottle of Pinot Noir on the kitchen counter and went to a cabinet for wine glasses. Once she stripped away the wrapper, she uncorked the bottle and poured the wine. Kayleigh handed Rebecca a glass before taking one for herself.

"I thought you might need some sort of a sedative and what better way to calm your nerves than with alcohol?" Rebecca winked before taking a sip.

Kayleigh laughed. "You're so right. By the way, I ordered you something for your store."

"Oh?"

"A massive neon sign. It's as big as the titanic. No one can miss it, not even the blind. You need to be more visible, for better business."

"Kayleigh, that's much too generous. Please, let me pay you something."

Kayleigh shook her head. "Nope. It's a gift from one friend to another."

Rebecca looked ecstatic. "Well, thank you, Kay. It's such a thoughtful gift."

She set her glass down and took Kayleigh's glass from her and placed it on the table. She stepped closer and pulled Kayleigh into a hug.

Kayleigh settled easily into the embrace. Her heart thumped wildly in her chest and it was hard for her to pull away from Rebecca's warm arms. With difficulty, she stepped back while trying hard to calm down her breathing.

"The guy will call you tomorrow and make installation arrangements with you. You'll see—business should pick up now." She went to the stove and stirred the pot of food. "Dinner's practically ready. Shall we go sit outside on the patio and relax for a bit before we eat?"

Rebecca moved closer to Kayleigh and tried to look into the pot. "What are we having? It smells wonderful."

Kayleigh shivered as she felt Rebecca's breath in her neck. "Chicken a la king. I hope that's okay.

"One of my favorites." Rebecca placed a hand on the small of Kayleigh's back. "The patio sounds great to me."

Rebecca quickly removed her hand and waved it in the air. "But you'll have to show me the way."

"Of course." They picked up their glasses, and Kayleigh led the way to the wooden deck that overlooked Wilderness. There was a cozy patio swing tucked in the far corner, and a small patio table with four wooden chairs neatly stashed in the middle.

"Oh, wow. This is one amazing view." Rebecca walked to the edge of the patio and leaned into the railing.

Kayleigh followed and stood beside her. "I love it here. I don't want anything to scare us away."

"You know, I was thinking of everything you told me. You said Sarah was sleeping when you heard her talking. Could it be that she was talking in her sleep?"

Kayleigh nodded slowly. "Yeah, I suppose that's possible. It's what I thought was happening at first but...."

"But what?" Rebecca asked.

Kayleigh shrugged. "After seeing the weird drawings, I really didn't believe it was possible that she was talking in her sleep." She looked at Rebecca welcoming any reassurance to make her feel better about her current situation. "How do you explain the shower incident?"

"It could be that your neck muscles tensed and it felt like a hand touching you."

"It felt like a cold claw actually, but go on." Kayleigh made a motion with her free hand as she took a sip of wine. "I'm listening. How do you explain Sarah's bizarre drawings?"

"Mind showing them to me?" Rebecca eyes were luminous in in the evening light.

"Sure." Kayleigh placed her glass down on the table. "I'll be right back. They're in the TV room where I stashed them earlier."

After retrieving the drawings, Kayleigh took a quick peek inside the living room where Sarah was still dancing while attempting to read the lyrics that came along with the CD. Kayleigh warmed at the sight and left for the patio.

"Thanks for coming over and being here for me. I could never tell Lindsay all these things. She'd think I've gone completely mad." She handed Rebecca the drawings.

"Anything for a free meal. At only a nominal small fee, I can also play ghost hunter." Rebecca took the pictures and started scanning through them.

Kayleigh relaxed a little and playfully smacked Rebecca on the arm. "You're such a brat. Doesn't anyone cook you dinner—ever?"

"Nope." Rebecca frowned as she studied the drawings. "These drawings are creepy—you got that right. You mentioned she was in a trance when she drew them?"

"Completely." Kayleigh stood next to Rebecca at the railing, examining the drawings with her. She felt Rebecca's warmth radiating from her body and leaned in a little to absorb some of the comfort she was emitting.

"Looks like some sort of a lid or maybe a square box. I don't know. What do you think?"

"Yeah, it does look like a box. But why would she draw so many of them?"

Rebecca frowned. "And you said that Sarah had no idea what they were either?"

"She was as shocked as I was about them."

The lump in Kayleigh's throat made it hard for her to breathe. She'd been anxious all day, but denial had kept her at bay. Now, reality was slapping her in the face.

"I can't really debunk these pictures, unless Sarah dreamt of something weird and subconsciously drew dozens of them," Rebecca said.

"Can I put them away now?" Kayleigh shuddered before she reached for the drawings in Rebecca's hand. Their fingers touched for a brief second, and she gasped as the sudden flow of energy between them caught her off guard.

Rebecca inhaled sharply and let her hand drop down to the railing.

There was a short moment of silence between them before Kayleigh left to put the drawings away. A few seconds later she reappeared, picked up her glass of wine, and returned to her spot next to Rebecca.

They stood still for a while appreciating God's creation—the view as well as one another's presence. The thumping sound of footsteps on the wooden patio coming up behind them made them both jump around. It was only Sarah.

"Mommy, when can we eat?"

"Oh, yes, let me go dish up," she said before glancing at Rebecca and laughing. Kayleigh leaned into Rebecca and whispered to her. "You were scared."

Rebecca shook her head.

"Yes, you were." She dug her fingers into Rebecca's side, trying to tickle her playfully.

"Yeah? So were you." Rebecca fought her off as they both giggled like school girls.

†

After dishing up, they returned to the patio. While they ate, Rebecca and Kayleigh spoke about business and how to advertise. The wine, or maybe even the company, made Kayleigh relax completely. She couldn't believe she'd been so nervous about the evening. After they ate, Sarah ran back to the lounge to listen and dance to her new CD.

Rebecca laughed at Kayleigh's facial expression when Sarah skipped the CD to the beginning again. "Maybe I should get her an MP3 player, so she can listen to her music on earphones."

She stood up and motioned toward the house. "Come. Give me a grand tour. Maybe I'll find something."

Kayleigh got up and followed Rebecca inside. Once inside, Rebecca motioned for Kayleigh to lead the way. As she walked, she could sense Rebecca's eyes on her. She stopped and turned around to face Rebecca, as she did so, Rebecca nearly crashed straight into her. Rebecca halted and swayed forward at the sudden stop.

"Traffic pile up," Rebecca muttered, sounding out of breath.

"I'm so sorry. I didn't realize you were so close behind me."

"Your brake lights don't work by the way."

"Keep a safe following distance," Kayleigh teased. "Shall we start with the shower?" She headed for the bathroom, and Rebecca followed. As they made it to the bathroom doorway, Kayleigh reached for the light switch. Rebecca quickly grabbed for Kayleigh's hand in order to stop her.

"Don't," Rebecca whispered, and in their closeness, her breasts brushed against Kayleigh's back as their hands met. Kayleigh was surprised at how the sudden contact made her heart flip. Rebecca's nipples were hard, and she could feel them poking her through their tops. She struggled to regain her composure as she stood still and absorbed the flow of heat from Rebecca. She closed her eyes for a second, not understanding the reason for the throbbing between her legs. She could feel Rebecca's breath on her neck, and with her eyes closed, she turned her head to the side slowly, absorbing Rebecca's closeness.

Rebecca took a step back and lowered her hand. She cleared her throat. "Keep the light off. If there's a presence in here, it might be able to make contact with us in the dark."

"Why do you think that is?" Kayleigh tried to calm her breathing.

"I don't know. That's the way it always happens on TV, isn't it?"

Kayleigh chuckled softly, and as she inhaled, she snorted. Rebecca burst out in nervous laughter as well.

"Don't make them angry now. Remember, you must still sleep in this house tonight," Rebecca reminded her. Kayleigh stopped laughing as suddenly as she'd started. Her eyes fixed on something inside the bathroom.

Rebecca, still looking at Kayleigh asked, "What is it?"

"Did you see that?" The fear was evident in her voice.

Rebecca followed Kayleigh's gaze to where she was looking and shook her head. "What did you see?"

"A large shadow, it looked like a man."

Rebecca brushed past Kayleigh and entered the bathroom, Kayleigh right behind her. As she walked, she felt the wetness between her legs from their earlier contact, wondering how she could be aroused and frightened at the same time.

"It's colder in here than it is out there, but it could be that the window doesn't seal properly." Rebecca was trying her best to reassure Kayleigh. "It could be the wind that blew the curtain and you saw the shadow of that perhaps?"

Rebecca stood in front of the shower and faced Kayleigh.

"Yeah, that must be it. Come on, let's get out of here." Kayleigh shivered. She wanted nothing more than to get away from the bathroom before she made a total fool of herself. Being so turned on and frightened, she feared what she might do to Rebecca in the close proximity of the small room.

"Sure." Rebecca seemed relieved to be leaving the room.

✝

They continued up the stairs. As they reached the top of the landing, Rebecca stopped and shuddered.

"What's wrong?" Kayleigh asked.

"I feel like I'm not wanted here for some odd reason."

"You are wanted here, all right? Don't get all sorts of stupid ideas in that head of yours."

Rebecca shook her head. "Not by you, it's as if the *house* doesn't want me here. Do you know what I mean?"

"No, not really... would you rather we stop?"

"I'm not backing out now and leaving you here all by yourself. I came here to help you, and that's exactly what I intend to do." Rebecca looked at Kayleigh's frightened expression and wished she could find a way to protect her from her fears. At first, she had thought Kayleigh was imagining everything, but seeing her in this state, she knew some of it must be real. When she had agreed to come to dinner, she only used the alleged ghost as an excuse to spend some more time with Kayleigh.

"This way to Sarah's room." She heard Kayleigh say while she followed her up the stairway.

As they entered Sarah's room, Rebecca winced. "My God, it's freezing in here. Maybe you should check the insulation?"

"I know, right? There was a contractor here today who sealed the roof and checked the insulation. He said everything was fine."

Rebecca walked over and sat down on Sarah's bed. She patted the space beside her and Kayleigh sat next to her. The room was dark, but the light from downstairs made it possible for her to see Kayleigh. Rebecca touched Kayleigh's arm gently and searched her eyes in the semi-darkness.

"I don't know what to say to make this easier for you. I can see that you're upset by all the strange things going on here. I really wish I could help you, but I'm not sure how. I get a very uneasy feeling about the place and I don't think the two of you are safe. Maybe you should find another house and just move out."

"No way. I love it here and so does Sarah. There has got to be another way besides us leaving."

Rebecca sighed and stood. "All right. Show me your bedroom then." She watched Kayleigh's perfect form move ahead of her and ached to touch her.

†

Kayleigh led the way down the passage and stepped aside to allow Rebecca to enter the room first. She watched Rebecca walk into the room and was amazed at how brave Rebecca was, knowing what she did of the unusual incidents happening in the house.

"Have you had any experiences in here?" Rebecca asked.

"None," Kayleigh answered quickly. Just the thought of what could possibly happen made her petrified. She still had to sleep here tonight. She started backing out of the room. "Shall we go back downstairs and drink our wine?"

"Pardon the pun, but you look like you've seen a ghost." Rebecca laughed at her own joke, trying to lighten the mood.

Kayleigh shook her head. "I don't want to do this anymore. It's making me feel very uneasy, and I still live here."

"You're more than welcome to come over and stay at my place until you've found another house," Rebecca said as she followed Kayleigh toward the staircase.

Kayleigh stopped and turned around. "That's a sweet offer, and as tempting as it sounds to run away from this thing, I'm a grown woman and I need to face whatever *this* is. Besides, I signed a very to-the-point legal contract which states clearly that I may not vacate the premises until the twelve months are up."

"Wow. That's unusual. Did the agent say why?"

"Apparently, previous tenants upped and left without notice, leaving the place neglected and in a bad state. The owner wanted to avoid that from happening again."

"Yeah... I wonder why...." Rebecca rolled her eyes. "We can find a way out of the contract for you if you want."

"No, Sarah and I will be all right," Kayleigh said, her voice not sounding very convincing.

Everything was as they'd left it downstairs, Sarah was still dancing to the music, unaware of what was going on. The only thing out of place was Rebecca's wine glass, which had fallen over and the wine dripped like blood through the spaces on the wooden tabletop.

"Oh, my God. It must have been the wind. Let me go grab a cloth." Kayleigh rushed to the kitchen. Rebecca took the cloth from Kayleigh and mopped up the mess.

Kayleigh poured Rebecca another glass in the hope that she could keep her there longer.

"Thanks," Rebecca said and took a long sip. She placed the glass down carefully in front of her. "How old is this house anyway? It looks like it's about hundred years old, at least."

"I don't have any history on the house. I've been meaning to ask the agent to give me the owner's number so I can find out what the back-story is. I don't think Graham will give me the name, though. It goes against their *confidentiality policy*." At the mention of the last two words, she raised her hands and made imaginary quotes.

"There's always the municipality or the library in George, you know. I can help you search for info if you'd like."

Kayleigh shrugged. "I wouldn't know where to start looking. The municipality will only give me the info if I'm the current owner."

"I'll try and help you in any way I possibly can."

"That would be nice. I need to find old newspaper clippings too, but I don't know where to start searching."

"We'll get to the bottom of all this, don't you worry." Rebecca sounded sincere. She examined her watch and sighed. "I can't believe the time. It has just rushed away from us. I'd better leave before I overstay my welcome."

"You could never do that."

"Thanks, but I really should go."

After thanking Kayleigh and Sarah for the meal, Rebecca left. As her car reversed out of the driveway, Kayleigh shivered. She wrapped her arms around herself and hugged tightly. She had no idea how she was going to sleep with everything that had happened. The thought of anything happening in her room scared her senseless and she feared what Sarah might be going through. She wished she'd asked Rebecca to stay

Chapter Nine

1896

Joshua kept his promise to treat Catherine like a jewel.

"Honey, what are you doing?" Joshua had been in the field all morning, working with his cattle, and when he came home, he found Catherine outside by the washing line.

She spun around when she heard his voice. "Nothing much, just helping with the washing."

"I told you, I don't want you doing these things. Come inside, let's go have some tea." He took her gently by the arm and guided her inside the house.

"I can't sit around all day and do nothing, I need to do something." She spoke while she walked beside him toward the kitchen.

"I know, but we need to think of the baby."

"You are a good husband, Joshua. I know you're just taking care of me, but please understand, I'm not used to people doing everything for me."

"Once the baby is born, you can do whatever you want around the farm." He sat her down by the table and asked the cook to make some tea. "I just want you and our baby to be safe."

She smiled at him. "I know, my love."

Chapter Ten

Present day

In the two weeks since Rebecca and Kayleigh went looking for answers to what was happening in her house, Kayleigh had no new weird experiences.

One morning, she was out of bed and in the shower a half–an-hour before the alarm went off. She was already dressed in a pair of jeans and black T-shirt when she heard the playing of the annoying alarm's tune. She put some color to her face and added eyeliner with mascara. She even sprayed on some extra perfume. It was just for luck, she told herself, but deep down she knew it was because she was seeing Rebecca later.

Whistling, she walked out of her room and started down the hallway toward Sarah's room. She was light on her feet and felt like singing and dancing. Sarah was up, her voice trailing down the hall. Sarah's bedroom door was partially opened, just enough for Kayleigh to pop her head in through the gap. Sarah sat on her bed and was busy talking to the space in front of her—to something that wasn't there. The hair on Kayleigh's arms rose, and chills traveled up and down her spine. At first she wondered if Sarah was talking to her doll again, but noticed the doll was on top of the toy box stashed in the corner.

"Who are you talking to, sweetie?" Kayleigh opened the door wider and entered the room. She sat down in the spot that Sarah was talking to a few seconds ago. The air felt cool, but it always did in Sarah's room so she wasn't concerned.

"Be careful, Mom!" Sarah jumped up and pushed Kayleigh off the spot. Kayleigh had to catch herself to keep from falling onto the floor.

"What?"

"You sat on top of her!"

"On top of whom?"

"Carrey!"

The goose bumps ran all the way down Kayleigh's neck, and the nausea she felt the other night in the shower overwhelmed her again. "Sarah, who's Carrey?" Kayleigh tried to steady her breathing and keep her voice gentle to not startle Sarah.

"The little girl," Sarah said and pointed to the edge of the bed.

"What little girl, sweetheart?" Kayleigh's eyes raked the room—nothing was different.

"That little—" Sarah looked very confused. "She was there just a second ago, I swear, Mom. I saw her—".

"It's all right, baby. I believe you." Kayleigh leaned in and gave her a comforting hug. "Did she say anything?"

"Not much." Sarah concentrated on her hands in her lap.

Kayleigh took hold of her daughter's hands. She was still so small and fragile. Sometimes Kayleigh forgot that Sarah was only eight years old and tended to treat her more like an adult. She leaned forward letting go of Sarah's hands and wrapped her arms around her thin shoulders. "I love you, baby girl, don't you ever forget that."

Why was this spirit being so damn pushy? Why couldn't it just leave them alone? What if it was evil? "Let's go and have some breakfast, shall we?"

The excitement Kayleigh had felt upon waking had now disappeared—as if someone had suddenly switched off a light inside of her. She went through her morning chores on autopilot, too afraid to ask Sarah more about this alleged Carrey. She just wanted to go to work and have the day she'd been anticipating—working and then having lunch with Rebecca.

After breakfast, Kayleigh cleaned up before driving Sarah to school. Sarah seemed very uneasy when Kayleigh leaned to kiss her goodbye.

"Are you all right, sweetheart?" Kayleigh asked as she hugged her close. She was at a loss as to what to ask about the girl named Carrey.

Sarah started crying. "No, Mom. I promise. She was there. I don't know where she disappeared to."

"I believe you, baby. I really do believe you." Kayleigh looked into Sarah's eyes and whispered it again. "I believe you."

"But you didn't see her. Why didn't you see her? She was right there and you sat on top of her. You went right through her," Sarah cried.

"I don't know, sweetheart. I'm sorry, I wish I could have seen her." Kayleigh shook her head. "I think you're just so special that only you can see her. Maybe she only wants you to see her."

That seemed to calm Sarah down and after one more hug, she climbed out of the car and walked into the school.

Kayleigh had to find out what was causing all the shit that had suddenly started to disrupt their lives, before things got any worse.

✝

Rebecca was at the store when Kayleigh drove into her parking spot. She hopped out of the Jeep and pressed the button to lock the doors when she heard the familiar deep, husky voice.

"Hi," Rebecca called from the door. "Do you have time for a cup of coffee?"

Kayleigh faked a smile and walked up to her. "Sure," she said before brushing past her and entering the CD store. "How are you today?" But before Rebecca could answer, she said, "You missed the commotion this morning."

"No. Not again…What happened?" Rebecca looked horrified.

"*Carrey* is what happened."

"All right…who the hell is Carrey?"

"Well, I'll be damned if I know. Ask Sarah." Kayleigh swallowed hard.

Rebecca shifted closer and wrapped her arms around her. "My God, you're in shock. You're actually shaking."

Kayleigh put her arms around Rebecca and held onto her. She eagerly absorbed all the comfort that Rebecca offered.

Rebecca positioned her head back far enough to look into Kayleigh's eyes. Rebecca's dark bangs were in her blue eyes. "Tell me what happened?"

"Sarah saw a little girl, even spoke to her. The girl's name is Carrey." Kayleigh's hands dropped to her sides. Rebecca let go of her as Kayleigh dragged herself to the red couch and plopped down onto it. "This has gone too far. They can mess with me, but not with my daughter," she said, punctuating each word by slamming her fist into the cushion of the couch.

"I'm really very sorry, Kay, but think about it. At least we have a name to go by. It may not be nice, but it's progress." Rebecca picked up her cordless office phone and handed it to Kayleigh. "Here, call the guy."

"Which guy? Who am I going to call, Ghost Busters?"

Rebecca laughed. "No, silly. Graham."

Kayleigh felt drained as she took the phone. With shaky fingers, she dug Graham's card out of her wallet and dialed the number. She tucked her right foot under her body as she made herself comfortable on the couch.

Graham answered after the third ring.

"Hello, Graham, this is Kayleigh. How are you doing today?" she asked politely.

"I'm doing well."

"That's good to hear. Listen, the reason I'm calling is I need the name and number of the owner of the house, please."

Graham was silent for a while. "Um, why, Kayleigh?"

"I want to… make an offer to purchase," she lied.

"I still don't know if the place is up for sale. I'll call my client and ask him if he minds me giving out his personal information. Or what I can do is give him your number, if you don't mind, then he can contact you directly?"

"That would be great, please ask him to call me as soon as possible. Thank you, Graham."

Kayleigh ended the call and looked up at Rebecca. "The owner will call me."

"Yeah, right," Rebecca said as she rolled her eyes. "When?" She must have noticed Kayleigh's discontented expression.

"Didn't you promise me coffee?" Kayleigh asked as she took the phone to the docking station before returning to her favorite couch.

"Of course." Rebecca poured two mugs of coffee from the percolator, added some milk, and handed Kayleigh a mug. She sat next to Kayleigh and placed her hand on Kayleigh's arm. "Everything will be all right," she added softly. "That I promise you."

"Thanks, Rebecca, for all your support." Kayleigh held up her mug. "Oh, and thanks for the brew."

"My pleasure. I like you. I'll do anything for you," Rebecca said, her hand still on Kayleigh's arm.

Rebecca's words, and her touch, made her stomach twist with excitement. Her breath caught in her throat. Kayleigh was very aware of how close Rebecca was to her. She drank her coffee slowly while she watched her office door—no clients yet. "I have to open at nine, because I have some booked surgery cases today. As a service to the community, I am neutering and spaying dogs and cats at cost."

"That's fantastic." Rebecca removed her hand from Kayleigh's arm. "Way too many homeless pets out there with all the accidental breeding going on."

Kayleigh drained her cup and handed it to Rebecca. "Sorry to drink and run but I need to go get prepared. I'll see you at lunch."

It was hard to leave, but the sooner she got started, the sooner she could see Rebecca again. She couldn't understand her need to be around Rebecca all the time. It had to be that all the fear she was feeling had turned her into a dependent person. Rebecca's presence eased Kayleigh's worries.

†

After her seventh patient, Kayleigh's phone rang. Hoping that it would be the owner of the house, she grabbed the phone on the second ring.

"Dr. Gibbs speaking."

"I know I said I'd wait for you to call, but please, can I take you out to dinner?" Damn, it was Kenneth.

She sighed silently. She really wasn't in the mood to go anywhere, especially with Kenneth. "I'm sorry, I can't. I don't have a babysitter at such short notice. Can I call you back later if I manage to arrange someone to sit for me?"

"I know you won't call me, so here's the deal. I'll call you again in an hour, and we take it from there."

She tamped down her anger at his presumptuous attitude. "Fine. I'll talk to you then."

After the call, she saw two more clients and then went to see Rebecca.

"How are you feeling?" Rebecca called from behind the counter. She was busy flipping through a music magazine.

"Hard to say. I was just invited out to dinner with a client, a date, actually." Kayleigh rolled her eyes. She peeked at Rebecca and swore she saw a hint of disappointment in her eyes.

Rebecca slammed the magazine down onto the counter. "Cool. Who's the dude?"

"His name's Kenneth. He's been bugging me for ages—"

"And he wouldn't accept no for an answer? God, that's one of the many things I hate about men." Rebecca interrupted while looking at the magazine she was paging through. "And?"

"And what?"

"Are you going?" The annoyance was evident in Rebecca's voice.

"I told him *no*. That I don't have a babysitter for Sarah, but he said he'd call me back."

"You know that's not true. You always have a babysitter with me around." Rebecca sighed. "Maybe you should go. It would do you good to get out of the house."

"Let me get this straight, you're offering to babysit?"

"Of course. I'd love to. What time do you want me over?" Rebecca's smile didn't quite reach her eyes.

"I'll tell him to pick me up at seven-thirty. Can you be there at seven?"

"I'll bring pizza for Sarah and me."

Kayleigh bit her lower lip. "Or maybe I shouldn't leave her at a time like this. She was so upset this morning."

"Nonsense, you need to get out a bit. I'll be there for her. You've told me what happened. I'll talk to her. You go out, have some fun."

"Thanks. You're the best friend I ever had. As far as having fun...I doubt it. He's not exactly my type." Kayleigh pulled a face as she lifted her cell phone and dialed Kenneth's number.

"Tonight, seven-thirty. Pick me up at my house. I'll text you the address," she said before he had a chance to say anything.

"You won't regret it," he said. She could hear him breathe and it made her stomach churn.

✝

After Kayleigh left, Rebecca could not function anymore. She sold a lot of CDs, but she still caught herself sitting and staring off into space. Customers came and went, and business had picked up since the installation of the neon sign. Her shop was now on the map, and school kids loved to hang out there after school, wanting to be the first to get the newest releases. Yet, after Kayleigh's visit, she couldn't focus. She grabbed her phone after the final customer left and dialed Judy's number.

"I'm screwed," Rebecca said when Judy answered.

"What's up?"

"I have feelings for Kayleigh, who I know is bloody straight." Rebecca sighed. "And please don't tell me you told me so."

"Oh, shit, Rebecca. Have you told her you're gay?"

"Nope. I don't know why, there just never seems to be a right moment."

"You can't form a friendship based on lies or misconceptions. What are you going to do? Wait. Why am I even asking you this? You *have* to tell her. She's my friend, too, remember?"

"I'm going to tell her. Tonight."

"Good. You do that," Judy said.

"But what if she likes me too?" Rebecca allowed her mind to wander for a second.

"She's straight."

"You know I'm awesome," Rebecca said playfully.

"She's straight."

"And I'm hot as hell."

"She's straight." Judy exaggerated a sigh.

"Cool beans, bud. Will chat later. After she's confessed her undying love for me," Rebecca teased.

"She's straight."

Rebecca giggled when she ended the call. A girl could dream, couldn't she?

†

Kayleigh was ready long before Rebecca arrived. She dressed and put on a little make-up, but while she was applying it, her thoughts were on Rebecca, not Kenneth. Why was that?

In spite of what had happened that morning, Sarah had been fine since she came home from school. She went to her room and played all afternoon, with the door open so

Kayleigh could keep an eye on her as she got ready for the evening.

Rebecca brought a pizza, as promised and refused Kayleigh's offer of money. Rebecca seemed distant. She hardly looked at Kayleigh when she spoke.

Wonder what I've done to upset her.

Rebecca sighed and glanced at her watch. "When is this guy coming again?"

Kayleigh raised her eyebrows at Rebecca's attitude. "I told him seven-thirty."

Just then, the doorbell rang—he was five minutes early.

Kayleigh opened the door and Kenneth stood there with flowers and handed them to her.

"Thanks. That's so sweet of you." Kayleigh took the flowers. "Come on in."

He followed her to the kitchen. "Kenneth, this is my good friend, Rebecca."

Tightlipped, Rebecca shook his outstretched hand. "Have her back by eleven, will you? I'm babysitting and I need to work tomorrow." She grabbed the flowers from Kayleigh. "I'll put these in water for you."

Kayleigh watched as Rebecca quickly turned to the sink and opened the tap. Why was she being such a bitch? Maybe she was afraid of losing Kayleigh's friendship? Kayleigh imagined how she would feel if Rebecca had a date with a guy, and she felt a stab of jealousy. *I don't want to lose my new best friend over someone like Kenneth.*

✝

"Is she your sister? Or better yet, your mother?" Kenneth asked as soon as they got in the car.

"She's my friend. She's just worried about me, is all."

79

"I don't like her. You shouldn't allow people to walk all over you like that."

And now I don't like you either, she thought. Not a great start to a first date, he was losing points within the first five minutes, and he didn't have any points to start with.

Kenneth took her to a steak house in Wilderness, where they could sit on the deck under a huge Milkwood tree. She felt annoyed, and hoped that the evening would be over soon. She wanted to be home early enough so she could spend a little time with Rebecca before she had to leave.

The waiter came and listed the specials. Kayleigh ordered a rare filet steak, while Kenneth ordered a large well-done rump steak with extra chips.

"You look very sexy tonight." He gave her a sly grin, while looking into her eyes. "I have to tell you, I'm an upfront kind of guy, I've been attracted to you since the day we met, and I can't wait until we're all alone."

"I...uhm...excuse me?" What the hell was she supposed to say to that? She wanted to leap out of her chair and make a run for it. Instead, she composed herself and searched for the right words. "This is a mistake. I'm sorry, Kenneth. I shouldn't even have agreed to this." Kayleigh shook her head while she started reaching for her handbag hanging behind her chair.

"Wait. I'm sorry. That was too forward of me. Relax. We haven't even received our food yet. You have to give me a chance at least."

"Kenneth, I don't have the desire to be alone with you and do whatever it is you have in mind, and I never will. I don't feel anything for you other than friendship. I'm sorry, I just don't."

He sat back in his chair. "I'm sorry you feel that way."

"We can be friends."

Kenneth instantly bristled. "Oh, spare me the we can be friends speech."

"Well, at least we tried this, right?"

"Yeah. Whatever." He sighed. There was a long uncomfortable silence.

The waiter brought their meals. A feeling of relief washed over Kayleigh.

The food tasted like rubber to Kayleigh and luckily, her portion was small. Both of them ate as if they'd never seen food before. Kayleigh mostly ate fast because she wanted to get home to Rebecca and Sarah. She didn't belong there.

When their plates were empty, Kenneth finally spoke again. "Wait. Wow, I think I know that girl who's looking after your daughter. I thought I recognized her when I saw her." He nodded thoughtfully. "Isn't she the chick who owns the new CD shop in town?"

"Yes." Kayleigh was happy to talk about Rebecca, but leery that he'd brought her up.

"I've heard some things about her that might shock you," he said. There was a gleam in his eye, reminiscent of a child with juicy gossip.

"And what might that be?"

"How can you leave your child alone with a person like that?"

"Like what? What are you talking about?" Kayleigh asked, suddenly afraid. She was expecting him to tell her some wild story like Rebecca was a serial killer or into drugs.

"You left your child alone with that gay woman. Aren't you scared she might influence your child?"

Kayleigh stared at him in shock. "What do you mean by gay woman? She's not gay." She waved her hand in the air. "Besides, there's nothing wrong with gay women. My best friends are all gay, but that isn't the point. I know for a fact that Rebecca is *not* gay."

"It's a small town, sweetie. People talk. Your so-called friend, Rebecca, is a lesbo. She digs chicks." He laughed out loud. "She's a carpet muncher. I can't believe you didn't know that?"

"First of all, I'm not your *sweetie*. Second, you're talking shit. Utter bullshit. Third, it has abso-fuckin-lutely nothing to do with you."

"Hey, we could have a threesome." He was still laughing at Kayleigh's shocked expression.

"Take me home. Now." She pushed her chair back from the table and stood. She eyed her glass of water, seriously thinking of chucking it in his face.

"Hey, I was just joking about the threesome."

"I said take me home, Kenneth."

"All right, all right. Hang on, I'm coming. I'm coming," he mumbled as he got up and paid the bill.

When his car stopped in front of her house, Kayleigh looked at him. "Thank you for dinner, but don't *ever* ask me out again." She slammed the passenger door before stomping to her front door.

She scanned her watch. It was only nine o'clock. The date might very well have been the shortest date in the history of all time.

Rebecca opened it before Kayleigh had a chance to.

"Hi. Early enough for you?" She brushed straight past Rebecca and into the kitchen.

Rebecca looked at her watch. "I'm sorry for being so rude earlier," she said following Kayleigh to the kitchen. "Can I make you some tea? Or shall I open a bottle of wine? Or how about a beer?"

"A beer, please." Kayleigh turned around once they reached the kitchen. Even though she was mad at Rebecca, she was glad to be home, finally.

She wanted to know if Rebecca had lied to her. Didn't she trust her enough? Was it even true? After taking a deep breath she spoke. "How's Sarah?"

"She's fine. She told me that Carrey doesn't scare her. Carrey is a four-year-old girl who used to live here." Rebecca cleared her throat, took two beers from the fridge. "There's more than one thing we need to discuss," she added nervously.

"Really? Like what?" She took the beer from Rebecca.

"In the bathroom, I swear I wasn't alone."

Kayleigh opened her beer and downed a huge gulp as she wondered if the evening could get any worse. "Shit. What happened?"

"I went to the toilet, and I heard a voice. It sounded like a man, whispering something. I'm not sure what he said, but it sounded something like get out. I know it sounds like something from a really bad movie, but I swear it's the truth." Rebecca looked horrified while she spoke.

"Seriously? Oh, my God." Kayleigh started shaking. "You're not hurt in any way, are you?" Her earlier anger was forgotten for the time being as she touched Rebecca's arm.

"Traumatized is more like it. Whatever is lurking in these walls is not very friendly."

"I'm sorry, Rebecca. I'm so sorry for dragging you here."

"I ran out with my pants around my ankles." Rebecca laughed, but Kayleigh could tell she was shaken up.

Kayleigh tried to join in the laughter. "Wish I'd been here to see it."

"I'm glad you weren't, and thank God, Sarah didn't see me either." Rebecca blushed.

"Was there anything else?"

"No, that was all that happened. Strange as hell. There I'm sitting with my pants around my ankles, minding my own business, then this cold rush of air settles over me and a deep voice starts whispering. God, all the hair on the back of my neck stood up straight. Mohawk style." She motioned toward the bathroom. "Just follow the urine drops from the toilet seat all the way to the patio. That's the path I ran with my pants around my ankles."

This time, Kayleigh didn't even try to laugh. She was too afraid to see any humor in the situation. "Let's go and sit outside. I've had one hell of an evening, and I want to tell you about it."

"Yeah. Why are you home so early? What did he do? Are you okay? You look frazzled."

Kayleigh didn't answer. Instead, she led the way to the patio. She sat down and shifted her chair so she could see the view.

Rebecca moved a chair next to Kayleigh's and turned it so she could face her. She sat down. "Something wrong?" She placed her hand on Kayleigh's shoulder and started to massage it gently.

The movement sent shivers down Kayleigh's spine and she felt herself warm between her legs like that other night they went ghost hunting. God, what was happening to her?

The air was warm and Kayleigh suddenly felt nervous at asking the question. She turned her face to Rebecca and stared straight into her blue eyes. "What was the name of your ex?"

Rebecca's eyes went wide with shock. Her hand that was massaging Kayleigh's shoulder stopped moving. "Why would you ask that?"

"Please just tell me, I want the truth."

Rebecca swallowed hard and answered. "Maria." As the word echoed from her lips, her hand dropped from Kayleigh's shoulder. She placed her hand in her lap like a child caught doing something terribly naughty. She avoided Kayleigh's eyes and turned her chair toward the view. "Did your boyfriend tell you?"

"He's not my boyfriend, but that's not the point. Why would you hide something so important away from me? I thought I was your friend. Don't you trust me?"

Rebecca stared down at her feet. "I didn't want to scare you away. I liked you and I needed a friend. I'm sorry. I didn't mean to betray you." She raised her head and met Kayleigh's eyes. "I'll leave if you want me to."

Rebecca moved to get up, but Kayleigh put her hand on Rebecca's knee to keep her from rising.

"You lied to me. On that first night we met, you told me you weren't gay. Why? Do you think I'm that shallow?" Hot tears filled her eyes. For Kayleigh, lying was one way of ruining a friendship.

"That wasn't exactly what I said. I never said I wasn't gay. I realize that I was wrong omitting the truth, that it's the same as lying. I'm so sorry, Kay. Please forgive me, I'm such an idiot."

"Please leave." Kayleigh sniffed, as she rested her forehead in her hands. "Please... just... go."

"Is this because I'm gay?" Rebecca asked, her voice rising. "Lindsay and Judy are also gay—for your information."

"I actually wouldn't have cared whether you were gay or straight. I trusted you, and you misled me. Friends don't do that."

Rebecca put her half-empty beer on the table, rose slowly to her feet, and left without another word.

Chapter Eleven

Rebecca spent the next two weeks running on empty. She took hours to fall asleep, and then when she finally got to sleep, she struggled to get up in the mornings. She'd spoken to Lindsay and Judy, and they'd confirmed that Kayleigh was very angry with her and didn't want to speak to her. At the store, she tried to catch Kayleigh's eye whenever she passed by, but Kayleigh looked the other way and ignored her. Rebecca finally decided to give up and to let their friendship go. Maybe this was what she needed to do in order to get over this impossible one-sided love affair.

†

Three weeks had passed since Kayleigh asked Rebecca to leave her alone. Work and Sarah kept her busy, but her mind always went back to Rebecca. Despite Rebecca lying to her, she missed her friend. On several occasions, she'd seen Rebecca try to catch her attention, but she'd refused to budge.

On Friday, she swung by school to pick up Sarah and they were on their way home when Kayleigh's phone vibrated in her pocket. She pulled off the road and checked the caller ID before answering.

"Hello, Bag."

"This name-calling has got to stop," Lindsay said with a laugh. "I've just ordered a huge platter of sushi, and we need help eating it. Come over for dinner, please."

"How can I deny my friend the help she needs? I'll be there at six."

"Great. See you then."

Kayleigh exhaled loudly when she ended the call. This was just what she needed. She looked over at Sarah. "How does dinner at Aunt Lindsay and Aunt Judy's sound?"

"Sounds like fun, Mom."

†

It was just after six when Rebecca pulled into the driveway and noticed the Jeep. What on earth were Judy and Lindsay up to now? They promised her there would be no one else at dinner. Part of her was hesitant about seeing Kayleigh, because her final words had really hurt her, but the other part ached to see her. It was the latter part that moved her feet to walk up the driveway. Her heart pounded in her chest, and her breathing was shallow.

Oh, Kayleigh, please love me back.

She swallowed the lump in her throat just as she reached the door.

†

Kayleigh looked up when she saw someone standing in the doorway. Rebecca. Her heart ached at the sight of her, but it didn't keep her from standing to leave. "That's my cue to go," she mumbled. "Sarah! Come on, honey. We're leaving." She called Sarah in from outside where she was playing.

87

"Kayleigh, you're going to sit down and listen," Lindsay said in a firm voice. "Sarah, honey, your mom was just joking, stay where you are."

Kayleigh dropped back in her seat and exaggerated a sigh. Lindsay was right. They needed to talk this through. She missed Rebecca too much to let the lie or omission bother her anymore. Rebecca's forlorn and vulnerable expression as she stood standing in the doorway had such a visceral effect on Kayleigh that she could hardly breathe.

Judy pulled Rebecca by her hand and shoved her down onto the other settee. "The two of you are being very childish. You're going to talk this out like adults, and after that, we'll have dinner. All four of us. Five." She looked over at Sarah through the huge glass doors, still playing outside, unaware of Rebecca's arrival.

Kayleigh watched as Judy and Lindsay walked toward the kitchen. Sarah came in from outside, her eyes beaming when she saw Rebecca. Before she could take off for the living room, Lindsay spotted Sarah.

"Sarah, come into the kitchen and see what I have," Lindsay said.

"Hi, Aunt Rebecca," Sarah called out as she ran toward the kitchen.

"Hi, Sarah." Rebecca finally met Kayleigh's eyes. "Are you still mad at me?"

"I don't know." Kayleigh swallowed back unwelcome tears.

"I miss you, Kay," Rebecca said in a soft voice. "I'm so sorry for not being honest with you. Please, can we try this again?"

"You were my friend. It didn't matter whether you liked men or women. I just don't understand why you lied to me."

Rebecca swallowed. "At the time, I didn't know you, and when you open with a line like 'I'm straight', I wasn't sure what to think. I know I shouldn't have let you think I was straight, but I didn't lie to you, I wouldn't do that. If you can give me another chance, I promise I'll never be anything but completely honest and up front with you. I really *do* miss you."

Kayleigh silently cursed the tears that spilled over and trickled down her cheeks. She wiped them away, stood, and walked to Rebecca, who also stood and wrapped her arms around Kayleigh. Kayleigh sniffed as she held onto her. "God, I miss you too, Rebecca. So much."

"That's much better," Lindsay and Judy said in unison as they walked in with the huge sushi platter. Sarah trailed close behind, and quickly joined her mom and Rebecca in a group hug.

"I missed you, Aunt Rebecca," Sarah said.

"Missed you too, honey." Rebecca bent down and hugged Sarah as Kayleigh pulled away from them.

"Now we can all have dinner and enjoy our evening together," Judy added.

†

Later, Rebecca followed Kayleigh home. After Kayleigh had tucked Sarah in, they sat next to one another on the patio swing as they each sipped a beer.

"I'm so glad we have this thing sorted between us. I hardly survived these three weeks without you." Kayleigh sighed feeling more relaxed than she had in…well…three weeks.

"Please don't ever chase me away like that again."

Before Kayleigh could speak, Rebecca held up a hand. "I do understand how wrong I was, but I thought I was going to die not seeing you."

89

They were quiet for a long moment until Kayleigh broke the silence. "I'm curious. What's it like...being gay, I mean?"

"I'm normal, just like you. I've tried being with a man, but I just ended up being unhappy. There's just no chemistry for me there." Rebecca took a sip of her beer and looked into Kayleigh's eyes. "I never felt anything for men. I thought I was unable to love. Then I fell in love with a woman, and my life changed. Look at it this way...who would know better what to do with a woman's body than a woman?" She waggled her eyebrows.

Kayleigh laughed. "Well, if you put it that way...."

"But it's not just about the sex. I could never feel for any man the way I feel about women."

"Tell me about Maria."

"We met at a party. She was there with a guy. We had too much to drink, and we ended up having a threesome."

Rebecca must have noticed Kayleigh's shocked expression. "Those were the days I was still experimenting. I was young—twenty years old." She sighed. "It was awful. Anyway, four years later, I saw her again at another party, we hit it off, and things just happened. Before long, we moved in together and ten years later, I found her in our bed with the guy we had a threesome with the first time we met. She thought I would be okay with her having sex with him, seeing as we had that three-way before," Rebecca said with a sarcastic tone. "Long story short, I was definitely not okay with it and she ran away with him."

"That's some seriously sick shit. What a bitch." Kayleigh placed a hand on Rebecca's arm.

Rebecca turned to face Kayleigh. "You don't know this, but I was a senior manager at a recording studio in Cape Town then. I spent six months chasing after Maria. It was when I got fired that I finally caught a wake-up. Promised myself I would never chase after a woman again. Sold my mansion and moved to Sedgefield."

Kayleigh was shocked. "Mansion?"

"Yes."

"Did you lose everything?"

"Most of it. But I did manage to invest some money when I sold my house, and I did manage to buy my current house for cash."

"My best friend is loaded." Kayleigh laughed.

"I didn't lie about that. I never once said I was poor." Rebecca defended herself.

"My best friend is loaded." Kayleigh said again, shaking her head in amusement.

"Gold digger." Rebecca teased. "I don't have enough money to keep me afloat for the rest of my life, which is why I need my store to generate at least some income. Music is my life. Buying my music store was the best decision I ever made."

"In Sedgefield? The one-traffic-light town where the tortoises set the pace."

"Hey. Watch it. My store is doing quite well, I'll have you know."

"Yes. It is. You should be very proud of yourself," Kayleigh said.

"I am. Thank you again for the sign." She leaned back into the cushions of the patio swing. "Tell me your story? Sarah's father. What happened there?"

"The same as yours, actually. Married a few years and caught him in bed with his secretary." Kayleigh rolled her eyes. "Such a cliché. Only it wasn't our bed. I received an anonymous phone call, telling me which hotel they were at. He was supposed to be travelling out of town on business. He was right there, two blocks from my practice. Fucking another woman. I left my job and our friends, just took my child and my Jeep. Left him with everything. In the end, he got what he deserved, though. He's married to her now, and she's the laziest leech I've ever seen. Doesn't do a thing. I understand she's pregnant now. But he seems happy. I guess that's what we all strive for. Looking back, I can't say I ever loved him. There was never that spark that everyone carries on about, you know?"

Oh shit. Do I have those kind of feelings for Rebecca? she thought, pausing.

"But he was my husband and we were supposed to spend the rest of our lives together," she concluded.

"Sounds exhausting. Spending your whole life with someone you aren't in love with."

"I'm glad it happened. If it hadn't, I wouldn't have Sarah and my practice in the best part of the country."

"Where the tortoises set the pace?" Rebecca imitated her and they both laughed. "Same here, actually. If Maria didn't do what she did, I wouldn't be here." Rebecca turned back to Kayleigh. "Then I wouldn't have met you."

Both went silent for a while. Kayleigh broke the silence. "Tell me about your parents. Do you have a family?" Her mind went crazy with thoughts of her feelings for Rebecca. She calmed her breathing and tried to listen to Rebecca.

"Sore subject. My parents had six children, five boys and then me. Funny how they tried until they finally had a girl, but then I was practically forgotten. My dad died when I was very little. Hardly remember him at all, and I guess my mom struggled to cope with us all." Rebecca lowered her head and picked at the label of her bottle. "She committed suicide when I was in high school."

Kayleigh touched her hand until Rebecca quit fidgeting with the label. "Oh, Rebecca. I'm so sorry."

Rebecca raised her head and offered sad eyes.

"Thanks," she said softly. "My oldest brother raised me until I left school. We don't talk much anymore. I guess he blames me for never achieving much in his life. Instead of going to college, he was stuck with me. I send him money every now and then, you know, to try make up for his losses." She took a big gulp of beer as if to drown out the memories. "Okay, your turn."

"I was the only child. My dad and I were very close. He passed away three years ago. Brain tumor."

"God, now it's my turn to say I'm so sorry to hear that. And your mom?"

"My mom took my ex-husband's side when I left him. She refuses to talk to me. I try calling her every now and then for Sarah's sake, but can you believe she will only acknowledge her granddaughter when she's at her dad's?"

"Wow. That's awful."

"The a-hole cheats on me, and my mom blames me for it."

"Family. Blood is supposed to be thicker than water." Rebecca stared ahead of her into space.

They sat silently for a while, and then Kayleigh decided to be brave. She cleared her throat. "You promised me you would be honest with me from now on. Can I ask you something and whatever the answer, I give you my word not to be mad and not to run?"

Rebecca nodded and she continued.

"Have you ever had any feelings for me?" As soon as the question was out in the open, she felt all the air squeezed out of her lungs. She wasn't even sure what answer she hoped for.

"I prefer not to answer that." Rebecca avoided eye contact and took a long gulp from her beer.

"Why?" Kayleigh asked, her heartbeat speeding up.

"That's not the sort of question you ask someone." Rebecca laughed nervously. "Why would you ask something like that, anyway?"

"I don't mean to put you on the spot and I have no idea why I want to know. I just want to know." Kayleigh could see her own hand shaking as she put the beer to her lips. The bottle top hit her teeth and vibrated against them as she tried to take a sip.

"I've thought about you, yes. A lot, actually. Why? Care to try it?" Rebecca asked with a challenging tone. She turned her face toward Kayleigh, and Kayleigh didn't miss the fire of desire that sparked in her blue eyes.

Kayleigh felt the blush warm her cheeks. She actually thought she heard the blood rushing to her face. "I don't know what I want, Rebecca," she managed to say in a voice barely above a whisper. *God, I want you to kiss me.*

Rebecca hurriedly drank some more beer. "You make me bloody nervous, you know. Look at me." She held up her bottle. "I'm downing this beer and I'm now sloshed."

"I like having you here. When you're not here, I miss you. Those three weeks apart were hell." Kayleigh placed a hand on Rebecca's leg and leaned into her. Touching Rebecca felt so good.

"You're right. They were hell." Rebecca put her arm around Kayleigh's shoulders and pulled her closer.

Kayleigh felt the warmth of Rebecca's throat against her face and turned to put her mouth at the base of her neck. Her lips found the soft skin there and opened her mouth slowly to allow her tongue to taste Rebecca's skin.

Rebecca moaned and pushed her back gently. "Kay, what are you doing?"

Kayleigh didn't miss the catch in her voice.

"Don't play games with me, please."

"I don't play games with people. Especially people I care about." Kayleigh felt the heat creep up her cheeks again. She had no idea what she was doing.

Rebecca pulled away from Kayleigh to look into her eyes, "You want the complete truth? Are you sure you're ready for it?"

Kayleigh nodded.

"The truth is, it's very difficult for me to be friends with you. I'm extremely attracted to you. I think about you constantly. I miss you when you're not around. I want to touch you and hold you all the time."

The words tumbled out so fast, Kayleigh had a hard time keeping up.

Rebecca drained her beer and got up. Kayleigh saw the anguish in her dark eyes. "And that concludes our session for today. I hope you're happy now."

Before Kayleigh could respond, Rebecca rushed for the door and left. Kayleigh stared after her. What had just happened? At least now she knew that Rebecca had feelings for her. Feelings that Kayleigh suddenly realized she could never return, despite the fire that burned down low when she touched her lips to Rebecca's skin. She had Sarah to think about.

Chapter Twelve

1897 Hoekwil

Joshua came home from the fields one day and found Catherine lying on the kitchen floor. She was bleeding and seemed to be in severe pain. He yelled out for help, and Evelyn came storming into the house from outside. She helped Catherine up and took her to the bedroom.

While Evelyn was busy with Catherine, Joshua marched up and down the passage waiting for the verdict. He was petrified that something bad would happen and he'd lose Catherine and the baby.

"Come now, nonna, you must try, push this baby out."

He heard Evelyn speaking low as she crouched by the bedside as Catherine lay moaning in agony.

"It's too soon, Evelyn. No, too soon…" Catherine cried out.

Joshua peered in through the doorway, and then he disappeared along the passage and down the stairs. He called for Stander, his fastest helper, to saddle up his stallion. Joshua leapt up on the horse to go fetch the doctor while Catherine was in Evelyn's care. As his horse chewed up the distance to the doctor with each stride, Joshua prayed for his wife and unborn child.

"Dear Lord God, please keep my wife safe. Please keep my baby alive and watch over them."

✝

Catherine was only eight months along and was worried that if the baby came this soon, a month early, it would die. She knew that once she'd started bleeding, there was no going back. Her contractions had started a few hours after the onset of bleeding, even as she prayed they would stop…it was too soon.

Another contraction wracked her body. Catherine hadn't thought it possible that a human could experience so much pain.

"I'm never doing this again." she cried and she started to push. Evelyn had her hands between Catherine's legs as she tried to guide the baby's head out of the birth canal.

"I can see the head, nonna. Push!"

Chapter Thirteen

Present day

A week had passed since that night on the patio, and Rebecca had spent very little time with Kayleigh. Rebecca showered, brushed her teeth, and stood in front of her bedroom mirror naked. Never in a million years did she think a straight woman would intrigue her as much as Kayleigh. The thought scared her to death, but she knew she needed to be strong and resist. She tried to ignore the constant ache inside. She longed to touch Kayleigh and she ached for Kayleigh to touch her too. She shook her head and grabbed her jeans from the bed.

She could never be with Kayleigh, no matter how attracted she was to her.

It would help if Kayleigh weren't such a damned charmer. The way she touched Rebecca... Kayleigh's eye contact, the way she walked, the way she drank her damned coffee. Everything she did was sexy.

"Get a grip, Rebecca," she said to the mirror.

†

While Kayleigh was working, she'd notice Rebecca's head bobbing up from behind her counter in an obvious attempt to get a glimpse at Kayleigh. She enjoyed the attention, but she was petrified of leading Rebecca on. Their friendship had taken a turn after that night outside on her deck. Knowing that Rebecca had feelings for her was a completely different ball game, and she wasn't sure how to approach the subject. Since that night, they'd kept conversations light and impersonal.

The bell of the door rang, and in walked Brenda Smith. *Damn....* Brenda was the town's own walking talking news channel. She knew everything about everyone and loved to gossip.

"Hey, Dr. Gibbs. How are you?"

"Hi, Brenda. I'm fine and how—"

"Did you know that Garry and Nancy are selling their house? That ugly house that's barely standing! Can you believe the nerve? Nobody..." Brenda rambled non-stop as usual. *Why even ask how people are when you don't listen to the answer? Double damn,* Kayleigh thought angrily.

Kayleigh nodded and acted like she was listening. She wished it were Rebecca who had entered the office instead.

"Doctor, please come quick! My cat!" Ronda Williams, flushed, with a tear-stained face, came storming in through the door. Kayleigh was glad for the distraction, but worried about the reason for it. Stepping around Brenda, with an apologetic smile, she went toward Ronda, the mother of one of Sarah's classmates. Kayleigh ran to her car where she found the cat lying on the front seat. The cat was in obvious distress. She was panting with her mouth wide open and mewing. Kayleigh gently picked the cat up with both hands and proceeded back to her surgery room. The cat was obviously pregnant and perhaps having difficulties delivering, her tail and lower legs were soaked in blood and urine. Ronda followed close on her heels after closing the car door.

"Please. You have to save her, she's my baby!"

"What happened?" Kayleigh asked as she pulled on a pair of gloves.

"I'm not sure. I found her on the side of the road just outside my house, she might have been hit by a car. She's expecting a litter soon, Doc." She was sobbing.

At times like this, Kayleigh really wished she had an assistant. Pet owners were always in distress in these situations, and in the way when they thought they were helping. Kayleigh needed all of her focus to be on the cat. She was terrified of not being good enough to save the kitty's life.

"She's bleeding, badly, and I need to operate immediately. Please wait in the waiting area for me," Kayleigh said as she shaved a leg so the veins could be easily accessible. She drew up a syringe with anesthetics, which she administered quickly to sedate the cat.

Kayleigh watched as Ronda, with slouched shoulders, hesitantly left the surgery. She saw Rebecca come into the office, and to her rescue. She must have noticed the commotion from her store. She took Ronda by the shoulders and led her to the waiting room, and had her sit. She gazed up, saw Kayleigh watching her from the surgery, and winked at her. Rebecca nodded encouragingly.

Kayleigh proceeded in doing the caesarean section and managed to save one kitten. It was a little black one, premature, of course. The two other kittens didn't make it. While the cat was sedated, she took some x-rays and found the cat had a fractured hind leg, which forced Kayleigh to operate for more than an hour longer. She had to put in some k-wires, and then round it off with a splint with thick crepe bandages. By the time she finished working, the cat appeared stable, although she'd lost a lot of blood and was very weak. Kayleigh tried to keep the kitten as warm as possible, but wasn't sure if it was strong enough to survive the ordeal. Once again, she berated herself for not having an assistant who would be able to help.

After cleaning up, she stopped by the waiting room. "Ronda, do you want to come and see your kitty?"

Ronda got up and walked toward Kayleigh. "Will Mittens be okay?" she asked, with a trembling voice.

"I believe she'll have a full recovery."

Rebecca had stayed. Kayleigh looked at her. "You can come and have a look as well, if you want."

Rebecca got up eagerly, and followed the other two women into the surgery. Mittens was half awake, but still very groggy from the anesthesia. Kayleigh took the kitten and tried to get it to latch onto its mother, but the kitten refused. Mittens mewed, and Kayleigh decided to give her a rest.

"You're going to have to leave her here for a day or two so I can keep an eye on her, but I think she will be all right."

"And the kitten?"

"We'll need to nurse him until Mittens is able to take over."

"You're an angel sent by God." Ronda thanked her and hugged her.

"Shall I go and fetch Sarah from school for you?" Rebecca asked.

"What about your store?"

"I already put a sign on the door: Gone fishing. It's fine. I don't mind."

"*You* are *my* angel sent by God. I would appreciate that very much, thank you."

Kayleigh spent the rest of the day at the practice, looking after the new kitten and its mom. She called around and managed to find a vet nurse named Faith, who could work the nightshift for her and Faith relieved her by seven.

Rebecca had taken Sarah home and said she'd stay there until Kayleigh got off work.

While Kayleigh tended to some other pets before she started for home, the conversation from the previous week played over and over in her mind. She still wasn't sure about how she was feeling. Was it really possible for her to be attracted to Rebecca?

Before leaving, she made sure Faith knew how to feed the kitten and asked her to call in case there were any problems. Kayleigh promised to be back the following morning at seven.

As she drove home, rain started to come down in buckets and she had to stop at the nearest gas station in order to put up the Jeep's top. She was soaked through and freezing cold by the time she finally had the roof top up and continued the rest of the trek home. It was dark by then. The heavy rain forced her to slow down, making the trip a much longer one.

While driving, Rebecca entered her thoughts again. She wondered what it would be like to be with a woman and before she could stop herself, she imagined Rebecca moving closer and touching her lower back and pulling her into her....

She thought of what it would feel like to stand against Rebecca, to have her body flush against her. She imagined Rebecca's lips meeting hers, tasting her sweet tongue, and feeling it massage her own. Her hands slid down Rebecca's back and found the bottom edge of her shirt, and she slipped her hands under that shirt. She slid her hands softly over Rebecca's bare back and felt her skin on her fingertips. Rebecca moaned and pulled her closer still. Kayleigh pushed her pelvis against Rebecca's, and Rebecca moaned louder.

As the fantasy played out in her mind, Kayleigh dropped her hand between her legs, imagining it was Rebecca's hand pushing up against her. The aching in her center was unbearable. She leaned back in the seat and thrust her pelvis against her hand. A soft moan escaped from between her parted lips and for an instant, she forgot where she was and closed her eyes.

The Jeep jerked. She quickly pulled her hand away from between her thighs and grabbed the steering wheel with both hands. In her carelessness, the Jeep had veered off the road onto the gravel. It was so close to the curb that she went over the edge. Twisting the wheel to right the Jeep almost made it roll.

She slowed to a stop to catch her breath and steady her nerves. How stupid of her to lose control like that. She was near home, and if she didn't stop fantasizing about the forbidden, she'd kill herself in a car crash and never make it there. Taking a deep breath, she shoved the images of Rebecca from her mind, pulled slowly back onto the road, and concentrated on her driving.

†

Kayleigh pulled the Jeep into the driveway and felt a wave of heat and dizziness rush through her. Her heart fluttered crazily and her stomach went into knots at the very thought that Rebecca was only about fifty yards away. She ran through the pouring rain toward the front door and went inside. Once inside, she shut the door behind her and couldn't resist calling out. "Hi, honey, I'm home!"

Giggles came from the kitchen, which she barely heard over the teenage music band blaring from the stereo. Rebecca popped her head from the kitchen doorway. "Hi, honey!" She laughed. "Very original. How was the rest of your day?"

"Hectic, but great, thanks. What are you two up to?" She reached the kitchen and saw Sarah was stirring something on the stove. Kayleigh gave her a warm hug. "Hi, baby. I missed you."

She kissed her on the top of her head and then glimpsed the witches' brew that was bubbling away in the pot. "Did you remember the newt's breath and the cat's claw?"

Sarah giggled again. "Maa, it's bean soup. You know, for the rainy weather? We can snuggle up in front of the fireplace while we have dinner."

Kayleigh looked around at Rebecca in surprise. Rebecca held a beer in her direction. "For you, ma'am." She nodded at Sarah. "We had a great day. I absolutely adore your daughter. You have done a marvelous job in raising her."

Kayleigh took the beer and warmed with the compliment. It was rare that anyone gave her important compliments. "Thanks, nice of you to notice." She took another step closer to Rebecca and winked. "And what's this about the fireplace?"

"Well, *honey*," Rebecca said with teasing eyes, "Sarah and I went to the store and got some wood. We then made a fire in the fireplace. It was a bit rusty and caused a lot of smoke at first, but it's fine now." Her gaze dropped to Kayleigh's chest.

Kayleigh felt her nipples harden even more—and it wasn't just from the cold rain.

"You should go put on some dry clothes," Rebecca whispered before turning away.

Kayleigh felt a flush of pleasure, knowing the effect she was having on Rebecca.

"Thanks for the fire." Kayleigh lifted her beer bottle. "Cheers." After taking a sip, she set the bottle down and proceeded up the stairs to her bedroom. After quickly changing into a dry pair of slacks and a sweatshirt, she went back downstairs to the lounge area where the fireplace radiated a warm glow. Rebecca followed her to the lounge and when Kayleigh sat down on the two-seater, Rebecca sat down next to her.

"How's the kitten?" Rebecca looked concerned.

"Refuses to drink from the mom. I had to start him on formula through an oro-gastric tube." At Rebecca's confused expression, she explained. "It's a hair-strand little tube that passes from the mouth into the stomach. I gave it one milliliter. Do you know how little one milliliter is? It needs a feeding every hour. Had to hire a nurse to take over tonight. Couldn't leave the kitten and his mom alone. Poor Faith is going to have a rough night."

"A fifth of a teaspoon per meal? Cheap round. Not only is the nurse going to have a rough night, aren't you heading for a rough couple of weeks ahead yourself?"

"I doubt Ronda is going to be able to raise the kitten all by herself. If she permits it, I'll have to take him home and nurse him. Once he's big enough, I'll have to find him a proper home."

"Why don't you keep the kitty?"

"That all depends on Ronda, I suppose. But if she doesn't want him, I might," Kayleigh said and warmed at the thought. "I've always wanted a black cat."

"Witches' cat," Rebecca joked and put her hand on Kayleigh's leg.

"It will go with the witches' brew that's bubbling away in the kitchen."

The hand on her leg made her muscles tense. The wild fantasies she'd had on the way home had left her defenseless against Rebecca's pull. The warmth flowed from between her thighs, making her ache for more. Desire took over, and she leaned back on the couch. Rebecca's hand sent tingles up her thigh, so much so, Kayleigh was sure she was going to explode with need. Her breathing quickened as she placed her hand on top of Rebecca's hand. Very slowly, she started to slide Rebecca's hand upward, toward the warmth between her legs.

Rebecca lowered her eyelids and looked like she was scrutinizing the hand that was moving up Kayleigh's thigh ever so seductively. She closed her eyes and groaned softly just as Sarah came in balancing a tray with three bowls of soup. Luckily, she was focusing so hard on the tray that she didn't notice what was happening. Kayleigh shifted away from Rebecca, and Rebecca put her hand back in her own lap before glancing sideways at Kayleigh. The look in her eyes was that of pure lust and it had Kayleigh biting her bottom lip before turning her attention to Sarah.

God, what had she been thinking, acting that way with Sarah in the next room?

Kayleigh quickly jumped up and took the tray from Sarah. "Careful, honey, don't burn yourself." She placed the tray on the side table. "Next time you should call one of us to help instead, okay?"

"Yes, Mommy. I just wanted to surprise you guys."

"Thanks, sweetie. This smells and looks great." Her appetite had gone, and she had no idea what to make of what she'd just done.

Sarah disappeared back toward the kitchen and returned with another tray. "Look, Mommy, we even baked bread."

"Wow. You guys are great." Kayleigh stared at the freshly baked bread on the tray. "Geez, Rebecca, you've really outdone yourself. All domesticated and all."

Rebecca shook her head. "Couldn't have managed without Sarah's help."

After dinner, they all helped to clear the dishes. Rebecca washed up while Kayleigh dried and Sarah packed them away. It didn't take long to finish and by that time it was Sarah's bedtime.

"Time to get ready for bed," Kayleigh said.

"But, Mom, I'm not tired."

"It is already past your bedtime and you have school tomorrow so get going."

"Okay." Sarah frowned and headed for the stairs.

"I'll be up to tuck you in in a minute."

Kayleigh heard her daughter grumble and she laughed. "She's afraid she'll miss out on something." She patted Rebecca's hand. "I'll be right back."

After tucking Sarah in and coming back down to the lounge, Kayleigh and Rebecca sipped on their beer in silence for a while. Rebecca sat on the single couch and Kayleigh speculated that she was afraid that she would make another stupid move.

"So... did you see or hear any ghosts this evening?" Kayleigh asked in order to lighten the mood.

"Nothing. Thank goodness," Rebecca said.

They sat in silence for a while.

"I'm so sorry. I don't know what came over me." Kayleigh spoke softly. She felt like a fool and really needed to hear from Rebecca that everything was all right.

"Please don't say you're sorry, but I'm not sure what you want from me. I must warn you, Kay. I've been burned badly once before. You know Maria left me for a man, and I seem to keep forgetting that I promised myself I would never get involved with a straight woman again. You don't have any idea what you're putting me through here."

"I don't understand what's happening, Rebecca. I have these feelings for you. But I've never been with a woman and…." Her voice drifted off.

"And?" Rebecca sounded calm.

"Nothing. Listen, thanks for everything you've done for me today. I'm really tired and it's getting late." Kayleigh swallowed as she tried to hold back the tears. She'd never been this confused before. She stood up and led the way to the front door. It had stopped raining. At least Rebecca would be able to drive home safely.

No matter how hard she tried, Kayleigh couldn't get to sleep. She felt so much for Rebecca, but starting a relationship with her might not be the best idea. What if they made love and Kayleigh decided it wasn't for her. Then she would hurt Rebecca by rejecting her and that would mean the end of their friendship. Or, the other scenario… what if Rebecca decided Kayleigh was too inexperienced for her? Before she gave in to sleep, she decided to back off and leave Rebecca alone. But still, her final thought was of Rebecca. What was she thinking of right now? About Maria, perhaps?

Chapter Fourteen

1897

Catherine screamed and panted as she pushed so hard, it felt like the veins in her head were going to pop. Something burned like fire between her legs. She yelped in pain. Then she heard a sloshing sound and felt a sudden release. She lifted her head and tried to see the baby. The baby was lying still, not breathing and not moving.

"What's going on, Evelyn?" she asked in a weak voice.

The doctor came storming in with his little leather suitcase. He immediately grabbed the baby and started to resuscitate.

Catherine cried out. "Please save my baby. I want my baby... please," she sobbed.

Joshua crouched down by her head and cried with her. "Please, Lord, save our baby. Please, God." He buried his face in Catherine's hair and cried.

Chapter Fifteen

Present day

Sarah had choir practice before school, so by seven o'clock, Sarah was already dropped off at school and Kayleigh was on duty. She kept looking at the CD shop, but Rebecca wasn't there yet. Faith appeared exhausted when Kayleigh relieved her, but she still offered to return again the following night to look after the kitten. Ronda's cat was far more awake and seemed stronger than the previous day.

Kayleigh called Ronda and told her she could collect her cat as soon as she was ready and in about fifteen minutes, Ronda was there. She cooed when she saw her cat and agreed that the kitten should stay with Kayleigh. It was too small for Ronda to handle and Mittens showed no interest. After she'd settled her bill, she left with Mittens in her arms.

Rebecca passed Ronda on the way in. Kayleigh's heart started racing again and she had to work hard to keep her composure.

"I couldn't sleep last night. I felt so bad after what happened. I was acting childish and weak and that's not me. I rushed over here this morning to tell you how sorry I am about my behavior." The words poured from Rebecca before Kayleigh had a chance to interrupt.

"I'm also sorry. I acted without thinking. I guess I got lost in the moment, and it was wrong of me." Kayleigh blushed and briefly glanced away in embarrassment. When she returned her gaze to Rebecca, her friend's face had reddened, too. Kayleigh liked seeing Rebecca blush. "I'd better go feed the kitty. Do you want to watch?"

"Ooh, yes please." Rebecca followed Kayleigh into the surgery where the kitten was sleeping in a warmer.

Kayleigh took the syringe, withdrew a small amount of stomach juices out to confirm the tube wasn't in the lungs. Then she drew up two ml of ready-made formula and inserted it into the kitten's stomach very slowly.

"Is that it?" Rebecca seemed stunned. "That seems so simple. Maybe you can take the kitten home with you and keep it there tonight?"

"That's a brilliant idea. It's warm enough." Kayleigh took a ball of cotton and dipped it into some warm water before wiping it softly over the kitten's perineum. It stimulated the kitten to pass urine and stool since Mittens wasn't there to lick her.

"Have you thought of a name yet?"

"How about Houdini?"

Rebecca laughed. "Houdini sounds like a great name. This kitten however looks like it's going to be a monstrosity. How about Rattex?"

"Rattex. Perfect." Kayleigh stroked the kitten.

"Coffee?" Rebecca offered.

"I would love some, thanks."

Rebecca disappeared off to her store and returned ten minutes later with two steaming mugs of coffee. They drank while talking about their businesses. Rebecca was happy that her business kept picking up pace, aided by the kids stopping in after school and hanging out at her store.

After they'd finished their coffee, Rebecca went back to work. Kayleigh slogged through another busy day. Since it was Friday, she decided to call Faith and cancel her shift for the night so as not to inconvenience her weekend. She also asked Faith if she'd like a permanent position as her receptionist and helper with the animals, which Faith accepted eagerly, saying she would start Monday morning.

Kayleigh wrapped the kitten up in a warm blanket and put him inside a carrier box. She'd feed the kitten at home for the weekend and bring him back to the office on Monday so that Faith could help with the feedings during the day.

At three that afternoon, Kayleigh locked up and went to see Rebecca. She waited patiently for Rebecca to finish with a couple of customers. As soon as they were alone, Kayleigh said, "I'm leaving now. Am I going to see you over the weekend?"

"Why don't you and Sarah come over for breakfast tomorrow?" Rebecca suggested.

"That sounds great. What time?"

"How about eleven," Rebecca said.

"Cool, see you then."

"Okay, goodbye and have a great evening," Rebecca said.

"Bye."

Feeling oddly sad, Kayleigh left the store to pick up Sarah from school.

†

Kayleigh made cheeseburgers for dinner, which they enjoyed on the patio. Sarah was excited about the new addition to the family, no matter how hard Kayleigh tried to explain that the kitten might not live with them permanently.

Sarah stayed close to Rattex and refused to let him out of sight.

After dinner, Kayleigh hopped into the shower, trying to figure out the last time that there had been any abnormal activity. It had been a month. *Thank God.* As she stood under the hot water, she thought of the hand that had touched her neck and wondered if she and Rebecca would have become so close had it not been for the incident. It was then that she heard a voice whispering. She tried to listen closely. It sounded like a man's voice. Kayleigh suddenly went ice cold, but decided to remain calm. If she were to get to the bottom of this, she would have to face the thing that was harassing her. She closed the taps and stood very still in the shower, shivering.

"Hello?" she asked softly. There was no response. Her heart pounded against her ribs. She was breathless with fear, but didn't move. She reached out for the towel and slowly wrapped it around her.

The whisper became more recognizable now. "*Catherinnnne…*" it said with a deep, desperate sound to the voice.

"Who's Catherine?" Kayleigh managed with a shaky voice. *My God, I'm going mad.* Kayleigh listened for another minute, but there was no response.

The voice stopped as quickly as it had started. Kayleigh scanned the room, but didn't notice anything unusual or see any shadows. The only sound was that of her rapidly beating heart in her ears and her own ragged breathing.

While looking over her shoulder, she hurriedly brushed her teeth before leaving the bathroom and then ran up the stairs to her room. Sarah had brought the kitten in its carrier up to Kayleigh's bedroom and was singing "Who let the dogs out" to him softly.

Despite what had happened in the bathroom, Kayleigh couldn't help but be amused. "Not a suitable song, sweetie pie. Run a quick bath, I'll look after the munchkin."

"Ah. No, Mommy. Please, can I bathe tomorrow?"

"Nope. Now. Move it."

Sarah jumped up and ran to her bathroom. Kayleigh had never seen her child so excited about anything before. Caring for the kitten would teach her responsibility, which was a great thing. She thought about Rebecca and that she would see her again the following day. Her heart skipped a beat. Only this time, it wasn't from fear. Her stomach made those weird and wonderful twists, making her belly feel tightly knotted. Then her thoughts went back to the shower and the voice.

First Carrey, now Catherine, she thought. *And the voice belonged to a man. How many ghosts are there within these walls?*

Chapter Sixteen

1897

The sound of a tiny little cough was followed by the sudden cry of a baby.

"It's a girl!" The doctor lifted the baby up in the air, upside down, and placed her in Catherine's arms.

Catherine sobbed. 'Thank you, Doctor. Thank you so much!' She looked at her baby and then up at Joshua. His eyes were red and filled with tears. "Isn't she beautiful?"

"Apart from you, she's the most beautiful girl I've ever seen." He touched Catherine's cheek and kissed her on the forehead. He turned to Evelyn. "Thank you."

"I'm afraid Miss Catherine did all the work," she said.

"And thank you, Doctor." He used both hands to clasp the doctor's hand.

It took the doctor another hour to deliver the placenta and then to sew Catherine up. She had a second degree tear and was still bleeding.

When the doctor was done, he washed his hands, and went to sit on the bed beside Catherine. Josh sat on the other side of Catherine, staring at his baby. The doctor looked at Catherine.

"It appears you had what's called placenta previa. The placenta was too close to the opening of your uterus and when you started having contractions, a small part of the placenta separated from the lining of your uterus, causing a massive rupture in the blood-rich tissue, which was why you were bleeding. You are lucky to be alive."

The doctor looked at Joshua. "If you hadn't found her when you did she would have bled to death, along with your baby dying." He touched Catherine's hand. "You must rest. Tell Evelyn when you need to use the restroom. She must assist you for a while. Just until you're stronger."

He then turned to Evelyn who was standing by the end of the bed. "You did a great job. Well done, Evelyn."

Chapter Seventeen

Present day

Sarah jumping on her bed awakened Kayleigh at nine in the morning. Kayleigh was exhausted. She'd been up every two hours the night before, feeding Rattex. She'd tried feeding the kitten with a miniature bottle, and he'd suckled well. So she had removed the gastric tube during the night and kept pushing the kitten to feed with the bottle. He managed five milliliters per feed already, so he'd be strong enough soon to go longer between feedings.

"I want to sleep. Why are you so cruel?" Kayleigh shoved her face into her pillow to avoid Sarah's foot in her face.

"Get up, Mommy. We're supposed to go to Aunt Rebecca's, remember!" Sarah cried.

"I'm up. I'm up." She dragged herself out of bed and went down to the kitchen to make some extra strong coffee. Sarah stayed with the kitten. Kayleigh took both cups— her coffee and Sarah's Milo—upstairs so they could drink it together while admiring their sleeping newborn. As she reached the top of the landing, she turned left to pass Sarah's bedroom when a rush of cold swept right through her and into the room. The handyman that had been there a month ago said there was no problem with the insulation. Kayleigh turned toward the room and saw a little girl looking out of the window. The girl was about half Sarah's size and had pitch black, long hair. She was too short to reach the windowsill and had to stand on a stool to see through the window. Kayleigh froze on the spot. She walked slowly into the bedroom as if afraid she'd startle the apparition.

"Carrey?" she asked softly.

The little girl twisted her head around and saw her and then as instantly as she'd made her appearance, she evaporated into thin air. Kayleigh, unnerved, took a deep breath to steady her pounding heart. The bedroom now felt warm. The cold had departed along with the little girl.

"Well, I'll be damned." Her heart still hammered away in her chest, and her legs felt weak with shock. She took a big sip of Sarah's Milo to get some sugar into her system because she felt like she was about to collapse on the floor.

"Mommy, come! The kitten's awake!" Sarah called from the other room. Kayleigh shook her head and walked on shaky legs back to her room, all the time looking behind her to see if the little girl had returned. Carrey was gone.

†

They reached Rebecca's house just after eleven.

She met them at the door. "Good morning, latecomers." She gave Sarah a tight squeeze. She turned to Kayleigh and took a step closer. She wrapped Kayleigh in a loving embrace. It felt to Kayleigh as if an energy field enveloped them and pulled them together.

"Where's the little guy?"

"Hmm?" Kayleigh was still tingling from being in Rebecca's arms.

"The kitten?" Rebecca asked.

"Oh, he's in the Jeep."

Rebecca carried the box containing the kitten into the house while she led the way up the stairs. Her house was located in Myoli Beach, just down the road from Lindsay and Judy. Only a small hill separated the house from the beach. It was roomy with more windows than walls, giving the place a light and spacious feel. The smell of bacon and coffee drifted from the kitchen and mingled with the fresh sea air. Kayleigh felt a pang of guilt as she realized they spent all their time at Kayleigh's house and never at Rebecca's, due to circumstances. It was hard for Kayleigh to be away from home, because Sarah had to be in bed at a certain time on school nights, and most weekends she had homework or projects to do. The strange happenings in her house also didn't help the matter.

"Penny for your thoughts?" Rebecca's voice brought her attention back to her surroundings.

Kayleigh shook her head and turned away. She wished she could make sense of it all. *Carrey... Catherine....* She had no idea how she would sleep tonight. For a month there had been no bad experiences, and then twice in one day.

Kayleigh tried to set that thought aside as she walked to the back of the house and looked out into the back yard. A swing made of rope was tied to a hulking milkwood tree. Kayleigh stared at the tire attached to the end of the rope.

She turned her attention to the kitchen. It was spacious, with blackwood countertops that matched the dining room table. It had a cozy feel to it. The backs of the chairs were very high. The chairs reminded Kayleigh of the chairs she'd pictured kings sitting on in the fairy tales of her youth. Kayleigh sat down in one of the perfectly hand-carved chairs and admired her surroundings. Rebecca brought two mugs of coffee to the table and sat next to Kayleigh.

"You look pale. Did the kitten keep you up all night?" Rebecca studied her with concern and put a comforting hand on her shoulder. Her hand felt warm and gentle on Kayleigh's skin.

"Sarah, honey-bun, go and put the kitten in the lounge, please." Kayleigh didn't want her daughter to be aware of what was really going on. After Sarah left the kitchen, she turned to Rebecca. "I had another experience in the shower last night." Her whole body shook as she told her story. "A voice whispering the name Catherine."

She shook her head. "First Carrey, now Catherine. I need medication. I think I'm going completely mad. Then I saw a little girl this morning in Sarah's room by her window. I saw her, every single little detail. She had long black hair and she was about half Sarah's age." She stared at Rebecca as dread filled her heart. "Am I going mad? You do exist, don't you? You're not a figment of my imagination?"

"You know perfectly well that I'm real. I really think we should investigate this further. Have you had any news from the owner?"

"None." Kayleigh sighed. "Prove to me that you're real."

"You need proof?" Rebecca leaned closer to Kayleigh. She lowered her eyelids and brushed a soft kiss on Kayleigh's lips before she pulled away gently. "Proof enough?"

Kayleigh noticed that her voice trembled, and so did her hands that rested in front of her on the table. Kayleigh was out of breath. The kiss had made every single cell in her body jolt upside down.

"Uhm. Not convinced. By God, please do that again." Her voice shook as she tried to control her breathing.

Very slowly, Rebecca moved her face closer to Kayleigh's. She paused for a short moment before their lips met again. Kayleigh's eyes closed automatically as she tried to drink in every detail of Rebecca's lips. Their tongues didn't touch, their lips didn't part. It was a soft brush of her lips, but so much electricity came with it that Kayleigh felt as though she couldn't breathe. Her eyes fluttered open as Rebecca pulled away.

"I'd better get the breakfast," Rebecca whispered as she stood and straightened out her jeans.

Kayleigh's body was on fire as she watched Rebecca move away. She had responded so suddenly, yet so completely that her whole body was weak with longing. All she wanted to do was surrender to her feelings. In her mind she could see them, skin on skin. Touching. Feeling. Tasting. Breathing. Grinding. Her center felt warm and slippery. Her stomach tied in knots. Her chest even felt tight, like an invisible band was around it, pulling her ribs in so that it was hard for her to breathe. Even her skin was warmer, and extremely sensitive. Regret filled her very being, because she knew that nothing more could happen. Ever. *Sarah would never understand.*

She watched as Rebecca's perfect body moved around swiftly as she continued preparing the meal. Her lips burned where Rebecca's lips had touched her just a few moments ago. She so longed for more. But how could she even consider having any sort of relationship with a woman while her daughter was there to take it all in? She was so afraid that it would scar Sarah for life, and she wasn't sure if Sarah's father could sue for custody once he found out. The thought of losing Sarah was too much to even think of.

Well, maybe just once—just to experience the sensations, the excitement of feeling Rebecca's body, of hearing her breathe and crying out when she climaxes. Feeling her hips writhe under my spell. Feeling her fingers dig into my back as she arches against me. Feeling her fingers slide inside me.... Stop it!

"Did you hear me, Mommy?" Kayleigh's head jolted up. It was amazing to think that life had gone on around her while nude, sexual images painted her imagination. Sarah's voice reached her from deep inside a long dark tunnel, echoing to the surface of her mind.

"I'm sorry, sweetie. What did you say?"

"I asked if I can feed the kitten. He's hungry."

Kayleigh hadn't even realized that her daughter had returned from the lounge and hoped that she didn't see any of what had happened. "Of course you can feed the kitty. Thanks, my baby, I'm pretty tired. I've prepared some bottles and they're in the kitten's box." Kayleigh had taught Sarah how to feed the kitten from a tiny bottle that very morning.

"Sarah, I have an idea," Rebecca said as she stood in the kitchen doorway with a pan of sizzling bacon. "Why don't we have breakfast first, then you can feed the kitty cat after?"

"Oh, yummy. I think the cat can wait. I'm starving." Sarah plopped onto a chair and poured herself some of the juice from a jug on the table, spilling a few drops.

"Here you go." Rebecca handed Sarah a little basket filled with golden brown toast. She dished bacon and scrambled eggs onto everyone's plates.

Kayleigh had lost her appetite for food. The only thing she wanted right now was another kiss. "Thanks, this looks delicious."

She took some toast which she buttered with shaky fingers. To her, every move Rebecca made was extremely sexy—even the mundane moves. Like how her mouth moved when she sipped her juice. How her hands worked as she buttered her toast and how her eyes lit up when she noticed Kayleigh watching her. Passion burned in her blue eyes, and her eyelids were heavy with desire as she stared back at Kayleigh.

They ate breakfast while watching one another silently. Sarah was the only one talking. If she noticed that she and Rebecca weren't responding, Sarah didn't seem to notice.

After breakfast, Sarah warmed a bottle of milk for the kitten and was about to take it to him when Kayleigh stopped her to feel the temperature of the milk. Just as she thought, it was a tad too hot. "Let me show you how to test the temperature. You drop the milk onto your wrist first. If it burns, it's too hot. Here, let me show you." She took Sarah's arm gently and dropped some of the hot milk onto her skin.

"Oops. That's maybe a bit too hot." Sarah snickered.

"Just wait a while now and test it again in a minute or so. Keep on swirling the bottle like this." Kayleigh showed her how to mix the milk to evenly distribute the mixture so that the milk's temperature was constant throughout. Kayleigh laughed at Sarah's look of intense concentration.

Sarah nodded and took the small bottle with her when she went to sit by the kitten in the lounge.

"She really loves Rattex doesn't she?" Rebecca said. "Gonna grow up to become a vet just like her beautiful mom."

Kayleigh was pensive for a moment. "Looks like we're going to have to keep it after all."

Kayleigh watched as Rebecca began clearing the table. Rebecca went to the basin and started running hot water into it. Kayleigh got up from her chair and helped. She took some of the dirty glasses from the table and progressed to the basin where Rebecca was carefully piling the dishes into the sink. Kayleigh shifted right behind her and reached around Rebecca's right side to stack the glasses carefully into the basin which was full of steaming water. She first let the glasses go and let them slip into the water, and then she pulled her hand back a little and rested it on Rebecca's right hip. She slipped her left hand onto Rebecca's left hip and closed the distance between their bodies. Rebecca tensed and exhaled slowly. A slight groan escaped from Rebecca's lips. Kayleigh's heart felt as though it was thrashing against her ribs like a wild animal in a cage, trying to escape out of her throat.

The smell of Rebecca's hair wafted up and she inhaled slowly. With her nose she moved Rebecca's hair out of the way, and pressed her lips to the nape of Rebecca's neck. She placed small, feather-light kisses against Rebecca's soft, warm skin. Her tongue darted from between her lips and slid down the neck. Her hands slipped up Rebecca's sides and back down again. She tugged into Rebecca's hips and pulled her into her. Rebecca's firm buttocks pressed into her center, and she moaned softly while trying to remember how to breathe. Rebecca's hands were still in the water in the sink, and the hot tap was still open. Steam twirled around their entwined bodies. The water had reached the top of the brim and had started running over the edge.

Kayleigh's chest rose and fell as she suddenly realized what they were doing and where they were at. "You'd better pull your hands out before they boil off."

Rebecca's hands were blood red when she lifted them from the hot water. The water sloshed over the edge of the sink onto Rebecca's jeans. "Oh, my gosh, I didn't even feel that," Rebecca gasped and quickly closed the tap. "Why are you torturing me like this, woman?" She turned around to face Kayleigh.

Their faces were very close now, their lips only inches away from touching. The aching in Kayleigh's groin throbbed, and she could feel the dampness growing between her thighs. Before she could say anything, Rebecca's lips were on hers. She enveloped Kayleigh in her arms and gripped Kayleigh's back, pulling her even closer. Their lips devoured one another. Rebecca moved her right hand to the back of Kayleigh's head to grip her hair. With her other hand, she pulled their hips together. Rebecca turned them around, so that Kayleigh's back was against the basin. She shoved her hips into Kayleigh's and pushed her up against the basin, grinding against Kayleigh in a slow rhythm. They both groaned.

Rebecca was the first to pull her lips away. She pressed her forehead against Kayleigh's. "Your... daughter... is... in... the... other... room," she gasped.

"What?" Kayleigh couldn't comprehend what she was saying.

"Remember Sarah?"

"God, what was I thinking?" It took a lot of strain for Kayleigh to haul herself away from Rebecca. She met her gaze and got lost in the swirls of blue desire she saw in Rebecca's eyes.

"Tell me you're not sorry," Rebecca said.

"I'm not. But this isn't the time for me to lose my head." Kayleigh saw a flash of worry cross Rebecca's face. "I'm *not* sorry, Rebecca," she repeated as she caressed Rebecca's cheek.

"Are you sure you've never been in a gay relationship slash fling? You seem very experienced."

"Never." Kayleigh felt her face warm with a blush. "I really don't have any idea what came over me. I've never ever done anything like that before in my life with another woman."

Rebecca trailed her thumb along Kayleigh's lips. "Hey, I'm not complaining." She gave Kayleigh a crooked grin. "We'll pick this up again?"

Kayleigh felt a jolt hit her body as she imagined doing just that... plus much, much more. "Oh, yeah," she said, her voice cracking.

"Good."

Trying very hard to concentrate on the task at hand, Kayleigh went back to retrieving dirty dishes from the table and struggled to avoid any more body contact with Rebecca as Kayleigh placed the dishes at the side of the basin. After she'd cleared the table, she grabbed a broom to sweep the floor.

Rebecca glanced at the broom. "Where are you flying off to now?"

"Ha ha." But Kayleigh was glad for the light humor. Anything to help break the sexual tension she felt crackling in the room. "You're a messy cook. I have to clean up after you."

After they'd cleaned up, they sat at the table as they drank coffee. Kayleigh had an overwhelming need to lean across the table and kiss Rebecca senseless again, but she refrained. She absolutely and completely loved the effect she had on Rebecca. It felt good knowing Rebecca was attracted to her, and that Rebecca could lose herself so easily in her.

"So, what do you want to do today?" Rebecca asked. "We can play a game or we can swim."

Sarah entered the room at that moment. "I want to swim."

"Well, let's hear what your mom wants to do as well."

"There's only one thing I'd like to do today, and it isn't swimming," Kayleigh said with a smirk.

"And what's that, Mommy?" Sarah asked.

"Sleep," Kayleigh lied.

"The cold water will cool you off and wake you up just fine, Kayleigh. There's a time and a place for *sleeping*. Believe me. I know *exactly* how you feel."

†

They spent the day by Rebecca's pool, which was sunken into the patio. A thatched deck covered half the pool and supplied shade from the threatening African sun. In the middle was a sunken bar, fully equipped with all types of liquor. Next to the bar were bar stools, attached to the bottom of the pool so that they wouldn't float away. Kayleigh sat on one of the bar stools so that the water cooled her hot skin, while Rebecca took the position of bar-lady. She lifted two cocktail glasses from under the bar and poured them each a cocktail of white rum and strawberry juice, complete with slices of fresh strawberries and topped with miniature umbrellas. Kayleigh was impressed. It was obvious that Rebecca was trying very hard to impress her. For the first time in a very long time, Kayleigh felt cared for and she enjoyed every moment.

Kayleigh watched Sarah in the pool. She swam like a dolphin, jumping and diving in and out of the water.

"You're doing a brilliant job with your daughter, but I think I've told you that before," Rebecca said, breaking the silence. "You've been very quiet since you attacked me in my kitchen."

"Well, you're lucky you got away this time. Next time you might not be so lucky."

"Ooh. I'm scared." Rebecca made a shivering sound and rolled her eyes.

When they finally got out of the pool, the sun had moved over the midline and was on its way down. They all had wrinkled skin from the extended exposure to the water and Rebecca and Kayleigh were tipsy from the cocktails.

While Kayleigh lit a fire, Rebecca prepared some steaks to grill, and together they made a salad and buttered some rolls. They ate their food out on the patio and watched the sun begin its descent in the sky. Kayleigh was glad that the food helped absorb the alcohol and she no longer felt lightheaded.

"I don't want to go home," Kayleigh admitted while Sarah was in the kitchen, clearing up after dinner.

"Don't go. Stay here. With me," Rebecca offered. "What if something happens to Sarah? I mean this ghost or spirit or whatever it is can possess your child, you know."

Kayleigh frowned. "I don't think it's evil. I mean, if it was evil surely bad things would have happened?"

"Look how scared you are there all the time. Is that not a sign that something is out of place?"

"Thanks for your offer, but if I sleep here tonight I'll most definitely end up in your bed. I don't think Sarah is quite ready to deal with that yet." Kayleigh produced half a smile at the thought. "But…to run away is not going to solve my problem either."

"Whatever suits you is fine by me. Just know that I'm here for you. Believe me, I'm more than willing to help you out any way you'd like." Rebecca added that bit with a naughty look in her eyes.

Kayleigh blushed. "Thanks."

Rebecca leaned closer and whispered, "Why are you blushing? Is your mind out there in the gutters again?"

†

That night, as Kayleigh reversed her Jeep out of Rebecca's driveway, she surveyed Rebecca's silhouette and felt totally complete. She didn't even question why—it just felt right. Halfway on their way home, she was already looking forward to seeing her again.

By the time the kitten was fed his meal for the night, it was nearly midnight. Sarah had enjoyed the day so much that she'd walked in the house, gone up the stairs on autopilot, and dropped down onto her bed before even saying goodnight to Kayleigh. When Kayleigh had unpacked the car, she'd gone upstairs to look for Sarah and had found her softly snoring in her bed. She'd tucked her in and kissed her on the forehead.

She made herself a mug of coffee and snuggled in bed with a book, all the while her senses were on hyper-alert for any strange noises in the house. Not a sound until her cell phone beeped a text message. She knew it could only be Rebecca, probably checking to see if they got home safely. She grabbed her phone and read the message: *I miss you already. Wish you'd stayed over. Sleep tight. Dream of me.*

Kayleigh sank back into her pillows and typed a reply. *Thanks for the day. We had great fun. I'll definitely dream of you.* She thought about the kiss for a while before she switched off the bed lamp and closed her eyes, slipping into a sound slumber.

✝

Feeling fully energized after an uneventful night, Kayleigh woke with a fresh mind. During the night she'd fed the kitten two meals, but he was drinking faster now and she could go back to sleep easily afterward. Upon awakening in the morning, her very first thought was of Rebecca. She wondered if she was awake yet and what she was doing. Stretching, she reached for her phone to find two text messages. She hadn't even heard the beeps announcing the messages. It was already ten and the kitten was awake, mewling for her food. Kayleigh read the first message: *G'morning. How did you sleep? I woke up thinking about you.* She scrolled down and saw that the message was sent at eight am. After yawning she read the next message: *No answer from you? Either you're still sleeping or you're playing hard to get. I'm on my way to come sort you out.* The second message was sent at nine fifty. Just ten minutes ago.

Kayleigh jumped out of bed and raced to the shower. She couldn't let Rebecca see her like this. Luckily, Sarah was up and ready with a bottle for the kitten.

"Morning, Mommy. Can I feed him, please?" Sarah looked like she'd been up for hours.

"You have no idea how much that would help, sweetie. Thanks and good morning!" She called over her shoulder as she rushed to the shower.

The water felt great, and there were no hands grabbing her this time. Kayleigh smiled to herself while she brushed her teeth in the shower. Through the steam in the bathroom, she closed the taps and opened the glass shower door, gazed up into the mirror, and froze. Written on the misted glass mirror was the name *Catherine.* It was as if an invisible finger was busy carving the name out in the mirror. Kayleigh swallowed hard and decided not to flee and it took all of her willpower.

"Who are you?" Was she hoping that the invisible finger would write out its name? Instead, the shower doors started to shake. Kayleigh jumped around in surprise. There was no one there, and yet the shower doors were rattling as if there was a massive earthquake.

"What do you want?" Kayleigh cried out desperately, forgetting that Sarah could possibly hear her.

As suddenly as the shaking of the shower door had started, it stopped. The bathroom door swung open, and Kayleigh jumped around, expecting to see something else scary, like with the shower doors. A panicked Rebecca stormed in. "What's happening? Why are you yelling?

What's that banging?" Rebecca's eyes were wide, and she folded her arms around Kayleigh's naked body in a protective manner.

"Look on the mirror." Kayleigh pointed. Rebecca turned around to face the mirror. The name *Catherine* was still there, although fading now with the steam evaporating from the shower. "And the shower doors were shaking. Truth, I promise you." Kayleigh held up her hand like she was swearing in at court. "I didn't touch them. They just shook."

"I heard it. Don't worry, Kay. I heard it. I'm here now. Shh... don't worry, I'm here." Rebecca soothed her in a quiet whisper, and then she kissed her on the forehead and held onto her shaking body. "Come. Let me help you get dressed." She reached over and pulled a towel off the railing and wrapped it around Kayleigh.

Rebecca led Kayleigh up the stairs. Sarah had taken the kitten to her room and was singing it to sleep after he'd finished his bottle. When they passed her room, Sarah showed no signs of having heard what had happened in the shower. She looked at Rebecca and put a finger to her mouth as if to tell her to keep quiet or else the kitten would wake up. Rebecca gave her the thumbs up, and nodded in understanding. She assisted Kayleigh to her room and closed the door behind them, locking it quietly. Kayleigh was still trembling. In the privacy of the room, Rebecca helped dry Kayleigh, using gentle strokes as if to calm her nerves. After drying her, she took the towel off and sat Kayleigh on the bed. Kayleigh reached her arms up and pulled Rebecca down to her. Rebecca kissed her gently for a few moments and then sat down next to her. She hugged Kayleigh for a very long time until she stopped shivering. Then she got up. "Let's get you dressed. You're naked," she whispered,

Kayleigh hadn't even thought of being nude in front of Rebecca. She was still shook up from her encounter with the ghost. She frowned, though. "How did you get in?"

"I knocked and knocked. Eventually Sarah opened the door for me before she hurried back to feed the kitten."

"Oh, I was just wondering."

"Can I get you some clothes? I don't mean to be a pest, but you're still naked and painfully irresistible." Rebecca grinned and waggled her eyebrows.

Kayleigh got up and walked to her cupboard without bothering to cover herself up. Rebecca followed her. Kayleigh picked out her clothes and started to dress herself. Rebecca helped her with the buttons and to tie her shoes when Kayleigh's hands couldn't manage.

"Might as well make yourself useful while you're down there," Kayleigh teased and then hurriedly added, "I'm just kidding." Kayleigh felt her cheeks fire up.

Rebecca glanced up at her. Her eyes glinted with mischief. "What? Want me to shine your shoes as well? Glad to see you didn't lose your sense of humor."

Kayleigh laughed and gently slapped Rebecca on top of her head. Rebecca straightened and kissed Kayleigh softly on her cheek.

"So, what do we do now?" Kayleigh asked.

"Sage." Rebecca sounded so sure of herself as she said it. As if the answer should've been clear from the start.

"I'm not in the mood to make pot roast right now. Is your plan to feed the ghosts and then they'll leave us alone?"

"Yes. Maybe they're hungry ghosts."

"What if they're vegetarians?"

"Okay. Seriously now. I went on the Internet this morning and Googled it. They say we must burn sage in the house. It gets rid of lost spirits. This is why I came over... besides wanting to see you, that is."

"All right. It's worth a try. Let's do it."

"I stopped at the store on the way over and got some, but we need to get Sarah out first. You know, just in case they get mad or something."

"I'll call her friend's mom and ask if she can go visit for the day."

Luckily Kayleigh's friend, Lisa, was happy to have her over. After Kayleigh had dropped her off at Lisa's house in Sedgefield, she headed back home to where Rebecca was busy preparing for the ritual. Kayleigh was scared.

✝

When Kayleigh reached her house, she put Rattex in his basket on the patio, making sure he was full and warm. She didn't want him to inhale any of the smoke.

Rebecca had taken out two pots and had laid out some sage in both. "One pot is for you, and one is for me," she informed Kayleigh right before she produced a lighter and lit them up. "They usually burn these in these tied up bunches, but these loose pieces were all I could find."

"Gives new meaning to smoking pot," Kayleigh said.

The burning sage generated a lot of smoke. While Kayleigh had dropped Sarah off, Rebecca had closed all the windows and opened all the closet doors. She explained that the smoke needed to spread throughout the entire house, including dark corners. This didn't make any sense to Kayleigh, but she didn't ask any questions. They each took their dish of burning bush and headed for the rooms. They started in Sarah's room. In the room it felt peaceful, but they walked around it and moved the pots around so the smoke would reach every corner. Rebecca waved her pot around inside the closet to let the smoke enter all the spaces. It was like fuming insects. Kayleigh wanted to laugh but managed to suppress it. Sarah would probably think they'd smoked dope while she was out with everything smelling of burning herbs.

They continued like this through every room, leaving the shaking shower door bathroom for last. When they finally reached the bathroom, an hour had gone by quite uneventfully. They both stepped into the bathroom and froze. The air was stale and cold. It felt sinister to Kayleigh.

With her face pale and drawn, Rebecca was the first to muster up the courage to speak. "We're not here to harm you. We want you to leave here. You don't belong here anymore."

Kayleigh got the general idea and continued. "You should follow the light. Your family is waiting on the other side of the light. This is not your house anymore."

The shower door started to have its seizure again as it had done that morning. Both Rebecca and Kayleigh stood rooted. Kayleigh wondered if Rebecca was thinking the same thing—to not run and show the spirit that they were cowards. The glass shook and rattled in the frame. It was shaking so hard that Kayleigh was sure it would break loose at any moment. But it stopped shaking as suddenly as it had stopped that morning. It was too quiet—eerie and creepy as if something was about to happen. They stood their ground. The only sound was their rapid breathing and Kayleigh was sure that Rebecca could hear the pounding of her heart as they stood there in the silence. They waited. As if something drew them at the same time they turned to face the mirror. There, in the mirror, was a reflection of a man. Kayleigh swallowed hard and started sweating. The perspiration slithered down her face. She wondered if Rebecca felt the same, because she seemed completely calm as she spoke.

"What's your name?" Her voice was merely a whisper.

He didn't answer. He acted as if he couldn't hear her.

"What do you want?" Rebecca asked again only louder this time.

"Catherine," he whispered before turning his eyes toward Kayleigh and disappearing.

Rebecca turned to look at Kayleigh, who had tears streaking down her face. She carefully took the pots from Kayleigh and placed them both on the floor. Rebecca straightened and wrapped her arms around Kayleigh. "It's all right, Kay. It's all right," she said in a soothing voice.

Kayleigh gently pushed her away so she could look at her. "It's not all right. Is this what happens to us when we die? We keep searching for the ones we love? I always thought we go to some special place where we're reunited with our loved ones."

"I'm sure there's a rational explanation for all this. Maybe he wasn't meant for that special place yet. Maybe this is his purgatory or something."

"I don't know. He doesn't seem evil to me. Just a sad man looking for Catherine."

"Well, he's gone now."

"Do you really think he is?" Kayleigh rubbed her arms trying to rid them of her goosebumps. "God, I hope so."

After they'd cleaned up all of their ritual items and opened the windows to ventilate the house, Kayleigh brought Rattex back inside. They sat at the table with mugs of strong coffee. Following the previous day's cocktails neither of them felt like anything alcoholic even though it probably would have calmed their nerves.

"We should invite our ghost for dinner, put sage all over the bloody salad."

Rebecca laughed. "Sounds like a plan."

"Next time we smoke the sage as a joint," Kayleigh said after taking a few sips.

Rebecca gave Kayleigh a thoughtful look. "Why don't we go to George tomorrow and see if we can locate some information about the previous owners of this house."

"I do have a light day tomorrow so I can get away."

Rebecca pushed her chair back. "Let's go outside."

As she got up from her chair Kayleigh noticed that the color had yet to return to Rebecca's face.

Rebecca followed Kayleigh outside to the patio, they sat down in the deck swing, and faced one another.

"How do you feel?" Rebecca's voice was full of concern for Kayleigh.

"Drained." She'd never been so scared in all her life. "Thank you for not thinking I'm a nutcase. You've really stood by me through all of this. If it were you who was seeing and hearing things, I have to say, I would've thought you were as crazy as a frog with mad cow's disease. I would've stayed as far away from you as possible. Yet, you've been very supportive. Thanks for sticking around."

Rebecca gasped and looked up in fake shock. "You mean to say that my cuteness wouldn't have led you to stick around anyway?"

"Well, you are sort of cute. I would probably have taken your madness for granted first. Used you up and then let you dabble in your lunacy."

"What do you mean, sort of cute? I'm hot. Full stop," Rebecca joked. "Besides, once you've had a go at me it would be too difficult to stay away. Some of my friends call me Beck, and you know what they say, once you go Beck you never go back."

"Oh, you don't say." Kayleigh playfully slapped Rebecca's leg. "For the sake of my well-being, it might be best to never start anything with you then. I mean, I wouldn't want to be stuck with being obsessed with you for all of eternity. Then *I* would be the ghost in the mirror whispering your name."

"Don't fool yourself, gorgeous. You're obsessed with me already. It's too late for you now." Rebecca fluttered her eyelashes and flicked her hair.

Kayleigh went silent for a few moments as she sobered, thinking about the two of them. "Where do we go from here? I mean you and me. I can't get you out of my head. That kiss. Wow. But I'm petrified, Rebecca."

"Let's go with the flow, what do you say? I promise not to do anything that you don't want to do. I'm not here to push you into anything."

"Yeah. Let's take things very slow. Baby steps."

Rebecca reached over and took hold of Kayleigh's hand. "I like that. I'm so scared of losing you. If it takes five years before we made love, I'd be happy with that. There's no rush whatsoever. Never any pressure. That's my promise to you. Please don't take five years, though. I beg of you."

Kayleigh's cell phone rang in the kitchen. She got up from the table and went to answer it. Rebecca, not wanting to leave Kayleigh alone for a minute, followed her inside, carrying their coffee. It was Sarah. Lisa's parents were on their way out and had offered to come and drop Sarah off on their way. After Kayleigh put the phone down, she turned to Rebecca. "What about Sarah? What if she knew how we feel about one another? I don't want to cause any damage to her."

Rebecca shook her head. "I've seen relationships where kids are involved. They are extremely adaptable, you know. They don't judge like adults do." She took a deep breath and walked up to Kayleigh. Rebecca put her arms around her and pulled her closer. They stood there and held onto one another for a few moments, breathing in the other's scent. They eventually went back to the patio where they awaited Sarah's return.

After Sarah came home from her outing, they cooked dinner together and ate outside on the patio while they watched the sun set. Kayleigh hated to see Rebecca go. She wished she could keep her there forever.

That night the house was peaceful and Kayleigh thought that maybe the sage had worked after all.

Chapter Eighteen

1899

They called their daughter Carrey and Joshua adored her as much as he adored Catherine.

In spring, 1899 when the Second Boer War started, Joshua was terrified his government would force him to fight against the English. Catherine was English and his two year old daughter was half English—he would be fighting against their people but he couldn't decline if asked to fight. When they did call him in early 1900 he had no choice but to join the war.

Catherine was hysterical. "How can you go? What will become of us, Joshua? I can't survive if you die," she cried. "One-by-one I've watched as my friends have lost their husbands in this bloody war."

"Darling, I have no choice. I must join the troops in the Cape," he said firmly when he got his orders.

On their final night together, they made love in the moonlight on the patio.

"If for some reason they take you away or we get split up, I will come back to the house and I'll meet you here," he said holding Catherine close. "I will always come back to you here, my love."

After Catherine fell asleep he got up quietly and went to Carrey's bedroom and looked down on the sleeping child. She was only two and, asleep in her cot, looked so innocent in her slumber. He cried as he planted a kiss on his fingertips and pressed it to her forehead. "I'll come back to you," he whispered.

Chapter Nineteen

Present day

Monday was hectic as usual and went by in a flash. Lunchtime came and Kayleigh asked Faith to answer calls for the rest of the day. Faith could send all emergencies to the other vet—even though Kayleigh didn't feel comfortable with that idea, she hoped the animals would be okay. She left Rattex in Faith's care for the day, seeing as he needed to be fed often.

Rebecca walked to meet Kayleigh as she was leaving the clinic. "Are you ready to go?" she asked.

"Yes. Let's go see what we can find out about our ghost."

They drove to the busy municipality of George where the library and public offices were. It took an hour before an older woman with graying hair finally helped them.

"What can I do to help you?" she asked.

"I'd like to find out some information about the property where I live," Kayleigh said, before looking at the woman's nametag. "Marge."

"Do you own the property?" Marge asked.

"Um, no I don't but I am interested in buying the property and would like to know more about it before I make the investment."

The woman eyed them both before shaking her head. "Very well. I'll need the name of the owner."

"Can I just give you the address?"

"Sure, but we don't usually work this way. This is your lucky day, we're way too busy for me to be following protocol. Shoot. What's the address?"

Marge passed Kayleigh a pen and paper for her to write the address down. Kayleigh quickly jotted the info down and slid it to Marge. Marge typed loudly on her keyboard. "The present owner is Martin Norton."

"Can you see who owned the house before Martin Norton perhaps?" Rebecca asked.

Again the woman typed and waited. "The owner before Martin Norton was a woman named Catherine Norton and before her it belonged to Joshua Botha," the woman said.

"Thank you so much, Marge. You've been a great help." Kayleigh smiled at her. She glanced at her watch. "Oh, I didn't notice the time. I need to call Sarah's school and have them keep her there at the aftercare."

"She didn't know you might be late?" Rebecca asked.

"I explained to her this morning I might pick her up late. I just hope she won't worry when I'm not there."

†

On the drive back to Sedgefield, they were both deep in thought.

Kayleigh broke the silence. "Martin is still alive, so the man in the mirror might be Joshua Botha. Why is he lingering searching for Catherine if she just bought the house from him? I don't know what to make of it all. This just doesn't make any sense."

"We need to find Martin Norton. He should be able to give us some answers. Maybe he was Catherine's husband or son. For all we know, Catherine could still be alive."

Kayleigh couldn't stop herself from admiring Rebecca's beautiful hands while she drove. The eyes that wandered over Rebecca's body didn't go unnoticed.

Rebecca looked sideways at her and winked. "You're gawking at me." She reached over, took Kayleigh's hand and placed it on her leg.

A current went up Kayleigh's arm and sent shivers of excitement right down her spine. Rebecca's leg felt warm and muscular. Ever so slowly she glided her hand up until it reached the top of Rebecca's thigh. Kayleigh's breathing was uneven as she closed her eyes, absorbing the moment.

Rebecca groaned. "I'm trying to drive here."

Kayleigh ignored her and curved her fingers and directed her hand toward the inside of Rebecca's thigh. Rebecca instinctively opened her legs a little, giving more space for Kayleigh's hand.

Kayleigh could feel the heat radiating from between Rebecca's thighs. She didn't push her hand upward to start pleasuring her but merely teased her a little with her fingers before she moved her hand away again.

"You really are trying to drive me as insane, aren't you," Rebecca whispered.

"I want to kiss you," Kayleigh said through trembling lips.

The car swerved as Rebecca pulled off the road and stopped in the emergency lane. She switched off the engine, leaned to the side and grabbed Kayleigh behind the neck. Their lips met with a hunger that Kayleigh had never felt before. Rebecca shifted over the gear lever, as close as she could and Kayleigh pushed herself into Rebecca's arms. They devoured one another with their lips, moving at the same rhythm. Rebecca slipped her hands in under Kayleigh's top and explored her warm, soft skin upward toward her breast. As fingers lingered at the side of her breast, Kayleigh groaned in anticipation. Rebecca's fingers slipped around her left breast and inside of her bra cup. Her fingers immediately found Kayleigh's hardened nipple. She gently rolled it between two of her fingers teasing it mercilessly. Kayleigh cried out with longing for more.

Kayleigh moved her left hand all the way up Rebecca's thigh until her thumb had reached the inside of her crotch. Separated only by a layer of jeans and panties, Kayleigh could still feel the hot moisture. She massaged with her thumb in circular movements, and Rebecca shifted her hips forward a little.

Rebecca pulled her hand away from Kayleigh's breast and ended the kiss. She lowered her hand onto Kayleigh's hand that was still moving against Rebecca's swollen flesh and stilled it. "God, I want you so badly that it hurts I'll be damned if our first time together is going to be on the highway, in my car, and in broad daylight." Rebecca moved Kayleigh's hand and took several deep calming breaths before she started the engine of the Mini Cooper and swerved back onto the highway.

"Oh, so you're a romantic." It was more of a statement than a question.

"Of course I am. I'm the inventor of romance."

"Good. Do you give lessons for free?"

"I charge very little."

"I pay in kind."

Rebecca grinned. "That's what I like to hear."

When they reached Sedgefield, Rebecca parked in front of her store and saw a group of students waiting for her outside the door.

Kayleigh pointed to the kids and laughed. "See. The people love you already."

Rebecca squeezed Kayleigh's hand before getting out and going to the shop to open the door.

Kayleigh grinned and immediately hopped in her Jeep to fetch Sarah from school.

Chapter Twenty

1899

Joshua dressed quietly into his newly assigned uniform and went back to the patio where Catherine lay sleeping on a mattress in the moonlight. The air was warm and he watched her silently for a few minutes. He couldn't shake the strong feeling that he would never see her again. The thought suddenly made his whole world crumble around him and he knew there was nothing he could do to change what was about to happen.

He knelt down by his wife, stroked the hair out of her face, and watched as a stray tear dropped onto her soft skin. *I can't say goodbye to her. It will be too painful to see her cry.* Without a word, he got up, took his backpack, and walked out quietly, leaving his life behind to fight for something he didn't believe in.

Chapter Twenty-one

Present day

The next two weeks went by with no paranormal events and Kayleigh was relieved. The sage must have worked.

Rebecca, Kayleigh, and Sarah had dinner together four times a week, alternating between the two homes. On Friday nights, they began the tradition of going to the Knysna market. The market was comprised of fifty stalls selling various types of food at reasonable prices. If they were lucky enough they'd find a table to sit at or they ate their meals on the nearby grass. Live music and open fires rounded out the ambiance.

More than two weeks after they'd been to the municipality in George, Kayleigh had a quiet evening at home with Sarah who was focused on her homework. After dinner Sarah had her bath and Kayleigh sent her off to bed. Kayleigh also showered, glad that nothing unusual happened.

After Kayleigh showered, she went upstairs and stopped at the top of the landing where the door that the previous owners must have used for extra safety stood partially open. Kayleigh liked keeping it open so she could listen out for any odd noises coming from downstairs. For a moment she wondered where the key was for the door because it wasn't part of the bunch Graham had given her—she'd tried them all.

Shrugging Kayleigh went into Sarah's room, to make sure she was covered and tucked in warmly. Rattex was sound asleep in his basket on the floor beside the bed. After kissing her daughter gently on the forehead, Kayleigh headed for her own bed.

She'd just fallen asleep when the sound of a window breaking downstairs startled her awake. She sat up in bed and listened with her hand on her chest trying to ease the pounding of her heart. Dizziness and nausea overwhelmed her. She jumped out of bed as quietly as she could and without making a sound, she tiptoed to Sarah's room as fast as she could. Sarah was fast asleep.

Creeping to the top of the stairs she could see flashlights at the bottom of the stairwell and shadows moving about. Perspiration pooled on her brow and started dripping down her face, making her eyes sting. She blinked the sweat away. She remembered seeing one of Sarah's baseball bats next to her daughter's bed and crept into Sarah's room to get the bat.

Just as she entered Sarah's room, the unused door at the top of the stairs slammed shut. Kayleigh jumped in surprise.

Suddenly, it sounded as if a World War III had started downstairs. She heard crashing and screaming from behind the closed door. There was hard banging as if all the furniture was flying around and crashing to the ground. She pictured splintered shards flying all over the place. The noise was deafening.

Sarah woke up with a start and jumped out of bed. She ran to her mom who was still standing in her doorway. Kayleigh grabbed her daughter and folded her arms around her. "Shh," she said as quietly as possible. "I think there are burglars in the house."

"Why are they breaking all of our stuff?" Sarah was in tears and shaking.

"I don't know, honey…" Kayleigh bent down so she could make eye contact with Sarah. "Sweetie, please listen to Mommy. I want you to go and hide in your closet. I must quickly run to my room and get my phone. Don't come out until I come and tell you it's all right."

"No, Mommy. Please don't leave me." Sarah shook with sobs as she flung herself against Kayleigh.

"I'm not leaving you. I promise. I just forgot my cell phone in my room. I'm fetching it and will be back in a flash. But I need you to stay hidden in here until I get back, okay, sweetie?"

"No, Mommy. No." Sarah held on even tighter.

Kayleigh pushed Sarah into her closet and reassured her through her own anxiety. "I'll be all right. Promise me that you'll do this for me." Before Sarah could refuse again, Kayleigh grabbed Rattex's basket next to her bed and handed the cat to her. "I need you here to look after Rattex. I'll be back in a few seconds. I must just go get my cell phone. Don't come out until I say so, okay? I'm going to call the police."

Sarah nodded through her tears as she clung to Rattex. Kayleigh closed the closet door, took the baseball bat as quietly as she could, and walked back to the bedroom door. She stepped into the hall. Glancing at it, she couldn't help her curiosity about the door that had slammed shut. She reached for the handle with a very shaky hand, still clutching the baseball bat in her other hand. Her palms were sweaty and slippery. She tried the handle, but the door was stuck—it wouldn't budge. She pushed it harder but it refused to give way. It was stuck tight. The crashing noises from downstairs continued. She pictured her furniture strewn about, everything in pieces. Glass was shattering and she distinctly heard a man's voice scream.

Kayleigh ran to her room and grabbed her cell phone. On her way back to Sarah's room she dialed the police. She opened the closet door, and clambered inside. After the third ring, a lady answered. "This is Ruth, what is your emergency?"

"Someone broke into my house and my daughter and I are in an upstairs closet," she whispered.

"Stay put," Ruth said. "The police are on their way and will be there in five minutes so don't try to play hero. I will stay on the line until they arrive."

These would be the longest five minutes of her life.

Much to Sarah's hysterical relief, Kayleigh stayed in the closet with her. In one hand she held her phone with the connection she had with the police and in the other she held the bat. The noises downstairs stopped just as suddenly as they started.

"The noise has stopped," Kayleigh told the dispatcher.

"Stay where you are, they may still be in the house," Ruth said.

"Okay, we will."

After some time, "The police are at your house now, ma'am. You may come out of your hiding place," Ruth said.

"Stay here until I say it's safe for you to come out," Kayleigh told Sarah before she crawled out of the closet. She entered the hall and walked to the closed door very slowly. Just before she could try the handle, the door slowly swung open. She gasped and jumped back in alarm—no one was there. "Hello. Is someone there?" Kayleigh asked.

From downstairs a man shouted. "Police!"

Slowly, with bat still in hand, Kayleigh crept down the staircase careful not to step on any broken glass or shards of wood. When she reached the bottom, she gasped at the sight of her house, and its furniture. Everything was shattered and strewn about the place.

Two men in uniform stood in her doorway. "Are you all right, ma'am?" the older of the two officers asked.

"I'm fine," she said, trying to tamp down her hysteria. "Are they gone? Did you catch anyone?" She leaned against the wall.

"There are two guys lying outside here in your driveway. They are still alive, but barely. Someone beat them into a pulp. Have you had Kung Fu lessons or something? Is your husband around?" The police officer asked suspiciously.

Kayleigh frowned. "Just me and my daughter are here, officer. We were hiding upstairs. I need to go get her."

Kayleigh went to fetch Sarah from her closet. "It's okay now, sweetie, you can come out." Shaken, Sarah took her mother's hand and followed her downstairs.

Sarah sat on the stairway while the police searched the rest of the house. They called an ambulance for the two burglars.

There was a broken window in the dining room where they must have gained access to the house. Nothing was missing as far as Kayleigh could see, but someone very strong had beaten the men by using her furniture.

"Looks like there was another one who got into a fight with the other two and beat them both up," the older officer guessed.

Kayleigh knew that was far from the truth. *How do I explain to the police that a ghost must have beaten them up?* She decided instead to agree with them.

"We will interrogate those two further when they wake up, anyway.

Kayleigh gave a full statement, leaving out the details about any ghost.

The burglars were semi-conscious and both needed to be hospitalized. The police had discovered weapons on the men, which meant that they could have killed Sarah or Kayleigh had they had managed to get to them. After the burglars were loaded into the ambulance, the police and ambulance left.

Kayleigh managed to clean up a bit of the mess, barricading the broken window with cardboard. She made them each a cup of hot chocolate and they went upstairs to Kayleigh's bedroom. Kayleigh finally got to sleep about four in the morning with Sarah snuggled next to her.

†

The next morning Kayleigh hugged Sarah close. "You don't have to go to school today. With everything that happened this past night I think we both deserve the day off. I've called your school and said you won't be going today and I called Faith to tell her I wouldn't be in and she said she'd take care of everything," She smiled at Sarah. "So we have a day just to ourselves. What do you think about that?"

"That sounds nice," Sarah said quietly.

"We are going to spend the day together, baking biscuits and listening to your CD."

Sarah smiled finally and hugged her mother.

A little after twelve, Kayleigh heard her phone ringing upstairs and ran to fetch it. It was then that she realized that she had a few missed calls and messages. One message was from a police detective called Bobby, asking her to return his call for an update. Another call was from a seemingly frantic Rebecca trying to find out why she'd never reached work. Kayleigh felt bad for worrying Rebecca by not telling her what had happened.

Since she'd met Rebecca, it had been one mishap after the other. Maybe subconsciously she was blaming Rebecca for all her bad luck. Maybe God was punishing her for being attracted to a woman.

She sent a text message. *We're fine, just had a bad night.*

What's going on? I'm coming over.

A short time later, the Mini Cooper drove up her driveway.

✝

It was suddenly hard to face her when Kayleigh saw that Rebecca's eyes were red and swollen. Rebecca had tried to call her five times during the day and had sent a slew of worried text messages, which Kayleigh only answered to one. It was understandable that Rebecca was worried and upset. Kayleigh stood in her doorway while she watched in silence as Rebecca climbed the three stairs up to her front door.

"If you really don't want me here, I'll leave right this instant. But I wanted to see with my own two eyes that you guys are all right," Rebecca said softly in a voice steeped in concern. Her eyes wandered past Kayleigh, and when she saw the mess inside, she stormed through to the lounge. "What the fuck happened here?"

"Aunt Becka!" Sarah called as she rushed from the kitchen. "I'm so glad you're here. If I have to bake so much as one more cookie I'm going to puke. We're already on our fifth bucket of biscuits." She started crying uncontrollably.

Rebecca hugged her before holding her shoulders to look her in the eyes. "What happened here, my pumpkin pie?"

"Oh, it was so bad," Sarah said around sobs. "They came...and noises...and Mommy left me...and so much…awful!" Sarah was crying so hard, Kayleigh was sure Rebecca couldn't make out everything she said.

Rebecca picked Sarah up and held her against her before walking to Kayleigh and putting her right arm around Kayleigh. "Whatever happened here? Why is your home wrecked? What's so bad that you won't talk to me about it? Are you hurt? Did someone hurt you guys?"

Kayleigh had a hard time keeping up with her questions, but she knew Rebecca deserved an answer. "Burglars," she said and swallowed hard.

"What?" Rebecca shouted in disbelief. "What happened? Did they hurt you?" she asked again.

"No, nothing like that. I heard a window breaking. Two burglars broke in through the dining room window. Then there was a wild racket going on down here. We hid away in Sarah's closet. I called the police, but by the time they arrived, two guys were lying outside in my driveway, beaten into a stupor. I don't really understand what happened, Rebecca. I'm sorry I hadn't called you. I didn't want to put this on you too. But now I'm so glad you're here. So is Sarah. Please don't go."

She wrapped her arms around Rebecca and held onto her while she cried softly. "I was stupid not to call you and let you know. I'm so happy that you're here now, Rebecca, because you make me feel safe."

"I would love to stay," Rebecca said with tears in her eyes. "I'm going to put you down now, Sarah. You're heavier than you look." Rebecca walked into the kitchen and observed the biscuits scattered all over the table. "I suggest you guys stop baking now."

Sarah nodded. "I know. There's like a gazillion of them."

Rebecca took a cookie and sampled it. "This is so good."

"Sarah, do you mind if I take your mom outside for some fresh air? I'd like to talk to her. Are you okay on your own for a minute?"

"Sure, Aunt Becka. You saved me from the cookie torture chamber. I owe you my life."

✝

Rebecca put a comforting arm around Kayleigh's shoulders and guided her to the patio. Once outside, she took a deep breath of fresh air. "Here's your chance to fill in the missing gaps. I know you too well by now and can see there's something you're not telling me."

"First, I heard a window breaking downstairs and then the door at the top of the landing slammed shut and locked itself. After that, all hell broke loose downstairs. I tried to open the door, but nothing I did could open it. The racket carried on for five whole minutes. Then everything went quiet and the door opened by itself again once the police came. When I went downstairs, everything was in shambles, and the burglars were outside, beaten up."

"Sounds to me like you have a guardian angel protecting you. I've never been so grateful for a ghost before in all my life. I think your ghost likes you."

"I know. I've just been in such a shock ever since. I'm exhausted, Rebecca."

"Come here." Rebecca pulled her into her arms. She held Kayleigh for a long time until she stopped crying.

Kayleigh took out her phone. "I'm going to call a guy I know who has a truck so he can come and clean up the mess. Then we're going furniture shopping."

"I'll drive."

After Kayleigh's call arranging the truck, her phone rang again. She answered before putting her hand over the receiver. "Police." She walked away from Rebecca while she spoke. After about ten minutes, Kayleigh ended her call. Sarah joined them from the kitchen.

"Aunt Becka, last night I was shit scared."

"If circumstances were a little different, young lady, I would wash your mouth out with soap," Kayleigh said with a stern voice. "You're lucky I'm having a very soft spot for you right now. In future, I suggest you watch your language."

"Sorry, Mom."

After Sarah went back inside the house, Kayleigh faced Rebecca. "The cops interrogated the burglars and both of them gave the same story. They broke in and were confronted by a man who started throwing furniture at them. The cops wanted to know who it was, and I couldn't tell them. The investigation is going to go on forever if they want to find the guy who beat up the burglars."

"This is all so unbelievable." Rebecca hugged her again. "Even though your ghost scares me shitless, I'm so thankful to him that you guys aren't hurt."

✝

After the man left, his truck filled with the broken furniture, everyone crammed into the Mini and drove to town for some furniture shopping. Kayleigh chose a new brown leather settee and a simple pine coffee table. Since it was late Friday by the time the furniture got ordered, Kayleigh was assured it would be delivered by Monday.

"Hey, guys, you hungry?" Rebecca asked when they were back in the car.

"Starving, we've only been nibbling on cookies all day," Kayleigh said.

"Yep, I could eat a whole cow, Aunt Becka. I'm a growing child and all my mom gives me is cake." She giggled at her own joke.

"I'm treating you both out to dinner. Knysna market or pizza?"

"Knysna market, please!" Sarah shouted.

"How about you, Kay? What do you want to do?"

"Oh, market will be great. I'm in the mood for their nachos, but we need to go home first to take a shower. I'm filthy."

"Knysna market it is."

Rebecca drove them home, and they entered the empty lounge. Kayleigh wondered if Rebecca was feeling the uneasiness.

"Sarah, you could also use a bath and clean clothes," Kayleigh told her. "I'm not taking you anywhere else while you're covered in cookie dough."

"All right, Mom." Sarah rushed upstairs.

"And no running in the house!" Kayleigh called after her. She started toward the shower and noticed Rebecca following her. She turned and raised her eye brows questioningly. "Yes?"

"I'm going to stay with you. I don't want to leave you alone again. I'm petrified of something bad happening to you. Whether you want me to or not. Period."

"Oh, you just want to gawk over my naked body," Kayleigh said, teasingly.

"You're damn right."

"Pervert."

"Yeah, I know," Rebecca said. "Now you'd better run or I'm gonna catch you!"

Kayleigh chuckled and started running to the bathroom with Rebecca right behind her. They laughed as they ran. Kayleigh tripped over her feet and crashed down to the floor, with Rebecca falling down on top of her. As Kayleigh tried to get back up, Rebecca refused to budge, and held her down. Kayleigh was positioned underneath Rebecca, their faces only inches from one another. Rebecca lowered her face, and kissed her gently on the lips, before getting up. She reached down and offered Kayleigh her hand to help her up. Kayleigh took her hand, and as she stood, she leaned into Rebecca, kissed her back, and Rebecca unexpectedly pinched her on the butt. Kayleigh yelped and continued down the passageway, Rebecca in tow, pinching her as they went.

When they reached the bathroom, Kayleigh started the water. With a confidence she didn't know she possessed, she undressed slowly, all the while keeping eye contact with Rebecca. Rebecca's heated gaze felt like tiny pinpricks on her skin. Kayleigh stepped into the shower and gasped as the hot water hit her.

After soaking for a bit, she felt someone behind her. She turned around and saw that Rebecca had also undressed and had decided to join her. Rebecca took the sponge, and lathered the soap over it. "Turn around. I'll wash your back," she said in her low, husky voice. "Don't worry. Like I told you before, nothing will happen if you don't want it to."

"Maybe I want something to happen," Kayleigh whispered as she turned and faced away from Rebecca.

"Oh, really... Well then maybe we should make a plan..." Rebecca rubbed the sponge over her skin gently. She stood close to her, so close that Kayleigh could feel her breath on her neck. She held onto the side of the shower so she didn't lose her balance as she absorbed the heat that penetrated her skin. Kayleigh arched her back and pushed her hips back until she felt Rebecca's pelvis touch her from behind. Kayleigh noticed that Rebecca was cleanly shaven. Her pubic area was smooth, soft and silky. She also felt how

Rebecca's body responded to her and welcomed the movement against her.

The sponge landed at Kayleigh's feet. Rebecca's lips touched the back of Kayleigh's neck. She slid her hands to the front of Kayleigh and stroked her nipples. Rebecca's hips thrust against Kayleigh's soft curves. Rebecca groaned as she lowered one hand down Kayleigh's stomach until she reached between her legs. She slipped a finger down into Kayleigh's wet folds.

"Oh, fuck," Kayleigh whispered breathlessly.

"You're so wet," Rebecca breathed into her ear. Kayleigh turned around, dug her nails into Rebecca's back as she pulled her closer and kissed her greedily, water running down their faces. Rebecca returned her kiss for a few seconds, but stopped abruptly and then bent down to retrieve the sponge.

"What? Why are you stopping?" Kayleigh asked, incredulous.

"Not here, Kay. Sarah is upstairs and can walk in at any moment."

Kayleigh, still throbbing between her legs, playfully slapped Rebecca on the shoulder. "Why do you start things you can't finish?"

"Hey, you started it." Rebecca chuckled. "Undressing in front of me like that." She inhaled slowly through her teeth. "You turn me on like no other ever has."

The rest of the shower was difficult. Rebecca was even more beautiful with her clothes off. They washed while looking at one another. She wondered if Rebecca was imagining all the things she wanted to do to Kayleigh's body. If her heated stare meant anything, Kayleigh would say she was.

†

After the shower, they went upstairs where Sarah was already fully dressed. When they were all dressed, they hopped in the car and drove to Knysna. It was still light at six in the afternoon, but the bonfires were burning, and the place was packed. They strolled around and visited the stalls, while Sarah went to play on the jungle gyms.

Sarah had already decided what she was going to eat. She wanted a vetkoek with mince—a ball of bread dough deep fried in oil which is then cut open like a bread roll and filled with savory mince. She also wanted some mini doughnuts with chocolate sauce, as if she hadn't had enough sugar for one day.

After looking at everything available, Kayleigh and Rebecca both had a plate of chili nachos and draughts. They sat on the grass while they ate their food, and watched the children play. The band was playing sixties music, much to Rebecca's dismay. Kayleigh discovered Rebecca enjoyed modern music the most, and Kayleigh agreed with her that old music was a bit overrated.

After the market they drove back to Sedgefield and bought ice-cream sandwiches at the all-night store. They'd eat them on the beach in front of Rebecca's house. The wind had turned cooler but felt heavenly after the hot day in the kitchen, baking. Rebecca was quiet on the drive back and then had an idea. "Why don't you ladies spend the night at my house and then go back home in the morning?"

"Yes, please, Mommy. Can we, please?" Sarah whined. "It's scary there."

The thought of going back to the house scared Kayleigh senseless. She knew the old saying that if you fall off a horse, you get back up on the horse again as soon as possible, but this was a different situation.

She glanced over her shoulder at her daughter in the back seat, then turned to Rebecca. "Well, if it's of no inconvenience to you that would be great," Kayleigh said. Not only was she not ready to face another night in her house, she also wasn't ready to say bye to Rebecca. "We just need to go and fetch Rattex first."

After eating their ice creams and walking on the beach for half an hour, all three of them drove to fetch the kitten, just like a family. Rattex was big enough to eat kitten food and had started playing and running around. He was growing very fast. His eyes were a luminous green and hair pitch black. Rattex had adopted Sarah, therefore he qualified as her cat. He refused to sleep anywhere else but on Sarah's bed.

When they got home, Sarah chose to stay in the car while Kayleigh and Rebecca went inside to get Rattex.

Rebecca searched the whole house for Rattex before finally finding him sitting in the doorway of the shower, growling, his hair standing up straight on his back, with his tiny tail fluffed out behind him. Suddenly, he arched his back and backed away crab-style, while growling like a dog. Something was most definitely scaring him or pissing him off big time. Rebecca crouched down next to Rattex, but when she saw how the kitten spat at something, she quickly scooped him up into her arms and fled from the shower. Running past the kitchen, she spotted Kayleigh packing food for the kitten and halted in order not to show her how spooked she was.

Kayleigh turned around and faced Rebecca and Rattex. "I have everything packed, including our toothbrushes. Ready?"

"Oh, I'm ready," Rebecca said way too quickly, rushed over and helped Kayleigh with one of the bags.

"Just so you know, I can see something spooked the both of you, but I'm not going to ask."

Once in the car, Rebecca passed Rattex to Sarah in the back before she keyed the ignition. Pulling out of the driveway, her eyes were drawn to the rearview mirror and to the ominous house of horrors. She couldn't get them out of there fast enough.

Chapter Twenty-two

1901

From their vantage point in the kitchen, Catherine thought the man hadn't seen them yet. She watched as he opened the screen door. He was dressed in a uniform, an English uniform. As he started to turn in their direction, Catherine crouched down to talk in a low voice so that only Carrey could hear. Tears flooded her eyes as she whispered. "Run, baby. Go and hide. Go...."

Carrey ran through the kitchen and out the back door.

Catherine tried to control herself. She stood up straight on shaky legs and faced him. "Can I help you, soldier?" She saw his face contort as he realized she was English.

"Traitor. Whore," he said in a cruel voice and then he spat at her.

The spittle landed on her left cheek. She wiped it off with her sleeve. She feared that there might be soldiers outside and they might have seen as Carrey went to hide. He slapped her across her face and she fell backward. Pain shot through her spine when her head bounced off the floor. The soldier bent down and gripped her by the hair and dragged her outside. There were five more soldiers there, all on horseback, clutching burning torches. She hoped that Carrey had gone to hide and was now out of sight and couldn't witness her in the clasp of these pigs. She knew she was going to die and she didn't want her daughter to remember her like this. Pain wrenched at her chest when she realized that she might never see her daughter again.

"Where's the brat?" One of the soldiers, a cruel looking man with evil eyes, asked through clenched teeth.

"Please leave her. Please!" Catherine pleaded.

"Burn it all," the one who held her by the hair said.

They rode up to the house, and threw their torches into the house. Catherine started pleading. "Please don't! Please!" she cried. What would happen to her little Carrey? She would die of starvation and cold if left there all by herself. She struggled to free herself from the soldier's grip. He gripped tighter when she tried to fight him off. He bent down, picked up a rock, and hit her over the head. The blow brought stars to her eyes.

Before everything went black for her, she felt the soldier pick her up and fling her over his horse.

Chapter Twenty-three

Present day

"Sarah, this is your room," Rebecca said after taking Sarah to one of the spare bedrooms. Kayleigh followed close behind them. After dropping Sarah off at her room, Rebecca led the way to another spare room right next to hers. "And this, my sweetheart, is your room."

She leaned close and lowered her voice. "Just for tonight you may sleep here. Next time I expect your naked body snuggled up next to mine." The corners of Rebecca's lips curled upward.

Kayleigh leaned back against the doorframe. "Lead me not into temptation, for my flesh is weak."

"Good night." After a quick glance over her shoulder, Rebecca gave her a long, deep kiss. Then Kayleigh disappeared into her room for the night.

✝

Kayleigh awakened at ten the following morning, feeling a little guilty about sleeping so late. She got out of bed and went into the adjoining bathroom. After brushing her teeth and making sure she looked decent, she went searching for Rebecca and Kayleigh. She found them sitting outside next to the pool, eating fruit salad.

Rebecca's face lit up when she saw Kayleigh emerging from the house. "Finally decided to wake up and join the world, I see. How did you sleep?"

"I slept very well, thanks."

Sarah ran to her mom and squeezed her hard. "Hi, Mommy. We missed you."

"Hello, child of mine. Did you sleep well?"

"Yes, Mommy. I love my room. It's so warm."

"Oh, yeah, little miss madam was up at six this morning," Rebecca said with a chuckle.

"I'm so sorry, Rebecca. You should have gotten me up." Kayleigh raked her gaze over Rebecca's body. She was breathtakingly sexy, wearing denim shorts and a white spaghetti-strap top. Her dark hair, shining in the sun, was hanging loosely, the bangs sweeping just above her eyes.

"No. You needed the sleep much more than I did," Rebecca said and dished some fruit salad into a glass bowl. She handed it to Kayleigh.

"Thank you. This looks good." Kayleigh sat down at the table. The sun was up, but the clouds were moving in. "Looks like rain." Kayleigh sighed. "Maybe we should watch some movies today."

"Yes!" Sarah gave her two cents worth. "I saw you have some good movies, Aunt Becka."

"Up early and snooping," Kayleigh said as she brushed Sarah's hair off her face. "This child from my loins is an embarrassment. I do apologize, Rebecca." Kayleigh forked a big red, juicy strawberry and popped it into her mouth.

Rebecca pointed at her with her spoon. "You've got to loosen up, chick."

"FYI, Mommy, Aunt Becka gave me permission to look."

"Watch your manners, Sarah." Kayleigh gave Sarah a stern look.

"Sorry, Mommy." Sarah slouched lower in her chair, and stared at her bowl.

Rebecca quickly chimed in. "Why don't we all take a turn to pick a movie?"

"Can I go first? Pleeeaaase?" Sarah pushed her palms together as she begged.

"Sure you may." Rebecca laughed. And with that, Sarah was gone. "Poor deprived child probably never gets to watch movies. Yet she bakes biscuits like there's no tomorrow. Slave driver for a mom and all."

"Actually we watch a lot of movies, but since the move we haven't had much time. The ghosts keep me entertained. More than enough."

While finishing her fruit salad, Kayleigh watched as Rattex played with the plants as if they were aliens trying to destroy the world and he just had to save the universe from total extermination.

Rebecca's eyes didn't leave Kayleigh. "So for real now, did you sleep well?"

"I slept like a baby, thanks to you and your hospitality. No nightmares. Nothing. Thanks for putting us up."

"I love having you around. Truth is, since I met you, life is just not the same. I used to be fine on my own, but lately I can't stop thinking of you."

Kayleigh searched her brilliant blue eyes. "I like you too. A lot. Just one teensy little thing bothering me."

"What might that be?"

"I'm worried about Sarah."

"I really believe Sarah will be fine. We won't be flaunting it in front of her and she'll grow up getting used to the idea. She'll learn that love can conquer all. And as far as I'm concerned, she already likes me more than you could even imagine and she loves being here. She's like family. We all feel like a family. You, Sarah, hell, even Rattex, and me. I don't expect to worm my way into your life and overnight become a part of your family, but I'd like you to give me a chance. And with regards to sex, that can wait. I like what we have right here. I really don't mind taking it slow."

"I want you so bad right now. It's torture. But in the same breath, I'm terrified of this. It's so new to me. And what if things don't work out in the long run? I don't want to ruin our friendship. I'd die if I had to lose you."

"It's too late for me. Whatever happens, I'm too far gone already, Kay. I'm so in love with you right now that I can't breathe." Rebecca turned her focus to her empty bowl and played with her spoon. "I said too much." She shook her head. "It's not your fault, entirely my own."

"Wow. You're in love with me?" Kayleigh stared at Rebecca's beautiful hands while she played with her spoon around the edge of the empty bowl.

"I'm sorry." Rebecca wouldn't meet her eyes. She pushed her chair back and got up. "Let's go see what movie Sarah picked."

Kayleigh reached for Rebecca's hand to stop her from leaving. "Before we go inside...I'm sorry. You caught me off guard. I want you, and you know that."

"Come, Sarah's probably waiting." She pulled her hand back and went inside. Kayleigh thought she saw tears in Rebecca's eyes as she turned for the back door. Kayleigh stood, took the empty bowls and followed her in.

Sarah had picked a movie, and Rebecca showed her how to load the disk into the machine and how to work the surround sound. Kayleigh heard their easy banter when she walked into the TV room from the kitchen where she had rinsed the bowls. She sank down onto the couch and tucked her cold feet in under her body. It had started raining. She wasn't exactly sure where her relationship was heading with Rebecca, but the fact that Rebecca was in love with her, for some reason, meant so much to her, but also scared her. Part of her was ecstatic and another part was absolutely confounded. Deep down she knew it was too late for her too. Even if making love to Rebecca scared Kayleigh, she wanted nothing more than to do just that.

Rebecca sat next to her on the couch, while Sarah flung herself down into a large bean bag in front of the large fifty inch TV. Sarah pressed the play button, and the movie started. Kayleigh had no idea what the movie was about —it was impossible to concentrate. She sensed Rebecca's warmth next to her, causing her stomach to flutter. Kayleigh's heart raced as if she was having withdrawal from a strong drug. She understood what Rebecca meant when she said she couldn't breathe. Was she in love too? Maybe this wasn't just a game of lust, but perhaps it was in fact love? Thoughts spiraled in her head, denial screaming loud cuss words in her mind. When had she let her defenses down? Yes, she admitted that she had some lonely nights, but those were just nights. She wasn't looking for another life partner. All she wanted were a few dates and then to spend her evenings with Sarah, but with Rebecca it was different. Kayleigh was petrified of *losing* Rebecca. Not *having* her. That was the truth, she knew it and it terrified her.

"Are you all right?" Rebecca whispered. Her low, sexy voice hit Kayleigh low in her belly. She closed her eyes and groaned. Rebecca turned to look at her. "Hey? You all right?"

Kayleigh turned her face toward Rebecca. "I'm fine," she said with a tremulous expression. She wanted to put her hand on Rebecca's leg, but fear made her hand as heavy as steel. Her blood rushed through her body, feeling as if it were traveling at light speed through her veins. She glanced over at Sarah before she finally moved her hand over and slowly climbed her fingers up Rebecca's leg until she came to a rest on Rebecca's thigh.

Rebecca looked down at her hand, took a deep shaky breath, and turned her attention back to Kayleigh. Rebecca's lips were full, and her eyes filled with longing. "You shouldn't do that," she whispered.

"I know, but do you mind?" Kayleigh whispered back.

"Kay, why would I mind? I want as much from you as I can possibly get." Rebecca put her hand onto Kayleigh's leg. The touch of her hand on her leg made Kayleigh's blood rush even faster. The tingling sensation went from where Rebecca's hand lay on her leg, right up her thigh, and into her center. Even her stomach went into knots. Kayleigh closed her eyes again and tried to steady her rapid breathing. She couldn't stop another groan from leaving her parted lips.

It took a whole lot of restraint for Kayleigh to sit still like a good school kid and watch the movie that she knew that neither of them was really watching. The awareness of Rebecca's nearness was unlike anything that Kayleigh had ever experienced before. She wanted nothing more right now than to be alone with Rebecca.

They watched movies all day while it rained heavily outside. Rebecca chose a movie, and so did Kayleigh. While watching the movies, they sat close enough so their bodies touched. Rebecca fetched popcorn and crisps, but neither of them had any appetite at all. Sarah was the only one crunching away.

"Time for bed, Sarah."

"But, Mom."

"No but Mom's, young lady. Off to bed with you."

"Okay," Sarah said with a pout.

"I'll come tuck you in in a few minutes." Kayleigh said as Sarah came to kiss her good night.

Kayleigh yawned. "For someone who slept so late, I sure am tired." In truth she was exhausted by wanting Rebecca so much all day. "I guess I'll turn in too."

"Sweet dreams," Rebecca said as she too got up. "I'll see you in the morning."

Kayleigh lay in her bed and stared at the ceiling wishing Rebecca would come into her room during the night. Rebecca never showed.

†

Sunday the sun was up and they swam all day and played cards during the afternoon. By Sunday evening, Sarah was reluctant to go home. Kayleigh secretly felt the same, but she knew that they had to go home eventually. She didn't want to run away from her problems forever. Besides, there was school and work to think about. They needed to face the problem hands on and deal with it. Since she had driven them to their house, Rebecca had to drop them off at home. It was with great difficulty that Kayleigh didn't invite her to sleep over.

The week flew by quickly. Rebecca had hired a full-time shop assistant at her CD store. Kayleigh had burglar bars installed over the windows on the first floor of the house, and the new furniture had been delivered. She wrote a letter to Graham, the estate agent, and explained the necessity for the extra security, and he agreed that she could pay for the burglar bars. She could then stop paying rent until the fee for the burglar bars was covered. The burglar bars helped them feel much safer, but Kayleigh took the extra precaution of

171

buying some motion detector alarm systems and placing them at every entrance.

On Wednesday, Sarah brought a letter home from school. They had a Red Hut summer camp that weekend, and Sarah told Kayleigh that she really wanted to go. There was horse riding, swimming, and lots of games at the camp. Kayleigh decided that Sarah deserved a weekend away, and she also desperately needed some time alone with Rebecca. The camp started Friday afternoon and ran until Sunday.

After dropping Sarah off at camp, Kayleigh stopped at her favorite CD store in town and said hello to her favorite CD store owner. Kayleigh walked to Rebecca and gave her a hug. "I missed you," she whispered.

"I missed you too," Rebecca whispered back. "Why are we whispering? There are no clients here."

Kayleigh searched the store. "You're right. Where's your new shop assistant?"

"Oh, Stephanie went to the Spar to buy herself a cola."

"Dinner tonight?" Kayleigh asked.

"My place." Rebecca nodded, looking pleased.

"Only you and me. No Sarah. She has camp this weekend."

"Hmmm. Gotta stop by the pharmacy and get condoms." Rebecca winked.

Kayleigh giggled. "You're so naughty. What time?"

"Six."

"What to bring?"

"Only your sexy self. Naked, preferably."

"What happened to no pressure?"

"Of course. Wear something then if you absolutely have to."

The new employee returned with a can of cola in her hand. She was young and very pretty. Kayleigh felt a twinge of jealousy.

"See you then." Kayleigh walked out and waved the royal wave as if she were the queen.

Rebecca laughed.

Kayleigh went home to start with her cleaning-of-self regime, happy to have the house to herself. Rattex played with the string that controlled the blinds and chased his own shadow. She took a bath in Sarah's bathroom and soaked for about half an hour before she finally got out. She'd also shaved all over. The thought of going bare was extremely sexy. She'd put her favorite CD into the music system and was singing along while soaking in the bath. After her bath, she brushed her teeth and dressed in blue jeans and a white, skin-tight shirt. Her black boots rounded out the outfit. She blow dried her brown hair until it fell in waves on her shoulders, giving her a wild look. She put on some eyeliner and mascara, bringing out the green in her eyes and making them appear larger. She applied some light brown lipstick.

When she went to the Jeep to put all her stuff inside, Rattex followed her, since he went everywhere with them. She helped him into the Jeep, and he sat on the front seat seemingly waiting patiently for her while she got her things.

†

Rebecca was waiting outside for them when they arrived. "I could hear your engine when you turned into my street, not to mention the music blasting the neighbors away."

"Hi." Kayleigh leaned in and gave her a hug. "Grab Rattex and I'll bring my bag."

"Bag, huh?" Rebecca raised her left eyebrow in surprise. "You're planning on spending the night?" She turned to the Jeep to get the cat.

"If it's all right with you, the night and the entire weekend." Kayleigh felt the familiar twist of excitement in her belly.

Rebecca took Rattex, who immediately purred and curled around in her arms. They walked up the steps and went into the house. "It's completely your decision which bedroom you want to put your bag in."

Kayleigh went up the stairs and set her bag down in Rebecca's room. She inhaled nervously before she went back downstairs again. "So, what's cooking, good looking?"

Rebecca, wearing jeans, with her hair still damp, was standing by the stove and stirring something in a pot. Rattex sat by her feet and played with her shoe laces.

"We're having pasta alfredo and salad."

"Mmm, delicious."

"Thanks. I've set the table inside tonight, because it smells like rain."

"It looks beautiful." Kayleigh admired the table that Rebecca had set. The wine glasses and candlelight made the atmosphere extremely romantic. She had acoustic guitar music playing on the stereo, and the lights were dimmed. Kayleigh was impressed.

"I chose a white wine to go with the pasta. Hope you don't mind?"

"Perfect. Thank you."

Rebecca poured wine into their glasses while Kayleigh went to sit at the table. After pouring the wine, Rebecca placed their plates of food on the table, and sat down opposite her.

"I'm so pleased to have you all to myself. This weekend is going to be fun. I want you to relax. I'm going to spoil *you* for a change. You have no responsibilities, and it's your weekend off."

"Yeah. No kids. No ghosts."

"Just you and me." Rebecca took a sip from her wine glass.

"That's so sweet of you, Rebecca. Thank you. And the food looks divine."

"Bon appetit."

"Mmm," Kayleigh said again as she took her first bite.

"Wait 'til you see what I have planned for dessert."

"You're such an amazing person. I'm so glad I met you."

Rebecca reached across the table and caressed Kayleigh's hand. "You're amazing too. You look very beautiful tonight, by the way."

"All these compliments. You're making me blush."

"You're pretty when you blush."

"Stop it."

Rebecca withdrew her hand and continued with her meal. "I'll never stop."

"I could possibly get used to this."

"Well, you may have to. I think you're perfect."

"I'm far from perfect, but I'm glad one person thinks I am."

They enjoyed the rest of the meal, talking about the camp and work.

"What's for dessert?" Kayleigh asked as she sampled the salad.

"You will just have to wait and see," Rebecca said. Her eyes shimmered in the candlelight. "But dessert is for later."

"Fine. Be like that." Kayleigh said and threw her napkin across the table at Rebecca.

"Children who don't behave, don't get dessert."

"Is that right?" Kayleigh got up and walked around the table to Rebecca. She pulled Rebecca's chair backward and Rebecca lifted her weight off the chair in order to assist. When there was enough space between Rebecca and the table, Kayleigh raised her leg over Rebecca's knees and sat down in her lap, facing her. "Doesn't behaving badly count?"

Rebecca inhaled sharply. "If you continue this you can have my dessert too."

Kayleigh closed the distance between their lips, and brushed her gently with a kiss. "Like this?"

Rebecca's voice shook. "Oh, yes."

"Great. Two desserts for me it is." Kayleigh got up and started clearing the table.

"You play dirty," Rebecca said as she got up and helped.

After clearing the table, they made sure Rattex was inside, then locked all the doors and closed all the windows. They headed for the bedroom and Kayleigh's heart pounded away in anticipation of what was to come.

Rebecca stopped in the doorway to her room. She turned around and faced Kayleigh. "So, where did you put your bag?"

"I'm following you there as we speak."

"Nice." Rebecca walked into her room.

Kayleigh silently took her bag and disappeared off to the bathroom to put on her night dress. She'd packed a little black number for the night—one that she'd had for years but had never worn before. She scrutinized herself in the mirror and wondered if it was too much—or perhaps too little—for their first night alone together. It was extremely short and silky. Her erect nipples were clearly visible under the thin material. She brushed her teeth again and sprayed on a little perfume.

Rebecca entered the bedroom from another bathroom down the passage when Kayleigh walked in. Her eyes went wide in appreciation when she saw what Kayleigh was wearing. "Wow," she said before taking a deep breath in and whistling on exhaling.

Rebecca had changed into blue silky shorts, with little pink pigs on them, and a strappy top which read *Young single and free.*

Kayleigh went to sit on the bed. "Young, single and free?" she mused.

"It's an old top." Rebecca closed the curtains before she walked up to Kayleigh. "I'm now old and hopefully taken."

Rebecca lowered her face to Kayleigh's and kissed her gently on the lips. Their lips parted and their tongues met one another's eagerly. While kissing her, Rebecca's hands slipped in under Kayleigh's night dress and quickly found Kayleigh's bare skin. She gently lowered Kayleigh to the bed and lay on top of her. Kayleigh marveled at how perfectly their bodies fit together. She'd never experienced a wanting that was so strong.

Their hips moved rhythmically against one another. Kayleigh reached up and pulled Rebecca even tighter against her. Rebecca found an erect nipple before gently squeezing it between her fingers. Kayleigh groaned and shoved her hips against Rebecca, feeling the beginning of a strong release. She tried very hard to hold back in order not to embarrass herself with such a low threshold, but it was no use. With each movement Rebecca made, Kayleigh came closer and closer to orgasm, the feeling between her legs becoming more and more intense. She dug her nails into Rebecca's back, never stopping the movement of her hips. Rebecca pushed harder with her movements, but at the same rhythm, bringing Kayleigh to a body shattering climax. Kayleigh cried out as she came, her body shuddering with pleasure. She felt the urgency in Rebecca's movement increase. "Oh, my God," she whispered.

Rebecca continued grinding into her. She cried out too, only moments after Kayleigh came, as she joined her in the climax. After Rebecca climaxed, she fell down next to Kayleigh.

They lay there breathless for several minutes before they started kissing again. Rebecca lifted her head and gazed into Kayleigh's eyes. "I'm sorry. I didn't want our first time to be this urgent. But the night is still young."

She sat up and slipped her top off, exposing breasts that were small and firm, with erect nipples. Then she slipped her hands under Kayleigh's gown and shifted the silky material upward in slow, tantalizing movements.

Before Kayleigh knew what was happening, they were both naked on the bed. This time, there would be no rush as they kissed and stroked one another with sincere passion. Before long, Kayleigh was wet and swollen and aching for more.

Rebecca slipped her fingers into Kayleigh's wetness while she rubbed her thumb against Kayleigh's clit. "Come for me, baby, I want to make you come again," Rebecca panted.

Kayleigh moved her hips against Rebecca's hand and felt the pressure building slowly, closer with every move. Her clit was pounding and swollen, and she crashed into another orgasm. Her hips rocked faster as Rebecca slid deeper into Kayleigh's center. Rebecca applied more pressure with the palm of her hand against Kayleigh's clit as her fingers continued to move inside Kayleigh.

"Oh, God, Rebecca. I'm coming again." Kayleigh breathed.

Rebecca kept moving as Kayleigh's body rocked against her until Kayleigh finally slumped down, spent. "You're fucking awesome," Kayleigh said, out of breath. "It's never been like this before for me. Never."

Rebecca met Kayleigh's lips in a passionate kiss.

"Teach me what to do. I want to do that for you too." She shifted until she was on top of Rebecca. Perfectly shaped breasts with nipples hard as rocks enticed her. Kayleigh leaned and started licking them.

Rebecca gasped. "Put your fingers inside me." She guided Kayleigh's hand to her wet folds. Kayleigh slipped her fingers inside. "Oh, yes, Kayleigh. Make me come, baby, please."

Kayleigh's stomach twisted in knots as she watched Rebecca getting closer and closer with every move. She pushed her fingers deeper inside Rebecca and pressed her thumb over her swollen and throbbing clit. Rebecca's hips arched rhythmically against Kayleigh's hand. Kayleigh felt Rebecca tighten around her fingers. "Oh yes, oh yes, I'm coming. Oh, God yes, Kayleigh! Oh! Fuck! Don't stop!"

Kayleigh moaned as she slid in and out of Rebecca. She loved feeling Rebecca's center throb around her fingers. She loved watching Rebecca's face as she came. She wanted to do this over and over... and over.

They made love all night long before finally collapsing next to one another, out of breath and satiated in the early morning hours.

Kayleigh was flushed and wet with perspiration. "I never knew a woman could orgasm so many times in one night. What have you done to me, Rebecca?"

"A few months of foreplay, and this, my dear sweetheart, is just the tip of the iceberg."

"You mean there's more? I don't understand how people can say it's wrong when it feels so damn right."

"That's because they've never experienced what you and I just have."

"I want you to teach me. I want to be perfect for you," Kayleigh whispered. She pressed her lips to Rebecca's and kissed her.

Rebecca pulled away after a long moment. "And I want you to teach me what you like too. I want to know all there is to know about your body."

Wrapped in one another's arms they fell asleep, sated and happy.

Saturday morning arrived all too soon but waking up next to Rebecca made Kayleigh feel warm and satisfied. She snuggled into Rebeca's body.

Rebecca wrapped her arms around Kayleigh and pulled her tighter. She kissed her forehead. "Good morning, sexy."

"Mmm, good morning, you sexy thing," Kayleigh purred. "I was just wondering what happened with the dessert you promised me last night after dinner."

Rebecca burst out in laughter. "You had it all last night, don't you remember?"

"Oh. You mean you were my dessert?"

"Yes, my baby. I was your dessert."

They lounged in bed a long while before finally getting up and showering. Wearing only T-shirts they made their way to the kitchen to make breakfast together—they were famished.

"We have some lamb sausages and eggs. Does that sound like a breakfast to die for?" Rebecca asked as she removed the vacuum packed sausages from the fridge.

"Yes. I'll make the toast. Do you have cheese and marmalade?" Kayleigh wrapped her arms around Rebecca and they kissed.

Rebecca pulled her face away and viewed Kayleigh through hazy eyes. "In the fridge."

After breakfast, they went outside to the pool. Rebecca pulled the T-shirt off over her head, chucked it aside, and jumped into the pool, naked. Kayleigh laughed as she followed suit. Once in the water, they swam to one another. Rebecca pulled her closer as she met Kayleigh's lips. Rebecca pushed Kayleigh to the side of the pool and pressed up against her. With her arms around Kayleigh, Rebecca gripped the edge of the pool and pushed her hips against Kayleigh's. Kayleigh wrapped her legs around Rebecca's hips and tried to match her rhythm. Kayleigh gripped Rebecca's back and held her tightly all the while moving with her.

Rebecca pulled her face a few inches away and gazed into Kayleigh's eyes. "I want to see you come," she panted. "Look at me when you come."

"Oh, yes." Kayleigh pushed deeper into Rebecca's hips, levering herself by arching her back and lifting her head up, leaning her head over the side of the pool.

Rebecca bent forward as she moaned. "Oh, God. Oh yes...." She started thrusting even faster. "Oh, fuck." She was breathless as her moans became louder with every thrust. Rebecca cried out as she came, her fingers digging into Kayleigh's flesh as she held onto her hips while thrusting against her.

Kayleigh felt the pulsating feeling climb up her center as she started coming. She opened her mouth and then clamped her jaws shut as she tried to stop from crying out. She dug her fingers into Rebecca's hot flesh as she pulled her closer. The orgasm shattered her body over and over as she came while Rebecca kept moving at a steady pace. Their lips met and they kissed passionately as they held onto one another. Then Kayleigh's whole body relaxed, thankful that Rebecca held onto her to save her from drowning. They looked into one another's eyes and laughed.

"Wow," Kayleigh finally managed to say.

"I love you," Rebecca whispered.

Kayleigh's heart stopped beating for a moment. She wasn't sure how to respond. Instead of speaking, she kissed Rebecca again.

They spent the whole weekend making love, sleeping, swimming, and talking. Kayleigh remembered lovemaking to be exhausting, but with Rebecca it was so different. They could make love for hours, and she never tired. Rebecca was completely selfless in bed. Kayleigh's ex-husband had no idea how to give a woman pleasure. All he ever cared about was his own pleasure never once caring about how she felt.

This was definitely something Kayleigh could live with for the rest of her life.

†

Sunday arrived too quickly. And before Kayleigh knew it, it was time to fetch Sarah from camp. She felt miserable, because she wasn't sure when she and Rebecca would have another weekend alone or when they'd make love again. She missed Rebecca even before she left. Her heart ached and her soul felt empty. A part of her belonged to Rebecca now, and she had no idea how she'd ever be able to return to her normal life again. Still afraid to say the words out loud she realized that she'd fallen madly, head over heels, deeply in love with Rebecca.

It was with great difficulty that Kayleigh said goodbye to Rebecca, afraid that Rebecca would disappear from her life forever, if she let go. She yearned for them to be together again. The pining in Kayleigh's chest formed a dry lump in her throat that threatened to suffocate her on the long drive to pick Sarah up from camp.

Chapter Twenty-four

Sarah was like a different child, happy and relaxed. She couldn't stop babbling about how much fun the camp had been. "You know, Mommy, they have camp every month."

Without a second thought, Kayleigh asked, "Would you like to go again? Maybe every month?"

"Oh, yes, Mommy, I'd like that a lot."

"Then I will sign you up." As much as she loved Sarah, she couldn't wait to be alone with Rebecca again.

Her bed felt cold and empty that night. She could only look forward to their routine of lunchtimes and dinners shared on alternative evenings. She missed Rebecca so much that it hurt. She wondered if it would be awkward to see her the next day, if Rebecca would've changed toward her after the weekend of tender lovemaking. Would they end up getting bored with one another like most couples did? She remembered how she loathed making love to her ex-husband, what a chore it had become after a while and knew that it would be different with Rebecca—Kayleigh craved more.

She was restless that night. It'd been so good sleeping next to Rebecca, lying in the comfort and security of Rebecca's arms. Most of all, Rebecca made her feel complete. All of Kayleigh's life, she had felt an emptiness that she couldn't explain. Since the day she'd met Rebecca, that feeling of emptiness was gone. Rebecca had filled that dark, empty hole that had always tormented Kayleigh.

After tossing and turning half the night away, she finally fell into a restless sleep. When morning finally came, Kayleigh felt alive again knowing she'd see Rebecca that day. Probably exhausted after her busy weekend at camp, waking Sarah was more difficult than usual. After dropping her off at school, Kayleigh drove to work, parked her car, and hopped out. For some odd reason she felt nervous and shy to see Rebecca this time. Taking a deep breath, she marched to the open doors of the CD store.

"Good morning, beautiful!" Rebecca beamed from behind the counter and then walked up to Kayleigh.

All the shyness disappeared and Kayleigh returned her greeting. "I missed you," she said just as Rebecca put her arms around her and pulled her close. After a short kiss, Rebecca pulled away and walked back to her counter. Kayleigh was a little bit disappointed at the quickness of the intimacy, but she brushed it off.

She lingered a moment, waiting for more. "Well, have a good day then," she said and walked out.

"You, too!" Rebecca called behind her as if nothing was wrong. "Oh, and by the way, don't be too surprised if Lindsay calls you later."

Kayleigh's cell phone rang. "Hi, my friend." Kayleigh said while walking to her clinic.

"What do I hear of you being fifty shades of gay? How are you doing?"

Kayleigh felt her cheeks warm up. "I've never been better, Bag. You should have told me many moons ago how fuckin' great lesbian sex is."

"I think I did. Are you okay? Any regrets yet?"

"God, Lindsay, I think I'm in love,"

Lindsay laughed. "That's fantastic news, Kayleigh. Judy tells me Rebecca is completely smitten."

"Is she? I mean, did she say she is?"

"I don't want to say too much, but sounds like she is."

"She makes me so happy, Lindsay. I hope I'm not getting ahead of myself."

"Just take it slow. That's the only advice I can give."

"Thanks. I've got to run, just arrived at work now. Say hi to Judy for me."

"Will do. Have a great week."

✝

The following week, they spent lunchtimes together like always, but it wasn't the same as it had been over the weekend. They could never touch one another in public for fear of what people might say. Kayleigh missed making love to Rebecca, but circumstances seemed to keep them away from one another all week. With every night, the longing became worse. By Friday, it was unbearable. Kayleigh wished she could find a way to get Rebecca to stay over without raising too many questions in Sarah's mind. Much to Kayleigh's dismay, Rebecca told her that she'd rather spend Friday night at her own house and not come over.

Kayleigh and Sarah had spaghetti and mince for dinner, which tasted like cardboard to Kayleigh. Sarah went up to take her bath and then to her room to play with Rattex. Kayleigh took a shower. It'd been very peaceful since the burglar event and she was beginning to wonder whether her ghosts had really gone. Not that she wanted them back. She was quite enjoying the peace and quiet.

After her shower, she climbed into bed with a novel and her nightly cup of coffee. She couldn't concentrate on her book when Rebecca was all she could think of. She was like a lovesick puppy. It was raining outside and the rain drops sounded like bombs on the corrugated metal roof. She checked her cell phone, but no messages from Rebecca. Her heart ached and she felt desperately lonely.

What if Rebecca had second thoughts about being with her? Why hadn't she made any plans to see her over the weekend?

For some reason she just couldn't get herself so far as to call her and ask, for fear Rebecca might have doubts about her feelings for her.

Suddenly, her curtains became light, as if a bright light shone on them from outside. She jumped out of bed, terrified after the break-in, and ran to the window. She pulled the curtain aside, just enough to look outside. There were two lights—car headlights. Her heart jumped into her throat. She hustled downstairs to the front door and peered out of the window. Much to her astonishment, Rebecca's Mini Cooper pulled up the driveway. Kayleigh ripped the door open. Her heart racing at the speed of light beat rapidly. If there were a speed limit for heartbeats, she would have a fine chucked in her direction…or possibly even a prison sentence.

Rebecca parked her car a few yards from the front door, got out, and stood in the rain. She raised her face to the sky and shouted. "I love you, Kayleigh Gibbs! I can't do this! I can't only love you one weekend a month. I want the world to know how I feel about you. I can't sleep without you. Gosh, man, I can't even breathe without you!"

Kayleigh laughed. "Shut up and come inside, you crazy lady." The deep, dark depression that had gloomed her life several minutes ago transformed into the strongest feeling of happiness that she'd ever experienced. Rebecca laughed too and ran up the driveway, shaking her wet hair before hurrying into the house.

Once inside, they grabbed one another and kissed.

"You're crazy, do you know that?" Kayleigh asked as she brushed wet strands of hair out of Rebecca's eyes. "I love you too, Rebecca, more than you could ever imagine."

"You do?" Rebecca had tears rolling down her cheeks. She kissed Kayleigh again. "Let's move in together then."

"Move in together? Seriously? What happened to taking it slow?" Kayleigh couldn't believe what she was saying.

"Screw all that. I love you, and I want to be with you all the time."

"Me too, but what about Sarah?"

"We can keep her," Rebecca said, eyes twinkling in amusement.

"You know what I mean, silly. What do we tell her?"

"Only as much as she needs to know."

Kayleigh grabbed a towel from the closet next to the kitchen and helped Rebecca dry off. Her short dark hair was dripping rain water.

"Here's the thing. I don't want to go home, so best would be to tell Sarah now that I'm not leaving," Rebecca said as she took the towel from Kayleigh and dried her face.

"Race you there."

They ran up the stairs like two teenagers chasing one another.

Sarah was on the floor, playing with Rattex. Her eyes grew wide with surprise when she spotted Rebecca. "Hi, Aunt Becka."

She was busy rolling a tennis ball on the floor while Rattex chased it around, attacking it and doing flips around the floor with it like he was a famous wrestler.

Kayleigh and Rebecca sat next to one another on Sarah's bed. Kayleigh cleared her throat, now a little nervous to begin. "Sarah, I love Rebecca, and Rebecca loves us, too."

Sarah stood up from the floor. "I love Rebecca too, Mommy."

"I'm happy that you do. You see, we love one another so much that we want to see one another all the time. We want to live together in the same house." She watched Sarah's face carefully as she spoke.

"That sounds great. I'd love for Aunt Becka to be here all the time."

"Best part is that we're going to be a family. We're going to live in the same house like a family. The three of us. Would that make you happy, sweetie?"

"Yeah! That would be so awesome." Sarah jumped up and down with excitement before she ran to Rebecca and hugged her. "Thank you, Aunt Becka."

"Let's all have a hot cup of cocoa, and then it's off to bed for you, young lady," Kayleigh said.

After having cocoa in the kitchen, it was a struggle to get Sarah to listen when Kayleigh told her to go to bed. But Rebecca helped with the persuasion, and a few minutes later she was in bed.

"I can't believe it. I don't have to go home tonight and miss you like hell," Rebecca said later when they were preparing for bed.

"I'm so happy. Thank you for coming into our lives," Kayleigh whispered as she held onto Rebecca.

"No, thank you, Kayleigh."

†

That night, after making love, they lay in bed in one another's arms, completely satisfied and flushed.

"It's so nice to have you in my arms again. I thought I was going to die if I had to wait another day. I missed you so much." Kayleigh traced her fingers across Rebecca's breasts.

"I felt the same way. It was absolutely awful when I had to act like nothing had happened between us these past few days. It's so unfair that we have to keep our feelings a secret just because other people don't share our point of view. Let's not raise our daughter to be so narrow-minded."

Kayleigh lay pensive in the dark. "I love that you said *our* daughter. Thanks. It means a lot."

"She's our daughter if we're going to be a couple. We need to discuss the options. Where are we going to live?" Rebecca asked.

"Well, I signed that twelve-month contract, so I'm stuck here unless we can find other tenants to take over until the twelve months are up."

"We could advertise both our places in the newspaper and see who responds. And take it from there then."

"Your house is right on the beach. During December we can make a killing renting it out over the holidays."

"True. Especially with the Easter holidays coming up, but in this house we have other issues."

"Do you know how hard it is to get tenants in this area?" Kayleigh asked as she leaned on one elbow and looked at Rebecca. Talking about their future was so exciting, she couldn't even imagine how wonderful it could be.

"How about we stay here until your twelve month lease is up and move to my house then. How bad can it be?"

Kayleigh laughed. "Very bad, but anything with you by my side is bearable. We'll have something to look forward to. Moving to your house."

"Which would be our house," Rebecca said and reached up to pull Kayleigh's face closer. She kissed her, deeply and passionately.

That night Kayleigh fell asleep with a huge grin on her face.

Chapter Twenty-five

1901

Catherine awoke a few hours later in the back of an ox-driven wagon.

"Carrey," she whispered as tears streamed down her cheek.

Where are you, Carrey? Are you safe? I hope Evelyn found you and is looking after you, my child.

"Are you okay?" Catherine's eyes moved toward the gentle female voice. "I'm Linda. You've been sleeping for a few hours."

"Where are we?" Catherine coughed as her dry throat scratched when she spoke.

"I heard them saying something about a concentration camp in Bloemfontein." Linda spoke quietly. "We're on our way there."

Catherine looked around her and saw two other women, seemingly older than them and four small children huddled behind Linda. "Who are these people?" she managed to ask through her burning throat.

"That's Lauren over there and Clara," Linda said as she pointed to the other two in the wagon. "And these are my children."

Catherine felt the warm tears flowing down her cheeks. "They're beautiful."

✝

The concentration camp was brutal and even though Catherine missed Carrey, she believed that her daughter was safe at home with Evelyn. She had to believe it, or else she would go insane with worry.

Then typhoid fever broke out, crushing any hope there might be for survival. Catherine thought of Joshua and Carrey constantly. Daily, she watched little children die of disease and starvation. It was hopeless.

Chapter Twenty-six

Present day

Three weeks had passed since Rebecca had moved in. Sarah had never raised any question about why her mother shared the same bed with Rebecca.

"Is there anything else that needs to get done?" Rebecca asked Kayleigh who was standing in the kitchen checking on the pork roast.

"No, I'm pretty sure everything is ready."

Just then the doorbell rang.

"I'll get it," Rebecca said. She gave Kayleigh a quick kiss and walked out of the kitchen.

Kayleigh heard their voices growing louder as they moved toward the kitchen. "Hi, Kayleigh," Lindsay and Judy said in unison.

"Hi, guys," Kayleigh hugged them both before accepting the glass of wine Rebecca handed her.

"Red or white, Lindsay?" Rebecca asked while pouring Judy a glass of red wine. "Here you go, Judy."

"Thanks," Judy said as she lifted the glass to her nose. "Did you let it breathe?"

"Oh, shut up, you numb nut," Rebecca said and laughed. "Who's got time for that shit?"

"In that case I'll have the white," Lindsay said with a big smile.

"So, how is the lesbian life, Kayleigh?" Judy asked while Rebecca poured Lindsay's white wine.

"Rebecca's great." Kayleigh wiped her hands and walked to Rebecca. She slipped her arm around her slender body and heard Rebecca inhale.

"She still takes my breath away," Rebecca said before she leaned closer and kissed Kayleigh. "Let's feed them so they can leave," Rebecca teased.

"I hope you're going to wash your hands before you pass me my wine," Lindsay said. "The way you two are all over one another. Yuck."

Judy laughed and reached for Lindsay's wine. "Here you go, my love. I didn't wash my hands after I touched you, though."

"You're a dirty, dirty girl," Lindsay whispered.

Just then Sarah walked into the kitchen, and everyone moved away from one another. "Aunt Lindsay, and Judy, you're here." She hugged them both.

"You're getting big, sweetie," Lindsay said while she hugged Sarah. "Is your mom still treating you well?"

Sarah giggled. "Life would be much better if my moms gave me more sweets." She turned to her mom. "Table's set, Mommy."

"Now that deserves a sweet, don't you think, Kayleigh?" Lindsay smiled at Sarah before reaching into her handbag and lifting out a box of Astros. "You can have these, but you may only eat them tomorrow, okay?"

"Thank you, Aunt Lindsay." Sarah took the Astros and held them like a newborn baby. "I love these."

"Dinner's ready," Kayleigh announced. "Shall we?"

✝

Lindsay and Judy stayed until late, and by the time they left Kayleigh and Rebecca were exhausted. Later that night, after Rebecca and Kayleigh had fallen asleep, something startled Rebecca awake. As she lay there in the dark, she tried to figure out what it was that had awakened her. She couldn't hear any sounds and couldn't see anything out of the ordinary.

After a few minutes, she decided to go back to sleep. Just before reaching dreamland, something tugged on her blanket. She grabbed hold of the blanket, thinking that it was Rattex playing with the edge. But whatever had tugged it, tugged at it again…harder this time. Rebecca knew that Rattex didn't have that amount of strength.

She shot straight up in bed, her heart pounding and rapidly gaining speed. She couldn't see anything, but she felt something was definitely with them in the room. The temperature had dropped by a few degrees and Rebecca shivered. She looked over at Kayleigh, who was still covered in the blanket and sleeping soundly. Whatever was pulling at the blanket was only pulling at her side. She was terrified, but didn't want to let fear rule her.

Not wanting to wake Kayleigh, she refrained from switching on the bed lamp. She just sat there in the dark with her eyes darting around the room. The air felt cold and damp. She shivered and pulled the blanket up to cover her shoulders. Suddenly, the invisible force yanked the blanket again so hard that it exposed her whole body. She reached over quickly to switch on the bedside lamp. Light flowed from the lamp and exposed the room. There was no one there. Rebecca's whole body shook, and she gasped for air.

Kayleigh rolled over and sleepily placed her hand on Rebecca's leg. "What's the matter, honey? Didn't you have enough of me yet?" she murmured.

"I think our ghost is back and he doesn't like me much."
Rebecca tried to swallow down her terror.

"Why, honey? What happened?" Kayleigh sat up and
put a comforting arm around her.

"He pulled my fucking blanket off me, that's what he
did." Rebecca's fear-filled voice echoed in the quiet house.

Kayleigh switched her bedside lamp on as well and
jumped out of bed. She walked around the room and
searched behind the door. She shivered.

"You feel it too, don't you?" Rebecca asked. "The
cold?"

Kayleigh nodded. "Where was he?" Her voice shook as
she began pacing the room.

"At the bottom of the bed, I think," Rebecca whispered.
"He scared the living daylights out of me." She took a deep
breath and tried to calm down. "How did you survive with
this shit, baby? Why are you still here?" Rebecca started to
cry cupping her hands over her face.

Kayleigh walked back to the bed and sat down next to
Rebecca. "Shh. I'm so sorry that he scared you. Don't cry,
my love." Kayleigh put her arms around her and soothed her,
but Rebecca was inconsolable.

They tried to fall asleep again after that, but Rebecca
didn't feel safe, and she was sure that Kayleigh didn't
either—especially since the ghost managed to beat up the
burglars. Rebecca only managed to sleep for short periods at
a time, waking up too many times to get a full night's rest.

†

The following morning, she went into the bathroom to
brush her teeth and wash her face. As she bent over the basin,
she cupped her hands and filled them with ice cold water in
order to rinse the exhaustion from her face. She closed her

tired eyes and splashed the water over her face a few more times. The air became cold and stale again, and Rebecca moaned into her hands.

"Please not now," she muttered. She looked up slowly at her reflection in the mirror and what she saw behind her made her scream out in terror. There was a man hanging from a noose, from an invisible shower railing, eyes open as if popping out of his skull. She let out a loud yell and leaped around in horror, but there was nothing there. If she could blame it on her exhaustion, she would, but she knew it was more than that. She was certain this spirit was trying to scare her and get rid of her for some reason.

Kayleigh stormed into the bathroom. She grabbed Rebecca by the shoulders. "What happened?"

"Listen here, Kay. You might be impervious to what's happening in this house, but I'm terrified. Can't we go and talk to Graham about this? I mean, surely he can release you from this contract if, say, the house just suddenly burnt down to the ground?"

"Tell me what happened."

"Man hanging by his neck is what happened." Rebecca laughed out loud. "The bastard actually committed suicide."

"What on earth is so funny?" Kayleigh didn't join in the laughter.

"I think I'm going mad." Rebecca carried on laughing hysterically. She ceased laughing as quickly as she started. In an angry voice she said, "You know what? We actually shouldn't allow this bastard to throw us out of our own house. He hanged himself, the son of a bitch. He can deal with it. Do you hear me, you fucker? Deal with it!" she shouted.

"We'll go see Graham today, I promise." Kayleigh hugged Rebecca close to her. "I don't like seeing you this way. Besides, we have a daughter to think about as well. Right?"

"Right."

Twenty minutes later, the three of them sat in the Mini Cooper, on their way to Sedgefield. Sarah sang one of her Afrikaans songs that she must have learnt at school, as if she were a CD player set on repeat.

Rebecca glanced over at Kayleigh. Kayleigh met her eyes, looking relieved that Sarah had no idea of what horror possessed the house.

Chapter Twenty-seven

Early 1900s

After the war ended, Joshua took the long road back home from Cape Town. He couldn't wait to see his wife and his daughter. The war was longer than they'd anticipated it would be, and Carrey would be much bigger by now. He wondered if Carrey would even remember him.

As soon as he saw his house, Joshua kneed his horse into galloping as fast as he could. When he reached the final bend in the road, he noticed the blackened walls and the burnt away roof.

"No!" he shouted as he dismounted. "No!"

He ran into the house, but there was nobody there. After searching everywhere inside, he ran to the helper's land, where he found Evelyn and her husband Stander, Joshua's farmhand.

"Hauw, Boss, we're so glad to see you still alive." Evelyn said.

"You too, Evelyn. Where are my wife and my child? What happened here?"

Evelyn started to cry.

"Tell me, please." Joshua pleaded, tears also rolling down his face.

"The bad man, he came, and he take your wife…and Carrey."

"No, no, no…" he cried out. "How could you do this to us, God?" He fell to his knees, his hands over his face.

"Me, I'm so sorry, Boss." Evelyn tried to soothe him, but he jumped to his feet and stormed toward the remains of his house.

Chapter Twenty-eight

Present day

Graham was only available at lunchtime. They'd meet him at his office at noon, but they decided to arrive a little early.

"What can I do for you two fine ladies?" Graham asked in his British accent.

"Graham, I'm not going to beat around the bush. I want out of my contract," Kayleigh said as she sat down in one of the chairs in front of his desk. Rebecca sat down beside her in the other chair.

"Why? Was there another break-in?"

Kayleigh knew that if she told him about the paranormal bullshit, he'd never believe her.

"Rebecca here has invited us to move in with her, and we think it's a great idea. Only problem is that I've signed a twelve-month contract, which you well know."

"I'm sorry, but your contract is a legal and binding document. There's no way out of it unless you can find other tenants. I also need to add, Kayleigh, that if you breach this contract, you'll have the owner's lawyers to deal with."

"I want the owner's details," Rebecca cut in. "If you refuse to contact him, then I will."

Graham's face hardened. "As his estate agent, I'm legally bound to keep his info confidential."

"Look, we already know the owner's name is Martin Norton," Rebecca snapped. "It's only a matter of time until we track him down. You might as well stop your bullshitting and give us his number."

Kayleigh placed her hand on Rebecca's arm in an effort to calm her down figuring that she was probably only impolite due to the lack of sleep from the previous night.

An angry red flush worked its way up Graham's neck. "I'm sorry, but there's nothing I can do for you. I suggest you track him down on your own. You seem to be getting along quite fine without my help. Now if you'll excuse me, I have work to do." As if to prove his point, he shuffled the papers that were on his desk.

"Oh, we'll find him, and then I'll tell him what a prick you are," Rebecca said through clenched teeth.

Graham didn't respond but fixed her with a dark glare.

Kayleigh could see this was getting them nowhere. She stood. "Come, honey, he's of no help to us."

She guided Rebecca out before she became physically aggressive and got herself into trouble.

†

After they left Graham's office, they went to eat lunch at the place where they'd had their very first lunch together. They still had two hours to kill before fetching Sarah from school. Kayleigh placed their order, reached across the table, and took Rebecca's hands into hers. "You really know how to stand your ground, don't you? I bet Graham didn't see you coming."

"He's such an asshole. What's up with him?"

"He has a business to run, just like you and I. I'm sure it's nothing personal."

"Our next step is to try and find tenants and then to track this Martin guy down. I've looked in the phone book. I've searched the Internet. I just don't know what else to do." Rebecca stared down at their entwined hands. "I love you, you know," she said softly, the anger now gone from her voice.

"I love you, too, sweetheart. More and more with each passing day." Kayleigh took a sip of water. "When did you look Martin up?" Kayleigh asked, surprised. For so long they'd thought only of one another that she'd forgotten about the search for the owner.

"Long ago. After we went to the municipality. Nothing came up. He must be unlisted or something." Exhaustion lined Rebecca's face.

Kayleigh tried to change the subject. "How is your sexy new shop assistant getting along?" She needed to get her mind off the ghost stories. Even if just for a while.

"Do I detect jealousy in that beautiful voice of yours?" Rebecca teased.

"Why didn't you hire someone plump and ugly?"

"Because sexy sells. I would have hired the sexiest chick in town, but she's already taken. She slices animals open for a living. I mean, how sick is that?"

Kayleigh laughed. "Weirdo."

"I learned from the best." Rebecca reached across the table to brush her fingers over Kayleigh's cheek. "My new employee is doing quite well. If it weren't for her, we wouldn't have had so much time together. I like spending time with you, in case you didn't already know."

"Ask her if she can slice open animals, maybe we can share her."

"I don't do threesomes—not anymore, anyway."

"Oh, that was bad, Rebecca. Even for you." Kayleigh smacked her on the hand.

"Hey, we needed to lighten things even more. Anything to get your mind from being jealous of my twenty-something assistant." The waiter approached with a full tray. "Oh, and here's our lunch. Mmm… looks yummy."

Kayleigh had ordered a rare filet with salad. Rebecca had ordered a medium rare sirloin.

While chewing on a big juicy bite, Rebecca said, "So, how are we going to break into Graham's office to find that darned owner?"

Kayleigh nearly choked. She quickly downed some water. "Break in? I was right. You have gone mad."

Rebecca swallowed and blinked. "Or else, there's always torture."

"I'd much rather torture him than break into his office," Kayleigh said as she cut another piece of steak.

"Invite him over for dinner. Your ghost will sort him out," Rebecca suggested with a sly expression.

"*Our* ghost." Kayleigh realized with dismay that they were back on the ghost subject.

"He doesn't seem to like *me* much. Maybe he's in love with you." Rebecca pointed at Kayleigh with her fork.

Kayleigh fluttered her eye lashes. "You know as well as I do that I'm irresistible. Who could blame him?"

"And right you are. I don't blame him for falling in love with you. You're a looker."

"So are you. I'm amazed he hasn't joined in for a threesome yet." Kayleigh cringed at her words, and her stomach made a sour turn by just the thought of what she'd said. She shook her head and went back to the job of carving her steak with the steak knife.

"He's not welcome in our bed. Gosh, this thing is really freaking me out." Rebecca dropped her fork on her plate with a clatter as her eyes welled with tears.

Kayleigh reached over and held her hand. "I noticed. You must be exhausted. I'm so sorry for putting you through all this, Rebecca."

"You know as well as I do that none of this is your fault." Rebecca gave Kayleigh's hand a quick squeeze before picking her fork back up and stabbing a crispy French fry.

After lunch, they popped into the newspaper office and placed an ad for the house, then they collected Sarah from school. She was waiting right by the school gates. She seemed upset when she hopped in the car.

"What's up, sweetie? That's not the face I expect to see the day before vacation starts," Kayleigh asked. "Besides, you'll be visiting your dad for two whole weeks."

"Kids keep asking me if you're gay. I hate them." Sarah started crying, looking out the window.

"And what do you tell these nosy ones?" Rebecca frowned at her reflection in the rearview mirror, her voice full of concern.

"I tell them to mind their own bees wax." She turned her gaze to her mom. "'But are you? Are you guys gay?"

Kayleigh glanced nervously at Rebecca, not sure how to respond.

Rebecca turned her attention back to the rearview mirror. "Sweetie, we love one another. You know that. But you can tell those nosy kids that Mommy and I are very close friends. They don't need to know more than that. There's nothing wrong with anyone being gay, but kids who hardly know you have no right to ask such personal questions, and so you don't need to give them any more details than what's necessary."

Kayleigh was relieved that Rebecca had an answer ready. She wasn't prepared for any such questions yet. Rebecca started the engine and took the winding road back to the house.

†

Rebecca unlocked the door. Kayleigh followed her inside and automatically went to the kitchen, straight to the kettle to make them some tea. Sarah ran upstairs to her room. A blood curling scream made Kayleigh drop the kettle in the sink with a loud clatter. Before she could react, Rebecca was already climbing the stairs three at a time. Kayleigh followed Rebecca's pursuit, terrified of what she would have to face when she reached Sarah. When she made it into the room, she found Rebecca holding a visibly shaken Sarah.

"What's wrong, baby?" Rebecca smoothed her hair as she hugged onto the child.

"There was a man in my room, but he just disappeared." Sarah managed to say between sobs.

Kayleigh raised her face to the ceiling and screamed. "Go away! Leave us alone! If you want to bug anyone, bug me! But leave my child and Rebecca alone, you sick bastard!"

Rebecca let go of Sarah and straightened. Sarah ran to her mom and wrapped her arms around her.

"Who was he, Mommy?"

"I don't know, baby." Kayleigh bent down and held onto her daughter. She didn't know how to deal with the fact that Sarah had also seen this thing. She felt completely helpless.

"He's gone now." Rebecca soothed them as she walked around the room and checked in the cupboards and behind the doors. "You know what? Let's go out to dinner. The school vacation is starting tomorrow, so I suggest we get out of here for a few hours."

Before leaving, they each took turns to wash up in Sarah's bathroom, too afraid to use the downstairs shower. Rebecca and Kayleigh stayed in Sarah's room while she bathed. Kayleigh didn't want any of them left alone at any time.

✝

"Let's go to the Blue Olive," Kayleigh suggested as they drove out of the driveway.

"Great idea," Rebecca said as she turned left at the corner.

"Tristan has a new girlfriend," Sarah said from the backseat.

"That's great news, sweetie. Are you happy about this?" Kayleigh asked.

"Very happy. Now he can leave me alone."

After Rebecca parked the car, they got out and walked toward the restaurant. "Kind of chilly, do you rather want to sit inside, love?" Rebecca asked as she took Kayleigh's hand.

"Definitely." Kayleigh let go of Rebecca's hand as they mounted the steps and entered the warm, cozy eatery.

"Good evening, table for three?" A very well dressed man welcomed them at the door.

"Please," Rebecca said and they all followed him to a table right by the window.

"Look, you can see the ocean from here. How nice," Kayleigh said as she moved to sit in her chair. She took the menu the waiter offered her.

"My name is Charles and I'll be your waiter for the evening."

"Thanks, Charles. Can you bring us a bottle of your house special?" Rebecca gave him one of her charming smiles. "And an apple juice for the little one. Thank you."

Charles nodded while he wrote it down in his little notebook. "Anything to eat? Or would you like a few more minutes?"

"What are you going to order?" Kayleigh asked Sarah who had her nose in the kiddies menu in front of her.

"Mac and cheese, please." She looked up at Kayleigh. "May I go and play in the play area?" There was a playroom for the kids with games to keep them occupied.

"Sure, honey. I'll call you when your food is here."

"I'm going to have your catch of the day," Rebecca said to Charles.

"And I'll have grilled calamari, thank you, Charles," Kayleigh said.

"With pleasure." Charles took the menus and disappeared off to the kitchen.

"We should have invited Lindsay and Judy to join us," Rebecca said before taking a sip of her water.

"I wonder how they would react if we told them about the ghost. I can't believe we haven't told them anything."

"I somehow don't think they would believe us, Kay. You know they're agnostic."

"Yes, which is exactly why I haven't mentioned anything."

"Your wine, my ladies." Charles showed Rebecca the bottle, she nodded and he opened it with a corkscrew before pouring a small amount into her glass.

Kayleigh watched with admiration as Rebecca sampled the wine and gave Charles the go-ahead. He filled both their glasses before placing the bottle in an ice bucket. He then ran off to the kitchen again.

"I love you, Rebecca, So damn much." Kayleigh didn't care who was watching them. She reached across and held Rebecca's hand.

Rebecca's eyes glistened. "I love you, too, my one and only true love."

After Sarah finished eating, she asked if she could go and play in the games area again with Angie, one of her classmates, who was also dining at the restaurant with her parents. As Kayleigh watched Sarah and Angie chat like old buddies on the way to the games room, she noticed Angie's parents looking in their direction. They had their heads together for a moment, then got up and walked to their table. Rebecca saw them coming and jumped up to greet them.

"Hi, I'm Rebecca and this is Kayleigh. She's Sarah's mom." Rebecca motioned to Kayleigh, and Kayleigh reached out her hand to greet them.

"I'm Bert and this is my wife, Jessica." He shook their hands and beamed at them. "Do you mind if we join you?"

"No problem at all. Please do," Kayleigh said.

Charles came over and offered more chairs, which Bert accepted. Bert went to help him while Jessica went back to their table to fetch their drinks.

"So where do you guys stay?" Bert asked as he took his seat.

"We stay in Hoekwil, just up the road." Kayleigh explained where the house was and saw surprise in Jessica's eyes.

"You mean old man Martin's place?" Jessica asked.

Rebecca frowned. "Do you know the place? And Martin?"

"Yes, we know the old guy. But isn't that house haunted or something?" Jessica raised her eyebrows when she asked the question.

At that, Kayleigh choked on her wine she had taken a sip from.

"Are you all right?" Rebecca tapped her back softly.

"Yeah. I'm all right."

"Do you mind if I ask a very straightforward question?" Jessica asked, seemingly letting off the hook about the house being haunted.

"By all means." Kayleigh was still coughing softly.

"Are you guys a couple?"

"Yes, we are," Kayleigh said as she took Rebecca's hand.

"I told you," she said to her husband and he rolled his eyes as he took his wallet out and handed her a note.

"Sorry," he said. "We must seem rude, but we had a bet earlier—"

"We don't have a problem with gay people. In fact, my brother's also gay." Jessica interjected.

"That's nice to know," Rebecca said, shifting in her chair. "Nice to meet you."

"I drive past your house every day and it looks so spooky. We live just behind you guys, in fact," Jessica said.

"So tell us about Martin. Do you know where he is now?" Kayleigh could barely contain her excitement that they found someone who knew about the owner.

"I heard he was at the Sedgefield Frail Care Center. He must be a hundred by now. He hasn't lived in his house for years," Jessica said and took a sip of her wine.

And there he was under their noses all this time. It had never occurred to Kayleigh to even look there.

Bert motioned at Kayleigh and Rebecca. "So how did you two meet?"

They talked for several minutes and got to know one another. Bert was a dentist in George, and Jessica was a full time mom. They'd bought their house the year after they got married, so they'd been staying in Hoekwil for ten years. Since they moved there, the house on haunted hill, as they called it, had been standing empty most of the time.

"I heard that people never live there for long," Bert said. "The last time anyone lived there was a few years back. Martin stayed there for a few months, but rumor has it he moved out fifteen years ago. He rented it out a few times, but the people always left in a hurry, only staying there a month or so."

"Do you know anything about the history of the place?" Rebecca asked.

"No. Unfortunately not much. Why? Have you seen anything?"

"We have had some strange experiences. Just tonight in fact. Which is why we came out to dinner. Sarah saw a man in her room, and the night before something tugged at my blankets."

Jessica's eyes widened. Bert seemed uncomfortable, but nevertheless, very interested. "What else has happened? I mean, you said you've had a *few* experiences."

Kayleigh cut in. "I heard a man's voice once. He said the name Catherine. Any idea who that could be?"

"I have absolutely no idea. Do you, honey?" Bert looked questioningly at his wife who in reply, shook her head.

"How do you know Martin, if he hasn't stayed in the house for fifteen years? You mentioned you've only stayed in Hoekwil for ten," Rebecca asked.

"Oh, he came to greet us right after we moved in. He wanted to let us know that he would maintain the lands. We were concerned that the place was empty, and then the estate agent contacted him. He came over for tea one day. He told us at that time that he was staying at the care center," Jessica told them.

"Well, as you can understand, we're pretty hyped up over the stuff happening and want to get in touch with him to find out what happened in the house," Kayleigh said. "Maybe if we know the history, we could sort of help the thing walking around the house to move on to the next world, or whatever it is, to get that thing to leave us alone. Look, I know we must sound crazy, but all of us have had at least one experience in that house. We just want it to stop."

Bert and Jessica obviously weren't skeptical. Bert said, "Maybe you should call a medium?"

"When I was a child, very weird things happened in my parent's house. They had a medium over and it worked. You guys should really try it."

"I don't suppose you still have that medium's contact details, do you?" Rebecca asked.

"No, I don't." Jessica shook her head.

"Just give me a second, I am going to call someone who knows a spiritual clairvoyant, I'm sure she would be able to help you guys." Bert retrieved his phone from his pocket and scanned through his numbers. He pressed on a contact, got up from the table and walked to Charles and asked for a pen. After a few minutes, he returned with a paper and a number scribbled on it. "Her name is Maggie Fletcher. My colleague says she's the real deal."

"Wow, this is such a great help. Thank you, Bert." Rebecca scanned the number for a second before saving it to her phone.

After a while Bert and Jessica left. Kayleigh looked over at Rebecca and reached for her hand. "I'm scared. Can't we go to your house, please?"

"I have a family in it for the Easter holidays."

"Dammit, I forgot. Let's stay a bit longer then. I'm not ready to go home just yet," Kayleigh said. "Oh, I forgot to mention earlier, I have a temp coming in for two weeks. He's a newly qualified veterinarian and here for the Easter holidays. He was looking for a temporary position and contacted me today. I told him he can come work for me for two weeks, and if he likes it, he's thinking of moving here permanently. It will be great having someone who can take over when I'm away. His name is Angelo. Apparently he finished first in his class two years back and has an excellent reputation. He worked for the animal clinic in Plettenberg Bay, but says he wants to open up his own practice. I'm thinking that if he's as good as they say, I can make him partner."

Rebecca's eyes lit up as Kayleigh spoke. "That's wonderful news, honey. You need a bit of a break."

"Yes, I do. It would be nice to spend some time with you once Sarah has gone to her dad."

"Ooh, the possibilities," Rebecca whispered.

Sarah returned to the table, waving goodbye to her friend.

"Finish your juice, sweetie, it's getting late. We should go," Rebecca said, then signed for the waiter to bring the check.

†

Kayleigh drove the Mini Cooper home. She thought again how safe it would've felt for all of them if they'd be driving to Rebecca's house instead. But because Rebecca had already booked a family into her house for the Easter holidays, that wouldn't be an option. Kayleigh listened to Sarah's excited chattering about her new best friend, Angie. It was as if she'd completely forgotten about the man in her room. Kayleigh mentally shook her head at the resilience of children.

When they reached home, Kayleigh turned to a pale Rebecca and asked quietly so that Sarah wouldn't hear, "Ready?"

"Let's do this."

They got out and walked to the house with Sarah taking Rebecca's hand and skipping along beside her. All the lights were on just how they'd left it. Kayleigh dug the keys from her jacket pocket and unlocked the safety door first and then the main door—it creaked open. Kayleigh entered first with Rebecca and Sarah following quickly on her heels. Sarah closed the door behind her before Rebecca took the key and locked the door. Taking a deep breath she walked into the kitchen.

"Mommy, can I move into the guest room, please?" Sarah asked while Rebecca switched the kettle on.

"I don't have a problem with you doing that, baby. Shall I help you?" Kayleigh turned to Rebecca. "Can you make the tea while I help Sarah?"

"Of course, babe." She gave Kayleigh a kiss and reached up in the cabinet for three cups.

Kayleigh and Sarah went upstairs to Sarah's room hand in hand, and got everything that Sarah needed for the night—blankets, pillow and pajamas.

Kayleigh kept the conversation light as they carried everything into the spare room. The room was on the farthest side of the hallway, on the other side of Kayleigh and Rebecca's bedroom. Kayleigh removed the dusty linen from the bed and replaced it with Sarah's pink duvet set. The duvet got lost on the huge king sized bed that was in the guest room. Sarah changed into her pajamas and jumped onto the big bed.

Rebecca came in, balancing three cups, "I think I messed a bit on the way up. I'll clean it later," she mumbled as she passed them their cups and sat next to Sarah on the bed.

213

"Thanks," Kayleigh and Sarah said in unison.

"Sarah, have you ever seen the little girl again?" Kayleigh sat on the other side of Sarah and put her hand on her daughter's leg as she spoke.

"Carrey? I saw her a few times, but not recently. She wasn't scary. She was nice. I liked her." Sarah seemed to think of something else. "She asked me if I knew where her mommy was. Her daddy was mad, because her mommy had found someone else, she told me. I think that man in my room was her daddy." She whispered the last sentence with big eyes.

Rebecca and Kayleigh looked questioningly at each other and nodded. "Hey, this bed is nice and big. How about we all sleep here—just for tonight?" Rebecca suggested. "If that's all right with you two?"

"You know what, I would like that. Let's get some more blankets."

Rebecca got the blankets from their bed and Kayleigh locked up the house and made sure Rattex came in from outside. They usually left the sliding door partially open and the safety gate locked so that he could come and go as he pleased, without any unwanted visitors breaking and entering the house while they were out. Tonight, she got Rattex in and closed the sliding door.

She'd also put in a safety gate at the top of the staircase and now kept it locked at night for extra security. After locking all of the what seemed like ten thousand doors and gates, she switched on the alarm system and switched off the lights and went to the spare room where her family was already lying comfortably, waiting for her return. Sarah had snuggled tight against Rebecca and was already fading into dreamland. Kayleigh climbed in on the other side of Rebecca.

Rebecca wiggled between them with a grin on her face. "Cool, I'm sleeping between two beautiful women tonight." She leaned to give Kayleigh a soft kiss. "Good night, my love," she whispered.

✝

Just as they'd hoped, the night went by without any strange events. Still, they didn't sleep very well. The following day was Friday, and the schools were closing early for the Easter holidays. With Sarah's bags in the trunk of the car, packed and ready for her trip to her dad, they dropped her off at school, and then both went to their respective offices. When Kayleigh arrived at her clinic, Angelo and Faith were sitting inside, talking like old friends.

"This guy is great," Faith said the instant Kayleigh stepped inside.

"You can tell that from only a few minutes of chatting?" Kayleigh smiled at her nurse.

Angelo stood from his chair and held out his hand to shake Kayleigh's hand. "Pleasure to make your acquaintance," he said. "I actually know Faith from Plettenberg Bay. We've worked together before." He looked around animatedly. "Quite the set up you have here. I love it."

"Thanks. So I take it Faith has shown you around?"

"She has. She's awesome." He smiled sincerely at Faith.

Kayleigh nodded. "I agree."

"Kayleigh, if you want to leave now, I am sure I can manage with Faith's help. You have absolutely nothing to worry about. Everything will be fine here. I'll make sure of that."

He was charming enough. Kayleigh was sure her clients would love him. "You sure?" She asked, and examined his face. He seemed quite relaxed.

"Absolutely. Faith can call you if there's a problem. Please, don't worry."

"Uhm. Okay. Call me if you have any questions."

"Will do. Bye Kayleigh. Rest well and have lots of fun," Faith said as Kayleigh turned to leave.

"Thanks. Bye," Kayleigh said as she left through the door and headed to Rebecca's store.

Just as Kayleigh reached Rebecca's store, Rebecca came out. "All sorted? That was quick," Rebecca said.

"Yes, he seems quite capable. In fact, I think the ladies are going to like him. He's quite the charmer."

"Glad to hear. He might attract some more clients for you. Not that you're not hot, but you know, some ladies prefer the guys." Rebecca spoke as they walked toward her car.

Kayleigh laughed. "You're not jealous?"

"I trust you, my love," Rebecca said, turned toward her and gave her quick reassuring kiss."

"Is Stephanie going to be okay without you?" Kayleigh asked as they approached the car.

"She'll be fine. She has the key and a list of instructions. She's been coping quite well without me a few times. She has my number on speed dial."

†

It was only a five minute drive to the Sedgefield Frail Care Center. At the reception, they asked for Martin, and the nurse showed them where to go. They found him sitting in his wheelchair and staring out at the garden. He did indeed look like he was one hundred years old. Kayleigh felt nervous. She wasn't sure how to start the conversation.

"Mr. Norton?" Rebecca asked, and he turned to face them.

"That's me," he confirmed with a shaky voice, confusion written all over his frail face.

"I'm Rebecca and this is my friend, Kayleigh. We're renting your house in Hoekwil."

"Why would you bug an old man like me, huh?" He sounded very annoyed. 'I told that damned Graham to keep my particulars confidential. I don't want to be harassed."

"We're so sorry for being a nuisance, sir. We were hoping you could perhaps tell us something about the history on the house?"

"I'm tired. I'm so sick of that house. I wish my mother had never left it to me," he grumbled. "Nurse. Take these people away." He turned back to them. "If you don't want to stay in the bloody house, you should just move out like everyone else did. Now leave me alone."

The nurse came in and led them away from Martin. "I'm sorry for his outburst, but he's an old man. It's best to just leave him be."

They left the care center with lost hope and frustrated as hell. This was their only chance of finding out anything that could help them. Kayleigh was tired and all she wanted to do was cry. Moving out would be easy, but they had to wait until the end of the vacation to get Rebecca's house back. Vacationers occupied every house and there were no houses available at this time of the year for them to move to.

They got into the car and drove back to school. It was ten o'clock, and Sarah would be coming out of class. They needed to drop her off at the airport soon. She was to spend the entire vacation in Johannesburg with her dad. Kayleigh was unhappy about letting her daughter go, but at least by the time Sarah returned, they could move into Rebecca's house. Martin did say they could move out if they wanted to, which was a relief, because they did want to.

Kayleigh finally gave into her emotion and cried all the way home after dropping Sarah off at the airport.

"She'll be all right, Kay," Rebecca said and patted Kayleigh's leg. "We need to get ourselves sorted now. Maybe we can start packing so we can move into my house as soon as the holidays are over. Graham, that asshole, lied about Martin Norton taking you to court if you breached the contract," Rebecca remarked with an irritated tone. "I just want to go and slap him silly."

"If we move out, he loses his commission. It's all about the money for him."

"Jerk."

"We just have to get through the next two weeks."

"I forgot to mention, while you were sorting Sarah out at the airport, Judy called."

"She did?"

"Yes. Her parents are here for the holiday. I was hoping that they had room for us, but they don't."

"Fuck," Kayleigh spat out before she could stop herself. "I was going to call Lindsay this afternoon and ask her if we could stay over for a few days. That was our last resort."

"It's just two more weeks. We've gone through longer phases with nothing happening. Maybe we'll be left in peace for a while after last night."

Back at the house, they made dinner together and ate it on the patio as they did when they first met.

"I need to go to the bathroom," Rebecca said, and she kissed Kayleigh on the cheek after getting up from her chair.

Kayleigh warmed. This was what she had always longed for—a happy and normal married life for her and Sarah. The fact that it was with another woman didn't matter to

Kayleigh anymore. She watched as Rebecca walked, imagining her beautiful body under those clothes. These past few weeks had been hectic, and they hadn't made love in a while. Kayleigh felt the need building up inside her.

†

Rebecca walked down the hallway to the downstairs toilet where the shower was. She hated using that bathroom but wasn't in the mood to run all the way up the stairs to their other toilet. She decided to take her chances as she quickly undid her jean button and sat down. Just as she finished emptying her bladder, she felt the sudden change in temperature in the bathroom. It was like a cloud creeping in and totally enveloping her.

She wiped, jumped up from the toilet, and pulled her jeans up as fast as she could. The air had become so cold that she could see her puffs of breath. She turned to flush the toilet and as she reached for the handle, something burned down her back. It felt as though she'd been cut or scratched. The pain was so intense that it incapacitated her for a moment. She bent over, losing her balance. The instant she realized what had happened, she screeched and turned, horrified that she might see what had caused the burning sensation. Just as she turned her head back, a deep, scratchy male voice screamed in her ear.

"*Get out!*"

Without buttoning her jeans, she ran out of the bathroom and down the passage to the patio where Kayleigh was busy picking up their dishes. Kayleigh's eyes widened with shock.

Rebecca ran straight to Kayleigh and grabbed hold of her. She held Kayleigh and sobbed making her whole body shake. "This is ridiculous! I can't take this anymore."

"What happened?" Kayleigh asked, concern evident in her voice.

Rebecca turned around and lifted her shirt to where it burned on her back. Kayleigh gasped.

"What?" Rebecca tried to get a glimpse of her back, but it was impossible.

"There are..." Kayleigh swallowed. "There are four parallel scratch marks all the way from here." Kayleigh gently touched Rebecca's shoulder blade. "To here," she said as she touched Rebecca's lower back. "And they're bleeding profusely. But your shirt? It's intact."

Rebecca felt her legs give out. Kayleigh helped her sit down on the chair and rushed inside, then returned with a first aid kit. When she returned, she made Rebecca lean forward and she cleaned her with saline solution and doused her with antiseptic ointment. She stuck on several large plasters in order to cover the wound. Rebecca's body shook while Kayleigh tended to her.

"He shouted in my ear, Kayleigh. He screamed get out right in my ear. We have to get out of here." Her voice shook when she spoke. She sniffed and swallowed hard.

"Where are we going to go?"

"Anywhere but here, please," Rebecca pleaded with her. But she knew they had nowhere else to go. At this stage, she would pack up and go back to Cape Town, for all she cared. She could never tell Kayleigh that, however. She knew it would hurt Kayleigh badly.

They sat outside on the swing, holding one another tightly, until midnight, until the weather started taking a bad turn. They were exhausted as hell, and they had no other choice but to go back inside. They decided to sleep in the guest room for the night.

They locked up downstairs and went back to the guest room, Kayleigh carrying Rattex with her. The instant they passed their room, Rattex went crazy. All the hair on his back raised until he looked as if he'd gotten a Mohawk cut. He scratched Kayleigh's arm and screeched, then raced for the door as he stormed back downstairs. Kayleigh started into their bedroom but quickly stopped. She shivered and rubbed her arms.

Rebecca went still and took hold of Kayleigh as Kayleigh backed right into her. She stared past Kayleigh into their bedroom and then froze. Something—or someone—had flung all of her clothes out of their closet. Rebecca got tears in her eyes as she pushed past Kayleigh and entered the room. She walked up to the closet and peered inside. Only *her* clothes had been removed from the closet with obvious anger and violence. Kayleigh's clothes were untouched. Rebecca yelled at the walls. "What do you want from me? Why are you doing this?" Tears were streaming down her face. "Ouch!" she yelled and took a massive step back.

"What's wrong?" Kayleigh asked, horrified at Rebecca's expression. She looked scared out of her wits.

Rebecca lifted her shirt and showed Kayleigh her back. "I think he scratched me again. It burns like hell." She sobbed as she spoke.

Kayleigh gasped as she saw four more red lines running down Rebecca's back, right next to the bandages she had stuck on earlier. "You've been scratched again!" Kayleigh cried. "Are you okay?"

"No." Rebecca shook her head, her body shaking as she did so.

"Wait. I saw on TV once, that we can use a tape recorder and record everything. Apparently we'll be able to hear them on the recorder when we play it back." Kayleigh explained about EVP or electronic voice phenomena. She searched around in her bedside drawer for a few seconds, and produced a digital voice recorder.

Kayleigh pressed the recording button.

"Is there anyone here who wishes to speak to me?" she asked. She waited a while and then continued, "What's your name?" A few seconds and then, "Why are you trying to scare us?" She waited again before continuing, "Why are you trying to scare Rebecca?"

Rebecca paced up and down the room as Kayleigh made her recording. Then, Rebecca walked to the closet, whipped out a suitcase from the top shelf, and started packing her clothes.

Kayleigh must not have noticed because she continued her conversation with the cassette recorder. "Was it you who beat up the burglars for us the other night?"

Shocked and unable to believe what she was hearing, Rebecca turned around to stare at Kayleigh. Was she giving this asshole of a ghost credit? He was deliberately trying to hurt her yet Kayleigh was talking as if she admired him for everything he did.

Rebecca hurriedly finished packing up all of her stuff from the floor into the suitcase and then turned back to Kayleigh again. "I can't do this. I'm out of here," she whispered. She wiped her wet face with the back of her hand and saw the remnants of her mascara on her skin. "You obviously think that this is a big fat joke, Kay, but I'm scared as hell."

Kayleigh finally looked up from the tape recorder, startled to see Rebecca had packed up her clothes. "Wait, what are you doing?"

"What does it look like I'm doing? I'm not staying here another night."

"Why would you think that I think this is a joke, Rebecca?"

"You with your ghost hunter's crap while I'm being attacked. I'm scared and you're talking to them, or him, or whatever this is that's messing up our lives. I can't do this, I'm sorry, but I can't be here right now. Are you coming?" Her heart beat rapidly when she spoke. Kayleigh just stared at her.

After a few seconds, Rebecca took her suitcase and stomped out of the room.

✝

Kayleigh sat there and stared at the door as she listened to Rebecca's retreating footsteps on the stairs. She couldn't believe Rebecca had just said those things. Worst of all, she couldn't believe that Rebecca could just leave like that. Was this how gay relationships worked? The minute things got tough, they up and leave? And where was Rebecca going? Her house was full of tenants.

After a few seconds of stunned inertia, Kayleigh jumped up and ran toward the stairs. She had to stop Rebecca. They could sleep in the Jeep for the night. She should have thought of that sooner. As she reached the top of the landing, the door slammed shut in her face. The force of the door was so hard that it knocked her off her feet. She fell back and crashed to the floor with a loud thud. Her head hit the floor so hard, that it bounced twice before it came perfectly still. Everything instantly went dark around her.

Chapter Twenty-nine

Early 1900s

While she was held captive at Bloemfontein concentration camp, Catherine and Linda became friends. Unfortunately, one of Linda's children died due to typhoid fever but Catherine had helped to nurse the child while he was ill, right up until he died. Catherine cried as much as Linda. She knew what the mother was going through. No pain compares to that of losing a child.

After the war ended, Catherine left the concentration camp with a mouth full of sores and with the body weight of a twelve-year-old. Catherine was weak and malnourished, but Linda's family took her in for a while and fed her until she was strong enough to travel back home. The family was kind enough to give her a horse. She left with a promise to repay them as soon as she returned home.

It took Catherine two weeks to travel back to Hoekwil from Bloemfontein. As she rode up to the house, she was on the verge of collapsing from exhaustion. She knew that the soldiers had burnt down the house, but she held out hope that she'd soon be reunited with Carrey and Joshua. As she dismounted her horse, her stomach dropped and her heart ached at the desolation before her. The only thing emanating from the remains of the house was a foul smell.

Chapter Thirty

Present day

Kayleigh awoke slowly from a deep, dark place in her subconscious. Her eyelids were heavy, but she felt as though she were lying in her bed under covers. Her first thought was that Rebecca probably never left and had helped her back into their bed. Then she felt a hand move upward on her thigh. She moaned softly and moved her legs apart. The hand trailed all the way up to her left breast, and she turned her head to Rebecca's side of the bed, expecting to see her lying there. Instead, the bed was empty beside her. She looked down, hoping Rebecca was crawling up on the bed from the bottom end. Nobody there either. She jolted up and assessed the room anxiously. No Rebecca anywhere. Her heart rate quickened and her breathing came in short rasps. Who the hell—or what the hell—had just touched her? And she'd responded so willingly. She vaulted from the bed and ran to the door. She yanked on the door handle, but the door wouldn't give way. She twisted around and ran to the window. If she had to jump, she would. The window wouldn't budge either. Kayleigh pulled at the window as hard as she could, banged against the glass, but it would neither open nor break.

"*Catherine…*" A deep, scratchy voice whispered from all the corners of the room, as if the voice was seeping through the walls.

She jumped around. "I'm not Catherine!" she shouted.

She searched for her cell phone but couldn't find it. She must have left it downstairs that night. If only she could call Rebecca and ask her to return. How the hell was she going to get out of this? She broke out in a cold sweat as fear oozed from her pores.

"Please let me go. I'm not Catherine," Kayleigh whispered. She could see the vapors of her breath in front of her face. She wrapped her arms around her body in order to get warm. Was he planning on keeping her prisoner in her own house, she wondered.

She backed up until her back reached the wall and slid all the way down to the floor. She sat with her knees against her chin and her arms wrapped around her legs. She was still wearing all her clothes. The ghost must have waited all this time for Rebecca to leave so he could take hold of her. He thought she was Catherine. Sitting there, she didn't dare move. She didn't dare close her eyes either. She just sat there as the hours slowly ticked by, staring at the room until the sun came up. The ghost remained silent.

By dawn, it was raining again, so the sun didn't brighten the room much. She was exhausted. When the room was light enough, she got up from the floor with much difficulty and walked to the window. Her whole body ached, probably from the fall and then sitting in the same position all night. Her bum burned from lack of blood supply until pins and needles signaled that blood flow was returning. She opened the curtains and glared at the view. In the beginning, the view took her breath away every time she opened her curtains. Now, she wondered what all the fuss was about. She held her breath as she attempted to open the window again. With a sharp yank, it slid open. She almost fell to the floor again—this time from relief. The fresh air that slapped her face felt like a million dollars. She took a deep breath in and exhaled before she turned toward the door. Slowly, she crept up to the door and tried the handle. The door opened.

In a flash she raced out of the room, into the hallway, and gripped the door handle at the top of the landing. It now opened, as did the security gate. The key was still in it. Hot tears flooded her eyes when she realized that Rebecca was the last one to move through the gate. Rebecca must have left the key in the gate so that Kayleigh could find it easily, lock it, and be safe on her own. Her heart ached, and she could barely swallow down the lump in her throat.

She needed to call Rebecca to see if she was all right. She desperately needed to hear her voice, talk to her, and try to persuade her to come back to her. There was no way she could ever live without her...well, she could probably live without her, but she didn't want to. Besides, Sarah would be so upset when she returned from her dad and found that Rebecca had left. Kayleigh tumbled into the kitchen and found her cell phone next to the stove. One missed call and a text message. Phone in hand, she staggered out the house, into the yard. The rain had eased into a mere drizzle.

With shaky hands, she inserted her pin. The missed call was from Sarah. The text was from Rebecca. It read, *what's happening to us? I loved you.* The fact that Rebecca had used love in the past tense made Kayleigh's heart cramp with pain. Feeling weak, she sank down onto the lawn. She dialed Sarah's cell number. It was eight o'clock and she was sure that Sarah would be up by now.

"Hello, Mommy." Sarah's chirpy voice boomed through the phone, and Kayleigh had to swallow hard in order to compose herself.

"Yo, kiddo! How are you? I miss you so much already."
She kept her voice steady throughout the conversation. Sarah
was fine. Her dad and his wife had had their baby boy. Sarah
was enjoying helping with the newborn. All the time while
Sarah spoke, Kayleigh dreaded what she knew would be the
next question.

"Mommy, may I speak to Rebecca too, please?"

"Oh, dear. Rebecca is still sleeping, baby girl. I'll get her
to call you later, all right?"

After ending the call, Kayleigh gathered all of her
strength to make the next and final call. *Rebecca.* Kayleigh
dialed Rebecca's number and waited.

"The number you have dialed is not available at
present," the pre-recorded voice informed her on the phone.
Kayleigh threw the phone down. Had Rebecca switched her
phone off just so she didn't have to speak to Kayleigh? Was
that how much their relationship had deteriorated? Where
had she missed the signs?

Suddenly remembering the recording device, she knew
she had to go back in to fetch it. Kayleigh entered the house,
and quickly ascended the stairs. Fear overwhelmed her when
she reached her bedroom door. She pushed the door ajar
before entering, waiting for any sudden burst of cold air that
would signify the return of the ghost. When it seemed it was
safe to enter, Kayleigh hurried into the room. The recorder
was on the floor, where she'd left it the night before. She
snatched it up off the floor, hustled out of the room, sprinted
down the steps, back out into the garden, and sat down on the
grass.

At that moment, she felt so drained and empty that she
started questioning her sanity. Did Sarah and Rebecca
actually exist? Or was she so far gone insane that she'd
conjured them up out of nothing. She'd seen a movie once
where someone had lived an imaginary life and made up all

sorts of people who didn't exist. Is that what Kayleigh had done? She shook off her dark thoughts and pressed rewind. She was afraid beyond belief, but desperation to get Rebecca back won out over her fear. Also, she had to admit she wanted to hear Rebecca's voice and Rebecca's voice would be on the recording. She hesitated for just a second before pressing play.

On the recording, she heard her own voice: "Is there anyone here who wishes to speak to me?" There was silence for a few seconds, but then she could hear the sound in the background of Rebecca's pacing. Kayleigh put her elbows on her knees and covered her eyes with both her hands. She wished she could rewind the time like she just did the tape cassette and go back to that night. If only she'd been more sensitive to Rebecca's feelings, she would still be there right now. Hot tears slithered down her face and burned her raw cheeks.

The next question came: "What's your name?" Kayleigh heard another sound and then a slight whisper. The sound made her head jolt up in surprise. She rewound a little and completely turned up the volume. There was the question again, followed by a whispered, "*Joshua.*" Her heart leapt in her chest.

She recalled the name Joshua Botha as being the first owner of the house. "All right, Joshua, you have my attention," Kayleigh muttered. "Don't stop now." She continued to listen. The next question was, "Why are you trying to scare us?" There was nothing but the sound of Rebecca's pacing and Kayleigh's breathing. She could hear the fear in her own voice on the recording. Her voice sounded shaky. "Why are you trying to scare Rebecca?" The volume of the recorder was still all the way up.

"*Get out!*" The deep voice that responded was angry. It came at such force through the voice recorder that Kayleigh jumped up from her sitting position.

She wished everything could just go away, and life could return to normal. She wanted Sarah back. She wanted Rebecca back. She would do anything to sit with them both right now, sip on hot chocolate, and listen to Sarah singing to her CD. Anything. How can life change so drastically in the blink of an eye?

She heard in the background what she now knew were the sounds of Rebecca taking the suitcase from the closet. She slowly sat back down again.

"Was it you who beat up the burglars for us the other night?" The scuffle in the background continued and then another whisper, "*Yes.*"

After the whisper, she heard Rebecca talking quietly to her. "I can't do this. I'm out of here. You obviously think that this is a big fat joke, Kay, but I'm scared as hell."

Kayleigh cried. Oh, how she wished she could reach into the tape recorder and bring Rebecca back.

She remembered being so shocked at seeing the packed suitcase. She heard her own voice as she questioned what Rebecca was doing and how Rebecca could possibly think that Kayleigh thought of the haunting as a joke.

Rebecca's angry and hurt voice came through quite clearly. "You with your ghost hunter's crap, and I'm being attacked. I'm scared and you're talking to them, or him, or whatever this is that's messing up our lives. I can't do this, I'm sorry, but I can't be here right now. Are you coming?" She heard Rebecca's feet as she walked past the recorder. Then the room was quiet. She heard her jump up and run after Rebecca. Kayleigh jerked at the sound of the door slamming shut at the top of the landing and the loud thump of Kayleigh hitting the floor. Her head still ached at the memory, which was really only half a memory.

What she heard next made her skin crawl. She could only imagine that she was lying unconscious on the floor, so there should be nobody else in the house. On the recording, clear as daylight, she heard heavy booted footsteps walking down the hallway. They stopped and then the floor creaked. It sounded like someone lifting something. The footsteps became heavier. They walked toward the recorder, and then passed the recorder. Then she heard the bed springs. All her hairs stood on end at the thought that the ghost must have picked her up off the floor and carried her to bed. Her skin crawled as she remembered how the touch of his hand had stirred her awake. She listened to the remaining of the recording, but there were no other untoward sounds.

Kayleigh sat there in stunned silence. She had no idea how long she'd sat there staring into space and thinking about the implications of what she'd heard. And thinking of Rebecca. She heard a car driving up her road. She jumped up in alarm. She didn't remember having invited anyone over, and people hardly ever dropped by without calling first. It had to be Rebecca. But as the unknown vehicle turned into her driveway, she was disappointed to see that it wasn't her.

Chapter Thirty-one

Early 1900s

Catherine didn't have the nerve to enter the house and went directly to Evelyn. Evelyn was shocked when she saw Catherine.

"Hauw, nonna, me I thought you is dead!" Evelyn exclaimed.

"I'm so happy to see you, Evelyn. Where is Carrey? And have you seen Joshua?" She searched frantically as she asked the questions, pining to see Carrey running around with the helpers' kids. Then she turned her attention back to Evelyn.

Catherine immediately saw the expression change on Evelyn's face. She dropped down hard onto the ground as her legs gave out.

"Master Josh, he's back, nonna. He came back five days ago, but he went into the house, and I haven't seen him since that day. I think he's too sad to come out."

Catherine stared up at Evelyn in disbelief. She jumped to her feet and gave Evelyn a hug. "Thank you, Evelyn. You have been most kind to me and my family. Where is Carrey?" She asked, still in denial.

Evelyn frowned. "I don't know, my nonna. Me I thinks she went with the soldiers."

"No, Evelyn, I told her to hide when the soldiers came. She must be here. You must be confused. Where is she?" Catherine shook her head anxiously while tears streamed down her face.

"Sorry, my nonna. Then I don't know. Me haven't seen her. Not since that day the soldiers fetch you." Evelyn wiped the tears that now flowed freely from her eyes.

Catherine sank back down again. Evelyn tried to console her, but Catherine shook her off and told Evelyn to leave her alone in her sorrow. Evelyn allowed her some time to grieve, but eventually came back to Catherine and helped her to her feet.

Catherine turned toward the house but stopped. "Please can you come with me, Evelyn?" Evelyn nodded and followed. The smell that came out of the house was unbearable.

"Joshua?" Catherine called into the house as they walked in. No response. Catherine hesitated for a short while and then followed the drift of the foul smell. It smelled like death itself. The odor became stronger as they reached the bathroom. Catherine put her hand to her nose as they entered. And there he was, hanging from the shower curtain railing.

She trembled as she walked closer to his decaying remains. His body had turned into a mixture of purple and yellow. His face was the shape of a monster's face. His eyes had popped and there was a rotten blackness inside his eye sockets. Maggots slithered in and out of the recesses. Catherine bent over and vomited. She retched until there was nothing left inside her. Joshua had killed himself. He'd left her all alone in this cruel world. If he'd only been braver and waited a few more days.

Evelyn touched her shoulder. "I'm so sorry, madam, I didn't know." She squeezed Catherine's shoulder and pulled her out of the bathroom.

Chapter Thirty-two

Present day

Kayleigh watched as a young nurse helped Mr. Norton out of the car into his wheelchair. She then seemingly struggled to push the chair up the rest of the gravel driveway. Kayleigh walked up to them, wondering what she must look like after her rough night.

"Please pardon my appearance, Mr. Norton, I wasn't expecting company."

"I felt bad," he mumbled. "An old man shouldn't die when he feels bad 'bout something. I had to pay her to persuade her to bring me over." He coughed. "Are you gonna make me sit out here in the cold all day and get pneumonia, or are you gonna invite me into my own house?"

"No, Mr. Norton. Of course. Please, let's go inside."

"It's Martin."

"Sure, Martin."

The nurse fetched a fold-up ramp from her car, and pushed him up with great difficulty. Kayleigh shivered as the nurse pushed his wheelchair into the house. Kayleigh led the way to the kitchen and switched the coffee maker on. She proceeded in fixing some freshly brewed coffee for her and the nurse and tea for Martin, who assured her coffee would make him hyperactive with his Parkinson's.

She sat down at the table next to Martin and passed him his tea. He ordered the nurse to wait outside for him. Kayleigh told her where the lounge was so she could wait there for him instead.

Martin began speaking without preamble. "My mom married an Afrikaner Boer before she married my father. She only told me this when I was a grown man, because she wanted to save me the embarrassment—as she called it. Those days, the English didn't marry Afrikaners. It just wasn't done. But my mom eloped with this guy. I believe his name was Joshua."

Kayleigh's head shot up at the mention of the name, but Martin didn't notice as he continued. "He loved her and she loved him. She had a daughter with him. Her name was Carrey. She disappeared during the war right after English soldiers took my mom to the concentration camp. I believe the girl disappeared at a young age. Three or four years old, I think."

He cleared his throat before continuing. "Joshua returned from the war. When he arrived home, my mom and Carrey were gone. He thought they were both dead, so he hanged himself in the shower."

Kayleigh nearly choked on her coffee. That was just what Rebecca saw behind her in the reflection in the mirror while she was in the bathroom that one day. A man hanging from a railing.

"When my mom returned after being released from the concentration camp, she found him in the shower. He had decayed by then. No one knew where her daughter had disappeared off to." He shook his head. "Ruined my mother's life. She never got over it, became an alcoholic after that happened. Never wanted us, neither me nor my father. I believe that he's lingering here, waiting for her to return. And so is she, Carrey. I saw her with my own two eyes. But she just shows up every once in a long while."

"Your mom's name was Catherine?" Kayleigh could scarcely believe she was getting confirmation of everything they'd seen and heard in the house.

"That's right." Martin confirmed with a quick nod.

"My daughter saw Carrey when we first moved in. We've had loads of experiences here." Kayleigh fumbled with her coffee cup.

"I lived here for a while right after I renovated the place. Almost the whole place had burnt down to the ground. Only half of it still stood, but I fixed it up and decided to live here. Not many things happened, but I did see the man walking around a few times and the little girl looking out the window at the top. Like she was waiting for someone. That was enough to scare me away. I had my own place anyway. And then I got this damn Parkinson's and ended up at the frail care center."

He took a deep breath and coughed again. "Like I told you before, you can move out any time you want. I won't hold you liable for the remainder of your contract. Place is paid for anyway, and I really don't need the money. The little nurse out there has no idea, but she's inheriting the place after I'm gone. She's done so much for me."

The nurse would be happy, but only if they managed get rid of the presence.

Martin reached into his coat pocket and removed an envelope with photographs of his mother and one of Joshua. He gave her the envelope and told her she could keep it. In one of the photographs, there was a picture of Carrey. She immediately recognized the little girl from the time she saw her in Sarah's room.

Chapter Thirty-three

Early to mid-1900s

Catherine stayed with Evelyn for a while, until after Joshua's burial. She searched daily, to try and find Carrey. There was no trace.

After a few weeks, she went back to stay with her parents for a while until her father forced her to marry an Englishman, Edward Norton. They had a son, whom she called Martin.

Edward Norton died at the ripe age of ninety-two, and in all those years, Catherine never returned to her farm in Hoekwil. She finally told her forty-three-year-old son about her life before she met his dad. Martin, until then, never knew that he had a half-sister who'd disappeared so many years ago. Catherine signed over all ownership of the farm to Martin.

Chapter Thirty-four

Present day

After he left, Kayleigh cleared the table. While washing the cups, she glanced up out of the window and—to her shock—Carrey stood in the garden, staring back at her.

Kayleigh removed her hands from the water and dried them off on a dish cloth. The little girl turned and walked toward the back of the house. Kayleigh frowned and decided to follow her. She went to the back of the house, and saw Carrey standing off in the distance, between the trees of the adjoining forest on the farm. Just as her gaze met Kayleigh's, Carrey proceeded into the woods. Kayleigh ran after her, trying to keep up. About a hundred yards through the trees, Carrey stood still again, staring at Kayleigh. Kayleigh slowed her pace and walked toward Carrey. Carrey raised her arm and pointed at the ground. Then she disappeared. Kayleigh rushed to the spot and frantically started searching the area. It was overgrown, with inches of dead leaves strewn all over the ground.

The spot where Carrey had stood was cooler than the rest of the area. Kayleigh's footsteps suddenly echoed under her boots when she walked. She stomped at the ground and felt it was hollow underneath her feet. She fell down on her knees and dug away at the debris. She continued to stomp with her boot, even harder now, to pinpoint the hollowed spot.

With shaky fingers, she managed to clear enough of the foliage and found a hinged handle underneath it. Hundreds of insects scuttled away when she cleared off the top of what resembled a hatch. There was a trapdoor. It was an exact replica of the pictures that Sarah drew months ago. Ignoring the insects, she lifted the handle and tugged at the door in the ground. It didn't open easily. It was rusted shut. She glanced around the shrubbery and spotted a branch. She used it to pry the door open. A stepladder led down underneath the ground. She dug her cell phone from her pocket and activated the flashlight before she descended the steps to a miniature room underneath. It wasn't deep, so she couldn't stand up straight. There in the little room, she found her. The beams from her flashlight captured the petite body of the girl that had gotten lost so many years ago, right there underneath the ground, hardly a hundred yards from her house. She bent down over the skeleton with long black hair and very old fashioned pajamas. And Kayleigh wept for all the pain the child's poor mother had gone through. For the cruel way in which this innocent child must have died. And for the child who never had a proper burial.

After a while, she went back up to the house and called Martin at the care center. Then she called the police.

After she'd called the police, she called Rebecca again. To her relief, the phone rang.

"Hello," Rebecca answered.

Hearing her voice was the best sound Kayleigh had heard in a very long time. "Please come over, Rebecca. We need to talk, and we need to get a medium or someone over. I've found the body of the little girl."

"Oh, my God, you did?" Rebecca gasped. There was a long pause. "God, Kayleigh, I'm so sorry for leaving you like that, but I wasn't… I wasn't myself. I'll be there in a few minutes. Everything's going to be all right. I promise," she said. "Are you okay? Are you mad at me?"

"I love you. I just want you back."

†

Twenty minutes later, Rebecca was there. She cried when she saw Kayleigh. They held onto one another for a long while, whispering apologies and how much they loved the other. Then they sat side by side outside on the patio swing while Kayleigh told her everything that happened after Rebecca left and about Martin who'd shared his story and left the photos. Together, they studied the photos.

"Catherine looks just like you, Kayleigh." And she did even in the black and white pictures. "So he thinks you're Catherine," Rebecca added in a murmur. "Then I must be the threat for him. He thinks Catherine's cheating."

She couldn't believe how much anguish Kayleigh had endured during the night and promised to never leave her alone again. They also listened to the tape together. Rebecca finally understood that running away would be easy, but they could never rest knowing that these ghosts used to be flesh and blood and just needed help.

"Do you still have the number for that medium Bert suggested?" Kayleigh asked.

"Yep. I actually called her early this morning. She said she'll come today."

"That's wonderful news. Thank you. If she brings sage, I'll strangle her myself."

"Or lock her in that bathroom of ours." Rebecca said, her eyes twinkling. "We'll be okay, baby." Rebecca placed a comforting arm around Kayleigh's shoulders.

†

The police came to remove the remains of Carrey and Martin promised to give her a proper burial right next to their mother. Kayleigh knew the little girl would finally be laid to rest. She hoped they could help Joshua cross over as well.

After the police left, the medium arrived driving a Harley. Maggie Fletcher looked scary with her spiky black hair, and her many piercings. Nevertheless, Kayleigh was grateful for the promised help. After introductions were made, the first order of business was to give Maggie as much information on the house as they knew, along with everything that had happened to them, so that she'd know how to approach the issue.

"It's important that you want the spirit gone and never even acknowledge that he ever existed. Talking about it will make the spirit think that you miss him and want him back. We have to let him know that he's not welcome here and for that you have to be sure that you want him gone," she repeated. "You have to be strong-willed. Spirits can feed off weak-willed people, and it gives them more strength. Can you both agree to all this?" she asked while chewing wildly on the gum in her mouth.

Kayleigh and Rebecca were both very eager to agree. Once everything was over, they never wanted to talk about it again.

"How do we go about this?" Kayleigh had to admit she was scared, but she wouldn't let her fear stand in the way. She wanted her life back, and she wanted everything back to normal.

"We sit right here, at the table." Maggie strolled casually toward the kitchen table, like this was an everyday experience for her. Kayleigh and Rebecca followed her diligently, and sat down on opposite sides of the round table. They studied one another anxiously, not sure what to expect.

Maggie chose the seat between them and reached her hands across the table so that Kayleigh and Rebecca could each take one. She nodded at their hands. "We need to hold onto one another's hands throughout the ritual. Whatever happens, don't speak and don't let go. We're stronger as a circle. Remember, whatever happens, never let go of one another's hands."

Rebecca reached over with her free hand and took hold of Kayleigh's on the table.

Before Kayleigh had a chance to chicken out, Maggie closed her eyes. Her eye shadow was dark blue-black. Then Maggie started to talk loudly. Kayleigh jumped at the unexpectedness of her loud voice but focused on not letting go. Her palms started sweating, and she wished she could wipe them quickly, but it was too late.

"I call unto you, restless spirits." Maggie repeated the same sentence continuously until she started breathing heavily. Her chest heaved, and her lips grimaced as she inhaled and exhaled loudly. It felt as though the temperature in the room dropped by at least twenty degrees. She saw Rebecca shiver across from her.

Maggie suddenly threw her head back, then she stopped breathing for a moment, and everything went quiet—eerily quiet. Maggie's head came down in slow motion, turned toward Kayleigh, and then her eyes flew open. She stared straight at Kaylcigh, and spoke in a deep voice. "Caaatheriiine..." the voice whispered in a gravelly voice. "Come with me." Maggie's hand gripped Kayleigh's fingers in a tight vise, causing tears to spring to Kayleigh's eyes.

Maggie's voice returned to its normal timbre. "This is not Catherine," she said. "You need to cross over to find your beloved Catherine."

"No!" The ghost screamed through Maggie, still staring straight at Kayleigh.

Maggie spoke again. "The other side is open. Catherine is waiting for you. You must go there."

The faint light in the kitchen started to flicker, and the table shook like a herd of wild horses galloping across a meadow. The noise was unbearable, and it took all of Kayleigh's willpower not to let go of their hands in order to close her ears to the noise. The kitchen cupboard doors started swinging open and shut, with glasses and cups sliding from the cupboards, and breaking as the doors slammed into them.

"You must cross over!" Maggie shouted this time. "You must go now!"

A cup flew past Rebecca's head, missing her by only a couple of inches. Kayleigh ducked and it missed her too. She held onto Rebecca's hand as hard as she could, or else she was afraid she would let go and run out of the house. She could see Rebecca's chest moving up and down rapidly as she breathed.

"Joshua, this is not Catherine. You have to cross over. Catherine is on the other side." Maggie repeated the words again and again, and just as Kayleigh thought it was a waste of time, the noise stopped. The room was quiet, the only sound that of Kayleigh and Rebecca's heavy breathing. Maggie was slouched in her chair, leaning over the table for a few moments. Then she let go of their hands and looked up at them as if nothing had happened.

"I love my job," she said with a tinge of sarcasm.

"Is it over now?" Kayleigh asked with disbelief. "It can't be that easy, can it?" She looked at Rebecca, whose hand was still clasped in her grip. Rebecca frowned and shook her head.

Maggie got up from her chair, but before she could say anything, she was pushed by an invisible force. She flew across the room and hit the wall with a thump. Her limp body slid down the wall. Both women ran to her and crouched down to see if she was okay. Maggie sneered at them. Her eye color had changed. She reached up with her one hand and pushed Rebecca. Rebecca tumbled back and hit the floor hard. Kayleigh turned and reached for Rebecca, but Maggie gripped Kayleigh's arm. The deathly grip was so tight, there was no way that Kayleigh could free herself.

"Come with me, Catherine," the deep voice spoke again.

His spirit had entered Maggie. "I'm not Catherine!" she shouted. Maggie's eyes, which were Joshua's eyes, looked sad. "You died many years ago, Joshua. Catherine and Carrey died too. You need to go to them. They're on the other side. I don't know what you must do. Don't you see a light or something?"

"I love you, Catherine," the deep voice said again, sounding confused.

"I'm not Catherine. My name is Kayleigh. Look at me." Kayleigh suddenly felt dizzy, her legs gave way and she slumped down onto the floor. Just as everything went black around her, she found herself in a different place. She stood in an endless white field. The air surrounding her was misty, and she couldn't see farther than a few yards. She just somehow knew that she was in the spirit realm located between the earthbound plane and the Other Side. It was the sound of his breathing that made her jump around. The man from the pictures, Joshua, stood behind her. He had tears in his eyes when he spoke again.

"I missed you so much, Catherine."

He was sobbing now, as he gently wrapped his arms around her. He was warm and felt like a living human being.

Kayleigh hugged him back for a short moment but then pulled away.

Kayleigh began to cry, too. "Joshua, I know you love Catherine, but look at me. I mean, really look at me. I'm not Catherine."

Joshua frowned as he focused on her for a long while. "Why are you saying that?" he whispered with confusion in his eyes.

"My name is Kayleigh. You died many years ago, and Catherine died, too. You have to cross over. Go to her. She's waiting for you."

Kayleigh saw movement behind him and looked over his shoulder. There they stood— Catherine and Carrey. Catherine was young again, and Kayleigh couldn't believe the resemblance.

"They're there." Kayleigh swallowed and pointed to the spot where Catherine and Carrey stood, hand in hand. Joshua turned and looked behind him.

"Catherine?" Joshua spoke softly. Kayleigh shivered as she watched him stumble toward Catherine, looking back at her, before continuing on. "My love? Catherine?"

"Yes, Joshua. It's me." Catherine cried as she hugged her husband that she'd lost so many years ago.

Joshua then let go of Catherine, bent down and held onto Carrey. He sobbed as he just held her for a long time. After a while, he lifted Carrey up and hugged his wife and child at the same time. Kayleigh swallowed back tears of happiness as she watched the family reunited.

When Joshua finally turned around, he looked at peace. "Thank you," he said, his voice now soft and tender. A bright light swirled around them, like a tornado of lights, and in an instant, they were gone.

When Kayleigh awakened from her vision, she found herself back in her kitchen, lying on the floor. Rebecca was above her.

"Are you okay, my love?"

Kayleigh tilted her head up at her. "He's gone," she said. "He's finally gone." Rebecca helped Kayleigh get up. When Kayleigh was back on her feet again, they held onto one another.

"Don't mind me, I'll help myself up." Maggie coughed as she used the wall as leverage to stand up. "What happened?" she asked with a frown.

"He's gone," Rebecca said while helping Maggie into a chair. Kayleigh told Maggie and a shocked Rebecca what she'd seen.

Maggie frowned at her. "Seems like you're in the wrong career, my dear. You did this all on your own."

"No, I prefer working with animals." Kayleigh laughed before continuing, "But I couldn't have done this without your help. Thank you." Kayleigh picked her purse up from the kitchen counter. "What's your price, by the way?" she asked as she lifted out her checkbook.

"A real medium doesn't put a price on her services." Maggie shook her head, but then quickly added, "We do however accept donations."

Kayleigh laughed. "We all have to survive, right?" She wrote out a check for Maggie.

Both Kayleigh and Rebecca couldn't believe it was the same house. It was as though light and warmth had entered and replaced the darkness. The house smelled of roses, and it felt filled with love and peace.

Kayleigh and Rebecca hugged Maggie goodbye and thanked her for all that she'd done and at such short notice, too. Maggie left with a look of satisfaction on her face.

✝

After Maggie left, Kayleigh and Rebecca cooked a light dinner. They took the meal to their bedroom, sat snuggled next to one another on the bed, and started in on their meal.

"So where have you been?" Kayleigh asked.

"I slept in my CD store, on your red couch. Well, I didn't sleep at all, actually. I sat and stared at the wall all night long, regretting leaving you here all alone. I hated myself."

"Why didn't you take me along?" Kayleigh asked in the most non-accusing tone she could muster.

"As soon as I walked out the front door, I turned around to fetch you. Just as I did, I saw the door slam shut. I thought at the time it was you shutting me out. I know now that it wasn't, and I can't tell you enough how sorry I am. I wish I could turn back time and take you with me," Rebecca said softly.

"It's all in the past now. Gosh, I can't believe how much has happened in the past twenty-four hours. It's like a whole lifetime has passed." Kayleigh took a deep breath in and exhaled slowly. She wanted to shut all of that out now. It was all over, and she knew with utter certainty it would never happen again.

After they finished their meal, Rebecca took their plates and left the room. Kayleigh leaned into the pillows, thinking of everything that had happened that day. She was so relieved that she had Rebecca back. A few minutes later, Rebecca returned and climbed in next to her.

"Promise me one thing, Kay. Even though everything is over, please, can we move into my house now? As soon as the vacation tenants are out, we should leave here." Rebecca placed her palms together, as if praying.

"When are they going?" Kayleigh asked.

"Next weekend. Another group of people were booked after them, but I told them there was a mix up of dates and refunded them. They were only too happy to get their money back." She laughed. Kayleigh felt giddy hearing that sound. She'd missed Rebecca's laugh so much. Even though they were only apart for a few hours, it had felt like a lifetime had passed.

"Can we start packing?" Kayleigh jumped up and made a beeline for the cupboard. She removed a suitcase from the top shelf and dropped it onto the floor.

"Let's pack tomorrow," Rebecca said and laughed.

"Sounds good. I am in desperate need of a shower, and I can't think of anything that would feel better right now." Kayleigh walked out of the room.

She got to the downstairs bathroom, which still had the lingering smell of roses. She undressed while she let the water run warm. She stepped into the shower and let the hot water soothe her tired muscles. She hadn't slept properly in quite some time and could feel the exhaustion laying heavy on her shoulders. A body behind Kayleigh made her jump around. She giggled with relief when she found a naked Rebecca behind her.

With a crooked grin, Rebecca apologized for scaring her. She lathered some soap onto the sponge and washed Kayleigh's back. Afterward, Kayleigh carefully washed Rebecca's healing back with the same sponge.

"You were so brave today," Kayleigh said.

"Oh, no. You're much braver than I am, Kay."

"No, I'm not. I didn't have the guts to leave," Kayleigh admitted. "I was afraid to move when you weren't."

They both were quiet for a few moments. "I miss Sarah. She's so much a part of us," Rebecca said. "What do you think she's going to say when she gets back, and we don't live here anymore?"

"She'll be happy. I think this has all been just as hard on her as it's been on us," Kayleigh said as she washed the rest of her body.

Rebecca squeezed some shampoo into the palm of her hand and worked it into her hair. "Were you able to speak to her today? With all the drama, we never called last night to hear if she'd landed safely. Bad mothers."

"I called her this morning. She was very excited that her new baby brother was born last week."

"That must be so amazing for her then. I'll call her tomorrow."

They finished showering and then ran up the stairs to get to bed. Their whole house still smelled of roses. Amazingly enough, they weren't afraid anymore at all.

Kayleigh dropped her towel and searched for pajamas in the cupboard. She bent down in front of the cupboard in order to find them. Rebecca came up behind her. She'd dropped her towel to the floor, too. She reached for Kayleigh and touched the lower part of her back softly. She trailed her fingertips along Kayleigh's back and slid to Kayleigh's front. She found Kayleigh's firm breasts and hardened nipples and stroked them until they were painful.

Kayleigh straightened and turned around to face Rebecca. Their mouths met, their lips parted, and their skin was still warm from the shower and got warmer as Rebecca pulled Kayleigh tightly against her. Rebecca's tongue came out from between her parted lips and they tasted one another. Kayleigh moved her hand up to grip the back of Rebecca's neck. She couldn't get close enough. She'd wanted this for some time now and her whole body ached for more. She moved her hips against Rebecca's. Rebecca groaned and lowered her hands to Kayleigh's hips.

They backed up from the cupboard and found the bed. Rebecca climbed onto the bed and Kayleigh fell on top of her. Kayleigh's hips found a slow rhythm, synchronized to Rebecca's thrusts. She trailed kisses down to Rebecca's breasts and sucked a nipple into her mouth. Rebecca cried out. "Yeah, my baby, make love to me with your mouth."

Kayleigh slid downward and sprinkled kisses along Rebecca's stomach. Her lips found Rebecca's mound. Rebecca parted her legs and invited Kayleigh's tongue inside her. Kayleigh licked and sucked slowly until Rebecca pleaded for more.

"Oh yes, baby, make me come. Please," Rebecca begged as she drove her hips upward to meet Kayleigh's mouth.

Kayleigh kept sucking and moved her head slowly from side to side. She could feel Rebecca's urgency grow with every passing second, but she continued at the slow rhythm with which she'd started. Teasing, torturing her. She could feel how swollen Rebecca had become and her warmth tasted sweet. She prodded with her tongue over Rebecca's swollen skin and then sucked again, playfully. Rebecca's breathing became ragged. She grabbed Kayleigh's head to move her even closer. Her hips moved at a rapid pace now. Kayleigh's mouth could feel Rebecca pulsating. Rebecca cried out as her body heaved and her hips thrust hard up against Kayleigh's lips. Just as Rebecca climaxed, Kayleigh inserted a finger inside her warm wetness.

"Oh fuck, that feels so good. Make love to me with your fingers. Yes."

Kayleigh slid her fingers in and out while her tongue darted over the swollen, throbbing clit. Rebecca thrust her hips against her mouth as she came again, her body shuddered, and her hands grabbed at the sheets.

"Fuck, I love you." Rebecca kept moving her hips against Kayleigh's mouth while gasping for air. After a few moments her body relaxed and she flipped Kayleigh onto her back. "I need to make love to you, too," Rebecca said as she searched out Kayleigh's mouth and kissed her passionately. She quickly kissed her way down to Kayleigh's wet center.

By now, Kayleigh was so hot that she could barely breathe. Rebecca's tongue slid slowly over her clit, only for a few short seconds, and Kayleigh already felt herself building up to a massive release. Her hips thrust high as she gripped Rebecca's head and held it between her legs. Rebecca pushed her tongue all the way inside Kayleigh and moved it in and out of her while she rubbed her clit between her thumb and forefinger.

"Oh, yes, don't stop, baby. Yes, just like that," she panted while Rebecca penetrated her with her tongue. "Fuck me, baby. I'm close. Oh yes! Fuck me! Please!"

Rebecca gained speed as Kayleigh convulsed underneath her. Kayleigh slashed and thrust wildly as she cried out with pleasure. Rebecca slowed her movement after a while and Kayleigh felt the pulsating fade. Then Rebecca kissed her on the inside of her legs and started slowly moving all the way up again, back to her mouth. Kayleigh kissed Rebecca and tasted herself on Rebecca's lips.

They continued to pleasure one another until their bodies were spent. They each collapsed into the other's arms and lay there in the dark, smiling at one another.

"And you were stressed I might dump you for your inexperience? Gosh, Kay, where did you learn all these things?" Rebecca was still out of breath.

Kayleigh slapped her lightly on the stomach. "I learned from the best."

†

In the week that followed, Lindsay and Judy came over and helped them pack everything into boxes. Kayleigh contacted the same guys that helped her move the previous time and by the time the weekend arrived, it took them only a day to move into their new home. By Saturday evening, they were done moving Kayleigh and Sarah's stuff to Rebecca's house, and they could relax by the fireplace with Chinese take-out and a bottle of champagne. There were still some boxes that needed unpacking, but there was no rush.

"Just another week and Sarah's coming home." Kayleigh sighed after they'd made love in front of the fireplace. "Then we can't make love all over the house anymore."

Rebecca laughed. "There's always camp." She kissed Kayleigh on her forehead. 'I love you more than life itself."

"I love you, too," Kayleigh said as she put her jersey back on. She turned to face Rebecca. "More than you know."

"How about we get married then?" Rebecca whispered.

"Married?"

"Yes." Rebecca looked serious as her eyes met Kayleigh's eyes.

"Imagine that." Kayleigh said, incredulous. "Is that a proposal?"

Rebecca also sat up and took Kayleigh's hands into her own. "I love you, and I want to spend the rest of my life with you. Let's get married."

Kayleigh laughed. Rebecca was perfect. "I love you, too, and I can't wait to grow old together. If we lived another hundred years, it would still not be enough time with you. Yes, let's get married."

Rebecca leaned and kissed her gently on the lips. "Let's do the whole nine yards then. Big wedding, honeymoon, everything. I want it all. With you."

"Are we really going to get married?" Kayleigh asked. "Two women? Is that even legal?"

"This is South Africa, honey. Of course it's legal."

Rebecca lay back down again, and pulled Kayleigh down with her. They slept in front of the fireplace, in their new home, both very content and happy.

†

The following Saturday, they drove to collect Sarah from the airport. She was excited to be back and had a whole photo album of her and her new baby brother, Marcus. All the way home, she talked non-stop. She kept chattering about how she helped bathe the baby and how she was sure the baby smiled at her once. She even got to watch how her stepmother breastfed the infant. Kayleigh felt a little tinge of jealousy at how much Sarah enjoyed it there.

At home, they unpacked all of Sarah's new clothes and toys into Sarah's new room. Sarah was thrilled with the move, just as Kayleigh hoped she would be. Kayleigh and Rebecca had hung her curtains, and Rebecca had bought Sarah her own music system for her room as a welcome to your new home gift.

A few days later, Kayleigh's phone rang. When she answered it, her surprised, 'Hello Martin' got Rebecca's attention. Kayleigh sat on the couch next to Rebecca, while talking, Rebecca whispered next to her, curiously, wanting to know what the call was about. Kayleigh motioned to her with her hand, trying to get Rebecca to be patient and quiet. After she hung up she told Rebecca, "The funeral is next week, on Wednesday. Just a small service and a quick burial. They're burying her next to her mother."

"Do they know how she died?" Rebecca asked.

"There were no signs of any injury, so the coroner thinks she died of dehydration. The trapdoor hatch was very heavy to lift and she was small. I think the door was too heavy for her to lift from the inside. Heaven knows whether she died of starvation, dehydration, or lack of oxygen. That room seemed pretty airtight to me. A pity her mother didn't find that underground room when she searched all over for her. She spent all those years wondering what had happened to her child. I can't even begin to imagine the suffering that woman endured."

On Wednesday, the funeral was small, just as predicted. The only people who attended were Martin, his favorite nurse, Kayleigh, and Rebecca. Kayleigh had one of the photographs enlarged and framed for the funeral.

At the gravesite, as the matchbox of a coffin went down into the ground, Kayleigh looked up. About fifty yards away, between the trees, she saw Carrey. The little girl stood between a man and a woman. To her left was her mother, Catherine, to her right, her father, Joshua. All three were smiling. Joshua nodded in her direction right before the three of them turned and walked away, slowly fading into the distance, until Kayleigh could no longer see them. Tears welled in her eyes.

Rebecca gasped next to her. "Did you see that?" she whispered.

Kayleigh nodded. "I sure did." She grasped Rebecca's hand.

"They're finally back together again. A family. Just like us." Rebecca squeezed Kayleigh's hand and smiled.

Kayleigh felt that smile reach deep inside and fill her heart. "Yes. Just like us."

About the Author

Charlene Neil

Charlene Neil resides with her children in Cape Town, South Africa.

As a child, she always had a wild imagination, and sometimes still finds her mind drifting in a parallel universe. She loved to write poetry in school and wrote a few songs for her music band—the band was just a rebel phase however, and luckily, she soon returned to reality.

Currently, Charlene is working as a specialized case manager for a medical company. In her free time, she loves to hike, read and spend time with her three children. She, however, lives to write. Once she starts, she finds that she can't stop.

A South African publisher, Memories SA, published her first novel, *The Prodigins*. It's a fantasy novel with the younger reader in mind. Charlene's passion however lies with romance, and her interest in the paranormal was inspired by events that happened to her in her own life. *The Presence* is based on actual experiences.

Charlene is currently working on her third novel, which she is hoping to finish by the end of 2015.

Feedback is always appreciated you can e-mail the author at: Charlene.neil@rocketmail.com

Other Books from Affinity eBook Press

Return to Me—Erin O'Reilly Renowned microbiologist Sydney Tanner left work as normal for her trip home but never arrived. Ellie Scott her wife of ten years franticly to the point of obsession attempts to find her—the only evidence there is something amiss is Syd's crashed truck then the clues go cold. Ellie refuses to believe that she will never see Syd again but realizes many months later with nothing solid to go on, it's time to attempt to move forward with a life without Syd. Leaving her home town she accepts a new job at Salvation aptly named for Ellie's predicament. There Ellie meets beautiful Maya Rojas who is the director of Salvation a rehabilitation hospital. Although she hasn't given up on finding Syd, Ellie finds herself increasingly drawn to Maya.Will Salivation bring just that to Ellie allowing her to find peace and happiness again or will it have her questioning all that she believes in? A wonderful romance cloaked within an intriguing mystery.

Terminal Event—Ali Spooner Tally Rainwater was born with the gift of second sight. A near fatal accident, at age twelve, brings her visions to her more clearly. As she matures, a spirit enters her visions to guide her in using her gift. When Tally uses her gift to locate the body of a murdered teen, she realizes her gift is to help lost souls find their peace. When it's discovered a serial killer murdered the teen, the FBI is involved. Blaire "Spooky" Cooper is the Agent in Charge assigned to the case, and a task force of local detectives and FBI forms to track the killer. Together with the team, Tally helps them piece together the puzzle of murders spanning twenty years throughout the Deep South.

Arc Over Time—Jen Silver Dr Kathryn Moss has job offers flowing in after her exciting archaeological discoveries at Starling Hill the previous year. Now she has choices to make that could jeopardise her relationship with Denise Sullivan, the fiery journalist, who has become her lover. For Denise the choice seems obvious. She thinks they have moved beyond the casual sex stage to something more like a true relationship. However, she's not sure how to handle Kathryn's continuing infatuation with Ellie Winters. Ellie's new career as a promising artist proves to be a catalyst for the simmering tensions in relations between her wife Robin, Kathryn, and Denise. Will Denise persevere in her pursuit of the reluctant professor? Does Ellie have anything to fear from Kathryn's fascination with her art, or is there another motive behind the professor's obsessive interest? This wonderful romantic continuation with the characters from *Starting Over* ties up loose ends. But the question is—does everyone have a happy ending? A must read.

A Walk Away—Lacey Schmidt Kat and Rand's daily worlds are 2,100 miles apart, but something about their meeting on the magical shores of the nation's oldest national park east of the Mississippi sparks questions that neither woman can just walk away without answering. Sometimes chance brings you to the right person to help you resolve some of your baggage, and you learn to like yourself a little more. Kat and Rand are smart enough to recognize this chance in each other, but they also find that there is a catch to every opportunity—walking toward something is always walking away from something else.

Love Forever, Live Forever—Annette Mori   No one forgets their first love. For Nicky, that's Sara, who abruptly disappears one day, leaving only a cryptic letter. That day scarred her soul. When the pain starts to diminish, Nicky begins to get her life back on track until it is derailed once again by an unimaginable twist. Changed forever, Nicky becomes a careless, womanizing nomad known as the Little Wild One, until she meets Annie. Thirteen years later, Nicky's finally settled and happy. Fate intervenes and puts her directly back into the path of her first love, Sara, and the corresponding events send her into a tailspin. Now she must decide—who will be the person she ends up living with and loving forever?

Possessing Morgan—Erica Lawson   New York City, in the height of summer. Crime seems to have taken a holiday, and Detective Morgan O'Callaghan is bored, bored, bored. Paperwork is mating and multiplying on her desk, and even a jaywalker is starting to look good. Anything to get her out from behind her desk! Enter Andrea Worthington, Charleston socialite and all-around rich girl, right down to the wealthy fiancé. She's also the new Assistant District Attorney assigned to Morgan's precinct. Their first meeting is like two freight trains crashing head on. Then a high profile, career make-or-break murder case throws them together again. The investigation has barely begun when Andrea becomes the target of a nearly fatal hit-and-run. But was it really aimed at her? Can she and Morgan find the common ground they need to solve the case and stop the attacks, or are the gaps just too wide to bridge?

Twenty-three Miles—Renee MacKenzie Talia Lisher has a long family history of lying, about anything and everything. With her father dead, and her mom gone on a quest to start a new life, Talia struggles to keep in touch with her only remaining family, her incarcerated brother. When Talia sets her sights on Officer Shay Eliot, she vows to stop lying. She starts watching Shay, waiting for just the right circumstances and amount of courage to talk to her. Talia might be watching Shay, but someone in a dark van is watching Talia. Is the mystery driver a dangerous part of her family's past, or is it all just a coincidence? Shay Eliot has left the police force because of what she perceives as a hostile work environment. When a brutal double-murder on the 23-mile-long Colonial Parkway puts the FBI's magnifying glass squarely on her, her alibi comes from an unlikely source – a young woman who has been stalking her. Shay wants to keep her distance from Talia, but once she gets to know the younger woman she can't keep feelings from developing. This is a story about community, and how it comes together in dangerous and devastating times. When you don't know who to trust, you better have friends who will rally around you. Will Talia and Shay find the answers they need to the mystery of the murders on the parkway, or will justice be elusive? Will they survive their quest for the truth?

Confined Spaces—Renee MacKenzie Andie Waters spends her days pulling waste samples for environmental testing and at night, she tends bar at The Cave, a popular hangout for straights in a small Georgia town. Serial monogamy has grown stale for her, so she's content working to pay off her debts and hanging out with her old hound dog. Or so she thinks, until a beautiful lesbian drops by The Cave. Andie suspects her involvement with the woman will be only temporary. Little does she know no part of her life will be left untouched. Kara Travis likewise anticipates nothing more than a brief fling upon meeting Andie, especially given her reputation as both a personal ice princess and a corporate hatchet wielder for Royal Environmental. What luck to find a hot lesbian bartender in nowhere rural Georgia. Andie and Kara spend a passionate weekend together and find that their notions of no strings attached are far from accurate. Their supposed short-term ideal diversion of a commitment-free romp hits a major complication when they come face-to-face with one another at Royal Environmental's offices Monday morning. While carrying out her duties, Kara discovers crimes being committed by and against Royal Environmental employees. Will Kara be forced to shut down the Georgia Division of the company? If she does, Andie will lose her job. Worse yet, Kara may lose Andie before she's really even sure she's got her. Corporate politics, complicated romance, and long distances conspire to keep Andie and Kara all boxed in. Can love triumph despite the Confined Spaces?

Reece's Star—TJ Vertigo Reece Corbett watches over the dancers in her gentleman's club with the blue, razor sharp eyes of The Animal. Few know that resting comfortably in her office is her newest love, a tiny MinPin named Smudge. What happened to The Animal, known for her rapacious appetite for women and danger? Faith Ashford is what happened to The Animal. Faith and Reece have been together a while now and they have settled into something resembling domestic bliss. This bliss alarms Reece. It's one thing for Faith to see her softer side, that's vulnerability enough, but to let her friends see it...no. Not the best plan. Under Faith's guiding, loving hand, will Reece successfully traverse the rocky road of emotion and embrace the positive changes in her life? Or will she panic and be unable to control that Animal part of herself? Will she take that next step to declare herself fully capable of love and devotion? This third installment in the popular series that began with *Private Dancer* continues the passionate and often hilarious romance of Reece and Faith as they both grow in love and in trust.

Flight—Renee Mackenzie It's 1983 and Kate Hunter is a student at a small, private college in Virginia. When Lana coaxes her onto the back of her beat-up scooter one night, Kate's education starts to encompass more than just her pre-vet studies. Kate has always done as expected of her, so when she starts staying away from home on weekends to spend time with her new lover it's way out of character for her. Lana is secretive, but Kate accepts things as they are and gives Lana her space. When she feels the sting of betrayal, will she be able to continue giving Lana her privacy? Kate's sister April is a high school student playing with fire as she parties with her older boyfriend, Boyd. After finding someone overdosed the morning after a big party, April grows weary of all the drugs and alcohol. Will she be able to convince Boyd that they should slow down? Will she be able to pull it together before it's too late? Kate and April are forced to face up to events from their younger years, their mother's desertion, and their long-deteriorating relationship with one another. Some lives will be lost and others changed forever when the sisters' lives intersect. Will they be consumed by the wreckage, or will they be able to pick themselves up and take flight?

Reflected Passion—Erica Lawson   Where passion, reality, and destiny combine. Dale Wincott is a 27-year-old woman born into Bostonian wealth and groomed to marry into the social hierarchy. Her mother is a hard-hearted society matriarch, but her father feels for his daughter and helps Dale find a life on her own as a furniture restorer. Françoise Marie Aurélie de Villerey is a 28-year-old Countess, born into the French aristocracy and forced to marry a count much older than herself. For ten years, she was his trophy wife, forced to endure his perverted desires, until the day he finally died. He had broken her emotionally and she no longer cared for what life had to offer, slipping from one sexual partner to another as often as she changed her clothes. Until... that one night when Françoise looked up during a sexual encounter and saw Dale watching her from the mirror. A veritable angel, full of innocence and curiosity, who touched her very soul. Through the mirror, Françoise embraces life anew, while for Dale it is a powerful awakening, forcing her to discover not only her sensual nature, but the inner strength she possesses.

The One—JM Dragon Phil (Philomena) Casters loves her work as a pilot, above everything else in her life except Ming, her married lover. Phil needs to enhance her status in the community before asking Ming to leave behind her wealthy husband. Rosa Moran a teacher, raised by missionaries in China after the death of her parents. She loves the country of her birth and the people. Her English grandfather desperately wants her to live with him to atone for the guilt he feels about the death of her parents. He sends her a letter requesting her to come home. When Phil flies to the mission to deliver the letter to Rosa, neither can envisage the chain of events about to take place. It starts as a collaboration to save four children, leading them to the surreal private paradise of Langshow. Could this be the perfect place for the children and Rosa to settle? Phil is not so sure. Chang, an old friend from Rosa's childhood lives in Langshow and makes no bones about the fact that he wants Rosa. All thoughts of Ming disappear as Phil tries to fight her attraction to Rosa. However there is the little matter of an innocent misunderstanding—Rosa thinks Phil is a man. *The One* is a romance with everything, love, intrigue, misunderstandings with a happy conclusion—the only question—who gets the girl?

The Chronicles of Ratha: Book 2 A Lion Among the Lambs—Erica Lawson It has been three years since Jordana Laren's path first crossed the Noorthi's - three years since she's had a drink, had sex and a life of her own. Her only excitement has been spent keeping up with her two year-old daughter, Rice, who is definitely a chip off the old block. All has been peaceful until one of the colonists becomes sick. Bad news shifts to worse news when the disease spreads through their community. Unable to get proper medicine, Jordana is forced to rely on the Noorthi healers to come up with a cure. Soon the herbs run out, leaving her with no choice but to search for more on the Noorthi home planet. What is supposed to be a simple pick-up flight turns into a nightmare. Can Jordana believe in herself like her Noorthi sisters do? Only then can she fulfill her destiny as The Chosen One. Follow the colorful cast of characters in this action-packed adventure sequel as they traverse the galaxy. Of course, nothing ever goes smoothly when Jordana is involved.

Cowgirl Up—Ali Spooner When the new ranch hand, Coal Bryan, arrives at the MC2, the last thing she's looking for is love. Her co-workers are surprised when Coal turns out to be female. Coal, used to the reaction, quickly earns the respect of the crew with her work ethic and skill with horses. Coal uses the strenuous work and friendship of the ranch hands to try and forget her broken past. Melissa Conway, owner of MC2, offers Coal a place to live in her home. They both are shocked to find they are linked in a way neither of them imagined. Mary Leah, Melissa's sister, arrives at the ranch to recover from a recent tragedy. The attraction between Mary Leah and Coal is instant and mutual. Can the three women survive their personal dilemmas? The love and friendship they develop certainly helps but will it be enough to bring them together. Ride along with the MC2, for boot scootin', butt kickin', dirt eatin', rodeo adventures, with a love story thrown into the mix.

If I Were a Boy—Erin O'Reilly Katie McGuire appears to have it all. A devoted husband, a job she loved, and a comfortable lifestyle. Helen Swenson is a successful financial director of a prominent investment firm, with an unfaithful husband, and few friends. Their husbands' annual trip to Padre Island National Seashore to reunite with their air force pilot squad becomes a pivotal point for the two women. Their lives take on a completely new meaning when an undeniable magnetism between them draws them together. Passion and secrecy becomes the norm, as they have no choice but to succumb to their attraction. Can the vacation love affair continue? When they leave for their respective homes, will they regret what happened? Life is not that easy to change and the people around them are the hardest to convince. There is no more powerful motivation than love. Except hate and there are plenty of people who want to see their relationship destroyed. Will Katie and Helen be able to make a life together work or succumb to doubts and the pressures of family? This story will fill you with the thrill of passion and the tenderness of love.

The Chronicles of Ratha: Book 1 Children of the Noorthi—Erica Lawson Jordana Laren is a hard-drinking, hard-fighting womanizer, who works as a freighter pilot in her spare time. Her latest customer drugs her, steals her ship, and abandons her on a desert hellhole called Rigeus, infamous penal planet for the worst women criminals. Her chances of survival aren't looking good. She has no food, water, or weapons, and the nearest bar is a million miles away. Just when she's ready to write her last will and testament, Jordana is rescued by a group of barely-clad women. Has she found nirvana? Her own personal harem seems like a possibility, until the intercession of their enemy, the Velkren. Their leader, Vel, remembers Jordana well, and not fondly. But why is Vel on this planet, surrounded by murderers, thieves, and bad-tempered bitches? Jordana knows Vel isn't a prisoner, so why is her nemesis on Rigeus mining mud, of all things? Jordana knows only one thing. She has to get off the planet before Vel kills her. Unfortunately, the women who saved her reveal themselves to be holy. They are the Noorthi, and Jordana's dream of endless debauchery becomes a nightmare of eternal servitude. The Noorthi make her one of them, marking her with a wrist tattoo, and leaving her no choice but to protect them with her life. The last thing Jordana wants is to become involved in galactic politics or heroic actions. But the tattoo ochre in her body is suddenly giving her morals and scruples, not to mention a better vocabulary! And she really can't pass up a chance to outwit Vel, whose megalomaniac plans are endangering not only the Noorthi, but the civilized galaxy itself. But Jordana is torn. Does she stop Vel at all costs, or does she get out from under the thumb of the Noorthi while she can? Some things were never meant to be easy…

Nesting—Renee MacKenzie Macy Stokes, a divorced mother who is struggling with her sexual identity, jumps at a once-in-a-lifetime opportunity to help her friends. She doesn't foresee it will put her in jeopardy of losing her son, Jeremiah. Fresh out of high school, Cam Webber travels to Augusta, Georgia, to reconcile with her aunt. When she learns that's impossible, she determines to gain acceptance from her aunt's partner, Sharon. Meanwhile, Cam sets her sights on Macy, but Macy has other ideas. Kenny Brewer is a good old boy who loves his wife, Dorianne, even when he thinks she's gone totally off her rocker. Dorianne gets it in her head that a local woman is her long-lost half-sister. But soon, her obsession with that is eclipsed by medical problems that involve them all. Set in Augusta, Georgia, *Nesting* explores the age-old issues of guilt, regret, and redemption, and the part they play in driving people to create and protect family-at any cost.

E-Books, Print, Free e-books

Visit our website for more publications available online.

www.affinityebooks.com

Published by Affinity E-Book Press NZ LTD
Canterbury, New Zealand

Registered Company 2517228